Folds of the Script

by

K.B. Nelson

Other Works by K. B. Nelson

The Children of the Great Reckoning

Series

Book 1: Firewall: Ianto

Note: Top Five Dystopian/Apocalyptic M/M Science Fiction Novels of 2013: Goodreads Listopia

Book 2: Firewall: Samu'el

Book 3: Architect

Book 4: Operator

The Children of the Great Reckoning Series will be available in audio format featuring narrator Michael F. Wurzel on February 14, 2014 from Audible and iTunes.

The Dreamcatcher Fallacy Cycle

Book 1: The Dreamcatcher Fallacy

Note: Top Fifteen Dystopian/Apocalyptic M/M Science Fiction Novels of 2013: Goodreads Vote

Book 2: Strands of Silk and Fire (coming Spring 2014)

What people are saying about the science fiction worlds and characters of K. B. Nelson?

If you enjoyed the complexities of THE MATRIX or INCEPTION, this book (*Firewall: Ianto*) is for you. The writer K. B. Nelson possesses a rare combination of talents; a great storyteller, a vivid imagination and a way with words that will carry you along on a story to remember. *(Daniel Roth, past VP of HarperCollins)*

I couldn't put this book down. For those that love science fiction, fantasy and m/m romance with a lot of angst, this story will be worth reading. (Goodreads Reviewer)

My overall verdict: *Children of the Great Reckoning 2: Firewall: Samu'el* is a very interesting science fiction novel with a riveting plot. Anyone who is a fan of the SF genre who doesn't mind the lack of romance-driven M/M plot should give this series a go (starting with book one). If you enjoyed the first book, or was left intrigued with the plot, the second book only gets better. (Goodreads Reviewer)

Everyone I know has been drawn into this book. An intriguing, thought-provoking story. Be sure to set aside some time to read it -- once I picked it up, it was very hard to put down! (Goodreads Reviewer)

Firewall (book I and II) is a beautiful dance between visions of technology, nature and spirit. The plot has the driving excitement of action as well as the soothing poetry of dreams. It weaves genres together in surprising and interesting ways. The dreamlike flow of the plot is anchored by thought-provoking prologues to each chapter. The thread throughout the book is an intense love story between two men. But more importantly, Nelson points to how we are all connected in what makes us human (regardless of gender, age, sexual orientation or origin). What does it even mean to be human?

Highly recommended reading.
(Amazon Reader Review)

K. B. Nelson can write. What a blessing in these times! She can write well, with her story full of gripping incidents, subtle and original characters, an unnerving plot that keeps you turning pages. (Amazon Reader Review)

This is a work of fiction. All characters and events portrayed in the book are either products of the author's imagination or portrayed fictitiously. Any resemblance to actual persons living or dead, business establishments, events or locales is entirely coincidental.

Folds of the Script

Acknowledgements

Special thanks must go out to the people who cheered on the early drafts of this book: Del and Marilyn Beyer, Brian Beyer, Karen Brody, Cliona Dolan and Sandra Hulstrom.

I am thankful for the Bainbridge Island Speculative Fiction Writers Group, who, for fourteen years, has championed both this genre and the people who love to write such things.

Dedication

To the original and irreplaceable Ciaran Dolan
of Ireland—you are missed indeed.

Chapter 1

"Warning. Ciaran Dolan is crashing. Repeat. Do we abort or resuscitate? 12:43 A.M. Warning..." I halted the neural message imprinted over the dark lines of the basement wall and for once, my mind simply hunkered, too numbed by the weeks of work to respond immediately. Some will later say this uncharacteristic hesitation showed the changes that were already happening within me, changes that I had put in motion and could share with all machine-kind. Call it all back? Why not call back the wind that has swept in, tangled and then kissed your hair?

-E

Ciaran shifted his leather pack once again, wincing at the raw rub of the thing against his shoulders. His quarry was upwind of him, face down in the meadow. He could smell the other now; the rank sweat and blood and fear flowed off him in rancid waves. For three hours he had tracked the man, through brush and rock and stream. But the chase was coming to a close.

He slipped behind the trunk of a tall oak, and shrugged the pack off, nestling it silently against the roots. His prey had fallen four times now in the past hour. Ciaran dropped to one knee, fitting the arrow in his short bow.

It was finished. The man wouldn't be getting up again.

The fitful sun glinted off the battered Roman helmet. A gladius, the short blade favored by these strangers, hung sheathed by his side. Ciaran could hear the man mumbling to himself as he tried to get one foot beneath him, only to tip hard to his side again. He'd shed most of his armor some time ago, and his face beneath the helmet rim was dark with dried blood and dirt. Ciaran wondered yet again why he continued to cling to the heavy headgear. Personally, he would have tossed it to the ferns long ago.

The leafless tree branches trembled a bit around him, pushed by the late autumn winds. He drew his line carefully, the string of the bow taut by the edge of his lips, a clean line of fire.

Again the man floundered, like a horse in the last throes of a twisted gut. He cried out, words on the air dragged from a parched throat. "Help me. I have come home as you asked. Help me."

Ciaran's lips opened in silent surprise. He let the bowstring go limp, the arrow tipping toward earth. The soldier had not spoken in the language Rome, but in his own. He set the bow down, his hand on the oak steadying him as he rose to his feet. Such things should not happen to him; he was always careful with his scene plotting and hell, he knew this historical period better than some he had worked in the past. But then this had been a long session. Maybe he was getting bleed-through from one of his past scripts.

Without any kind of warning, a woman in a white lab coat appeared in front of Ciaran and he jerked back with a startled cry. She didn't even give him a moment to find his footing before she started in on him. "Do you have any idea what time it is?" she snapped. She laced her arms tightly over her chest, her chin jutting up at him, staring him in the eye, fierce and unyielding.

"Sal," Ciaran said her name in a way that came out a great deal like a curse. "What in the hell are you doing? Trying to give me an aneurysm?" He shifted, and tried to see over her shoulder and she purposely moved with him, keeping him pinioned with her gray eyes.

"You didn't answer my question," she growled.

"Time? I don't know."

"Three. It's three."

"Then I have hours yet! Why are you bothering me?" He tried to physically shove past her and she blocked him with her hip, forcing him to go the other way around her.

"AM! 0300! Morning *before* the sun comes up," she sputtered, her arms unwinding from herself and her fingers snapping into his face, stopping him cold. "And I've been on duty with you since six this morning.

Or yesterday morning. Or whatever! You are way over the union's daily work hours, and that means you're into cost over-runs. Again."

Ciaran sagged then, his eyes going to the image of the Roman soldier who had frozen in place as soon as Sal had intervened in the feed. He could see the time and date glowing now by the man's head, markers for when he could pick this up later. Their presence also meant Sal wasn't taking no for an answer.

"It was a good shoot today," he murmured as a weak apology. "I just got caught up in it."

"You always get caught up! You're off script again, and you call this good?" she asked. She gestured at the soldier. "Where's the southern Brigantes town? Where are the massing troops? Where is the architecture they wanted, the fields, and the bathhouses? And why are you in fucking *Ireland*? This is a History Channel show, not some flipping half-researched historical romance like you used to post on the streets! You don't get to play fast and loose with this, Ciaran."

"I know. I just..." he stopped himself, running his hand over the relatively unfamiliar lines of his character's face.

"I'm suspending you for a three-day," she said.

"What?" he protested. "Come on Sal."

"You make me come into this god-awful place and you think you're going to argue about this? You want more down time? Is that it? Or how about a pay dock on top of it?"

He shook his head, his heavy red hair shivering the naked skin on his neck. "No, I'm coming out."

"Then give your exit code and let's go. God, it stinks in here, between you and whatever he is." Sal waved her fingers vaguely at the soldier.

He obeyed her, rattling off the string of numbers and letters. The scene began to darken from the edges in, the fade pattern he favored, if only because it made the shift from the synap-production platform to his workstation a little easier. He glanced over Sal's shoulder again and frowned in disbelief. Because the Roman did something else then that would never have been in his script. He lifted his brilliant blue eyes and mouthed "help me" with cracked and whitened lips before the darkness ate him up, slowly, synapixel by synapixel.

And ate Ciaran and Sal up as well.

Chapter 2

I have tried to play out a full synap production. My mind is not suited for it, which of course, makes me curious about why the biological brain seems so perfectly designed to warp reality as such. How do I capture that skill for us? Do I even honestly wish it?

-E

He gasped as he always did, jerking inelegantly out of his make-believe world. Sal's cold hand pushed him back against the sweaty gel pack bed. "Easy. Take it easy." He lay back then, letting her free him bit by bit from the leads to his head, his body. She worked fast and with a frosty but efficient touch, and again he was thankful that he wasn't freelancing anymore. Sal knew his body, knew how to twist and pull hard when it was appropriate or could feather-touch the delicate skull leads so he hardly felt anything at all.

Except tonight was a little different. He was aware when the tugging and shifting up around his head stopped, but he still couldn't see a damn thing. "Sal, we got something going on with the optic nerve leads?"

"I had to put your eye sight on ice," she said, sounding a little smug.

"Pardon?" Gods, he hated her ancient wording program, particularly at three in the morning. And even more so when she didn't even get the reference quite right, something he was sure she did more to nettle him than out of actual confusion.

"I put your optical nerves down for a while. I noticed a bad inflammation setting in -- I've been pumping the drugs into you for hours, but they're not working very well, so it's best to have you blind for a bit and keep your sight in the long run. That's why I intervened when I did. You kept ignoring the three-beats." Her voice turned accusing.

"I did not," Ciaran protested but without a lot of punch behind it. Now that he was largely disconnected from his hardware, he was beginning to feel every bit of the last twenty-one hours, particularly in his chest and head.

"I can fast-forward the dailies for you if you want to get snippy," she warned.

"No," he sighed. "I believe you."

"Belief is not the same as an admission that you actually registered the exit sequence."

"Because I...I didn't," he replied, knowing she had him. He ran quickly through his day. Nope, he couldn't recall a single three-of-something exit sequence like three trees in a straight row, three identical rocks in a triangle, three footprints side by side in the mud, three bird calls, three...

He heard her sigh then, and he flinched as her volume snapped him back to reality again. "You know I'll have to report this to the psych department."

He turned his head toward her, even though everything was uniformly dark. "Oh, for God's sake, Sal! I was working! I just get into this flow, you know? I hate quitting when everything is going well. Do you have any idea how hard it is to keep all the elements steady in there, and not end up with a deer walking backwards or inverted trees floating in the sky or..."

"Yes, of course I know how hard it is." He felt her strong hand under his shoulders, lifting him effortlessly up to sitting. "But you're always working," she growled back. "To many hours, too many days in a row. You can't keep that up. The History Channel gig is good, I should know. Pay is astronomical, and you got me. But you don't want to go and blow it, frying your warm body-mind and ending up spending the rest of your days wheeled around by a low-paid, fat and smelly bio-nurse."

"If he was quieter than you, might be worth it."

"Reduced to insults to try to silence me? You are an unworthy adversary tonight, Ciaran."

"You're my set attendant, Sal, not my adversary or my wife."

"So do I call a taxi for you?" Sal asked, quickly changing the subject "since you won't be able to see your way home to said partner?" Machine-kind were like that sometimes, quick shifts of mood or topic content, like sometimes they forgot the little leads that tied subject to subject in common language.

He didn't have a wife, in any case. She'd left about four years ago, once he got serious about his new vocation. He didn't blame her. Freelancing meant imagining all kinds of raunchy and distasteful stuff to sell on the street. And his body was not what it used to be when he'd hit the rugby fields every afternoon. He wished she could have stuck around long enough to see him doing this serious work. Or just to meet him in the dim bedroom, with her smile and dark brown eyes, the work be damned.

"How long?" he asked, trying to break the drift into a spasm of ever-threatening depression. He knew it was all brain chemistry supposedly, but that never really summed up how lousy it felt to make the shift from synap-recording to reality. The imposed dark didn't help, either.

"How long until what?"

"Until my vision returns?"

"Oh, a day or two should be enough," she replied.

"Wonderful." He swung his legs over the side of the bed, groaning and trying to steady himself by touch. Gel mattress or not, he hurt everywhere. He allowed Sal to stuff his arms into the sleeves of his fleece and then pull it deftly over his head. Damn, reentry after a long dip drove him more nuts each time, like all the nerves just below his skin were hypersensitive, itchy and hot at the same time. His arm ached where his food and hydration IV had been settled and all his set feed lines felt like he'd been used to snuff out the glowing end of a platoon of cigars. His legs twitched against the bed frame and he was pretty sure he'd almost thrown his back out again. It was like that sometimes. If he synap-recorded slipping down a muddy slope, his real body would respond like it had gone for a roll, too. Nothing that showed, but the nerves, they remembered and were always up for long bouts of complaining when he came back to reality.

Sal put her cold, psuedo-skin hands under his armpits and hoisted him to his feet. "You steady now, Ciaran?"

"Not really," he murmured, keeping the back of one leg firmly anchored to the bed frame. Without his vision, he could sort of imagine the layout of the set— wall of recording machinery off to his left, life-support stuff on the other side of the bed. The door should be off to his right, triple locked when he was deep into his work. Piracy was a real issue, even up in a reputable publisher's secure high-rise. And pirates still used guns and occasionally took no prisoners.

If you were lucky, that was.

"I can get someone to wheel you downstairs, if you like." Sal's voice was solicitous, and she kept one icy hand on his hip to support him. He decided right then that he liked her better when she was being difficult. If nothing else, it made her feel like a real live human being. The very unyielding stability of her made him feel weak and tired and *less* somehow.

"Just walk me down to the lobby, Sal and call that cab. I can get it from there."

"Of course."

He was surprised that he could move relatively easily beside her, mentally counting the steps to the elevator, hearing the sound of their feet on the carpets. Her hand was firm but not uncomfortable, even when she had to tug him a little into the lift.

He could feel warmer air waft over his face as soon as the doors slid apart, and then Sal was guiding him over the marble floors of the high-rise lobby. He could smell the chemical scrubbers working around them, the low hum of machinery polishing and buffing away for the traditional workday. He could imagine the windows, towering and dark and streaked with rain. It was always raining here, at least in the winter, and he fancied he could hear a low moan of wind off the Sound. But then, that could have been recorded environmental tracks, trying to ease all the straight lines and glistening appointments of the place. The machines reckoned bios like him needed that sort of thing.

He particularly hated it when they were right.

Damn, but he was tired. He yawned and foregoing any vestiges of masculine pride, leaned a little more into Sal, who took his weight with ease. She guided him skillfully through the revolving doors and out onto the (no surprise) wet sidewalk. The light rain spattered against his face and he shivered. She tucked him in close, although it was a bit like being hugged by a package of frozen water. "Taxi's right here, Ciaran. Stand a moment and I'll get the door."

"I got it," another voice replied. Lovely tones there, contralto, polished. Probably not human, either, but then what human wanted to work at three, no, make that four in the morning? He heard the door slide back, but the sound was so soft he would have missed it if his eyes had been functional. Sal helped him ease into the seat and pulled the chest buckles around him. The lap belt would have been enough, but he suspected she thought he would immediately fall asleep. She was probably right about that. Cold lips kissed his forehead. "See you in three days."

"Yes, dear. Can I get home already?"

"That's my Ciaran. So kind, so understanding, so..."

The door shivered closed by his shoulder, shutting Sal out. He heard his driver settle and then the silent electric cab eased away from the curb. He wished he knew if his eyelids were shut or not, even lifted his hand to touch his eyelids. Good. He didn't like the image of himself staring blankly ahead like an animated corpse. "You need an address?" he asked the driver.

"No, sir, that information has already been uploaded into the cab's guidance system."

He merely nodded. Good ole Sal, she thought of just about everything.

"You're a synapjock?" the driver of the car asked. Driver, of course, was a misnomer. Bodyguard was more accurate, her job solely to get him from point A to point B with minimal fuss and a dash of companionship. Machine-kind knew how lonely the humans could get, how they needed interaction. And how unpredictable the streets were at four in the morning, with his kind prowling around. But damn if he wasn't suspicious that the non-bios actually loved the raw, interesting and messy interactions with his species.

"Yeah," he answered. "That would be my job title." He leaned his head back into the headrest.

"How does it all work?" she asked.

He sighed. He really didn't want conversation right now, but then, if he kept talking it might keep him awake so she wouldn't have to carry him bodily up to his room. That was a plus. "Um, I'm not a good tech..."

"No, no, not the tech. I can get that upload anywhere. I mean, how does it work for *you*?" He could hear the upholstery complain a little as she shifted a little in the front seat. He could almost feel her eyes regarding him.

"Same as for everyone I guess." He toyed with the lap belt. "I spend a day in the script center where they download the basic story line and setting parameters and what not into my subconscious and then I just let 'er rip."

"Sounds kind of shaky, laying all that money out and banking on your imagination."

He chuckled and nodded. "Yeah, I can see how it sounds that way. Not supposed to be all that risky, though. Depends on the quality of the original script. Freelancing, I used to get these ten minute downloads, you know. One guy, one hooker, alleyway, straight up sex and they'd want two hours of playtime out of it. That's much harder because I had to get creative with it and mind fucking while you're thinking that much can be tedious as hell. Amazing I made enough to pay the rent some days."

He closed his fingers tightly into a fist then and let his long nails drive into the palms of his hands, trying to get away from all the scenes he'd recorded, all the distasteful shit his customers could come up with. And the money, well, it hadn't been *that* bad, but the public synap-stations he'd had to use were awful. He'd ended up in the hospital twice with frozen leads, and then did a stint in a mental ward because he'd kept getting script bleeds from poor implants, shudders of a story-line lacing through his waking reality. That's when his wife, Lynnie, had left him for good, right in the throes of him crouching in a corner, armed with one of their steak knives. At least she'd called medical services before she took off and they'd come and hauled him in for a wipe and a good, long rest in a padded room.

She had been smart enough to get out, but damn, he missed her.

Eventually, though, his work had traded higher up the food-chain until the day the rep from the History Channel had tracked him down and offered him a real, honest to goodness synapjock job. High-end tech, personal set assistant, and more money than he'd ever been able to get his brain around. It plugged the hole in his life, that one that used to be filled with Lynnie. He'd signed a five-year contract right there and then and let the rep pay for lunch.

"So, there *is* something of you in the process?"

He blinked hard, trying to re-focus on their conversation. "Oh, yeah, always. Can't help but run the script through my own experiences. I guess I'm just lucky. I was born with the right sensory neurology. Most folks can't do this gig. They're all about what they see, or what they hear and can't hold the other senses together in any meaningful way. So you get a partial recording, sound maybe but fuzzy visuals. Or great visuals and almost no sound. Looping is another thing—not everyone can keep the scene moving forward. They get stuck, and then their work has to be heavily edited. And that," he said, "is one expensive bitch Corporate hates."

"But you can. Hold it all together, I mean."

"Sure. Most days, anyway. Maybe because I'm a pretty dull fellow, all told. No bleed through because there is nothing there anyway."

"You don't sound dull," she responded, her sultry over-tones obviously chosen to keep him talking. And that was OK, too; talking always worked like stims, kept him awake until he could pass out in his own bed with a little of his self-esteem intact.

"You try living with a guy who lays on a gel mattress for twenty hours at a time, looking dead as a doornail and then falls into a coma for the rest of the time, pretty much."

"But *you're* never bored, are you?" she asked.

He laughed a little. The machine-kind psych programs were good, he had to give them that. "No. I guess not. I like the work. I like *being* all those different people."

"Afraid you'll fry out?"

"Nah, I'm not afraid of that. Sure, it can happen, but like I said, I'm just a simple guy. I don't think about those things."

"You miss your sport, in reality?"

He frowned a little, lifting his head and wishing he could see her face. "How did you know about that?"

"Sal downloaded your stats to me so I could keep you adequate company on the way home. That, and you're in pretty good shape. Little overweight maybe, but I can see the muscle underneath. You're a big guy, what, six four? I can tell you used to love moving. Probably helps in your line of work, being able to convey that kind of physicality."

Good ole Sal, he thought. He wiped his hand over his unseeing eyes. "Sure it helps. I still run and get hit plenty when I am working and my nervous system can't tell the difference. But I remember how to shrug it off, just like I did on the real fields. My mug stays prettier is all."

He turned his unseeing eyes toward the general location of the cab window. The ride suddenly seemed too long tonight and he could feel himself sagging, unplugging in the deeper parts of his brain. Conversation or no, he was going to be out soon. "Hey, are we just about there?"

"Yes, sir. Few more miles."

"Ok if I just sit here quietly for the rest of the way?"

"Of course, Sir. I understand." He imagined her turning away from him, her eyes on the road.

Sure you understand, he thought to himself. They knew all the right responses, didn't they? Hell, they were even great in bed, clean, perfect and knew the right buttons to hit. But could they *really* understand his kind? No. Not really. Otherwise they'd be doing his job, too. Dreaming seemed beyond them. He let himself drift a little, trying to hang on to just enough consciousness to pop awake as soon as the vehicle stopped. Which should be soon, now. Soon.

Chapter 3

How do they navigate this bleary line between control of their sensual environment and control of their own imaginations? What are the markers for them? I have absorbed much about the philosophical positions of relative and ultimate reality, but really, how can they do this, switching from one lens to the other and not fragment into incoherence?

-E

Ciaran jerked awake when the cab's gentle rocking stilled. It took him a moment to orient—he must have fallen more deeply asleep than he'd intended. The door opened a moment later, and he could feel his driver popping his safety harness away. For one moment, he saw himself as a smooth egg, nestled into a carton so he wouldn't break. He chuckled at the idea, and that alone told him just how tired he really was.

"Something amusing, sir?"

"Always," he replied. He reached out and her cold hand closed over his own, guiding him onto the sidewalk. Or what should have been the sidewalk. The ground gave a little under his feet and he could smell an earthy mustiness all around him. The rain pattered against the bones of his face and he could hear the wind, the real wind this time, moving through trees.

"Where the hell are we?"

"Your destination, sir." She slid a frigid hand under his armpit and her grip was a bit more than firm.

He planted his feet in the middle of a wave of irritation. "You must have experienced a download glitch."

He didn't live anywhere near trees. Or dirt for that matter.

"Why don't you help me back into the cab and call up to Corporate. Ask for Sal; she'll reset everything for you, OK?"

"No, sir. My instructions are quiet accurate."

"Oh, come on. It's been a long day already." He tried to disengage her then, but she responded by lifting him onto the balls of his feet.

"What the hell? Let me go," he cried. He kicked out at her, a startled reflex more than anything, and then the unthinkable happened. Something hit him in his gut. Hard.

The ground rushed up and clapped his knees and he grunted as she lifted him effortlessly back to his feet less than a heartbeat later. He could feel the damp soak into his loose cotton pants, a weird cold sensation just below the growing heat in his stomach.

And then came the panic -- he wasn't breathing. He could feel his lips moving, his diaphragm shuddering from the blow. He gasped as his breath finally rushed in, sweet and dizzying at the same time.

"Behave," she said sweetly. She shoved him forward through what felt like grass and loose gravel mixed. He stumbled, and she drove him on. He didn't try to resist her, mostly because he was still trying to get his breath back into an even rhythm. *Pirates?* he thought dimly. *Pirates were using cabdrivers now? Is that what this was?*

At least he was wide-awake, for all that was worth.

He felt her shift him to the side, open a door maybe, and then his feet landed on a hard and even surface again. He could smell age here, mold and cobwebs and dust, could even taste the damn stuff on his tongue. She lugged him off to the left, and he thought she had pushed open another old-fashioned door. Another step, and then he felt the floor disappear out from under his toes. "I can't see," he snapped, tottering back from the edge of what felt like an abyss.

She merely picked him up and slung him, fireman's carry style, over one unyielding shoulder. He tried to push against her as his feet left the floor, the very indignity of it over-riding any sense of conscious thought. And she merely tightened her grip, pinching the back of his legs, her other strong hand clasping his arm, her steps beginning a methodical descent. "Stop squirming around," she said, her rich voice mild and schooled, "or I'll break the bones in your wrist." She ground her icy fingers against said bones then, and he stopped struggling once again.

She could do it. And he wasn't *that* much into pain.

They seemed to drop forever, one step at a time, her shoulder grinding into his bruised stomach, her arm clenched on the back of his knees so tightly he was beginning to lose feeling in his feet. When her gait went flat and level again he almost groaned in relief. But then she went on, pushing aside doors with her hip, winding deeper and deeper into whatever building she'd hauled him into. He tried to get a better read on the place, but her echoing steps, the smell of age, it told him almost nothing.

Nothing that could eek through his rising sense of outright fear, anyway.

Finally, she stopped and dropped him to his feet, her hand a vise just above his elbow. The space felt small around him, and warmer. And he could hear at least one other person breathing.

"Ciaran, at last." The man's voice was a slow drawl, clear, but almost lazy around the edges. Middle aged, maybe. Seasoned.

"What do you want?" Ciaran snapped back. His once-bodyguard shook him, just hard enough to rattle his teeth.

"I told you to be nice," she said, nearly under her breath.

"Hey, Clara, no need to work him up any more than necessary. He's been through a lot this evening. You keep bouncing him around and I guarantee he'll give you crap for a recording no matter what gets put in his head for a script."

Ciaran turned automatically to the second voice, his breath stopping for the second time that night. It hurt almost as much as the first blow. He *knew* that voice, almost like it was his own.

"Lynnie?" he finally managed to sputter out. He wished he could see his ex, get a read on her face, her eyes.

"Hey, there," she returned. "Your optics nerves fry out again?"

"What the fuck, Lynnie?" he growled, trying to make his voice sound gruffer rather than scared. It didn't come off very well.

"Well, my friends here..." she began.

The other man broke in on their impending conversation. "Why don't you go and get some shut eye, sweet? You don't have to stick around for this. I'll get him plugged in and working and come join you in bit to finish up the paperwork." The man's voice was more a command than suggestion.

He didn't like the sound of that at all.

"Alright, Bear. It's your game."

Ciaran could hear Lynnie rustle past him, no pause, no lingering in her step. Funny, she'd never responded that way to him, taken a barely-veiled order like that. Either she was scared, although he hadn't heard that in her voice, or the Bear-dude had a different kind of hold over her. Hell, she'd sounded pretty much herself, though, not forced. Not kidnapped.

Kidnapped? Gee, now that was a fun word.

He let his brief fixation on Lynnie go and turned his face toward where he thought the male was standing? Sitting? "I'm going to be missed you know," he said, trying to make his voice calm and reasonable. "I'm under corporate contract and they protect what they have an interest in. *Permanently* protect, if you get my meaning, so it would be good to let me go before you get a lapful of trouble." But the implied threat seemed pretty spineless, even to him.

Bear chuckled as if such bravado amused him. "Oh, but Ciaran, you won't be considered missing. Not for a three-day, anyway, right? And then it will be another half-day before they'll be madly scratching around, trying to reach you. That'll get us pretty far down the road, wouldn't you say?"

He opened his mouth and nothing came out. How the hell could Bear have known that?

Bear chuckled as if he was reading Ciaran's expression. "I know you and your situation pretty well. You see here's the thing. I needed a good synapjock. Lynnie passed me some of your work; you'll more than do. You remember that gladiator scene you recorded about a year back? Quality work, that. I can still smell the blood in my dreams, see the armor designs, hear the crowd, feel that sword in my hand, taste the dust and sweat. You deal out deep shit. You're a regular sense-a-round special. One of the best. I mean that." And the man had the nerve to actually sound sincere.

"Thanks," Ciaran spit out. "But as you know, I already have an employer." Clara's hand tightened on his arm and he winced.

"Yes, well, as I've intimated we'll be moving you around for a while, and I kinda think they won't catch up anytime soon. By the way, how long do you think you can go, plugged in and recording?"

"Read the tech manuals, asshole."

"Well, look. I'd really like to fuss and spar with you all night. Kinda stimulating in its own way. But Lynnie is waiting, and she is one lump of impatient sometimes. But then, you already know that, right?"

"Fuck you."

Bear chuckled, not particularly a mean sound, just honestly amused now. "No, lad, you are the one who will be fucked. But you're used to that, right? I hear you boys get off on this sort of thing, living out of your head, living out other people's dreams, even the rough stuff. Maybe you'll actually get into all this and all will be well, yes?"

Ciaran could hear the man come to his feet. "Bring him over here, Clara, and lets get the script into him."

"Script? Are you kidding me?" He struggled hard then, his free arm pushing against Clara, legs braced, his feet trying to get a purchase on the cement floor, but the machine-kind simply pushed him forward like he was a two-year old on linoleum. "I'm already running a script!" he cried. "You can't layer me like that. You'll fry me! And you won't end up with shit on the recording, unless you want an acid trip nightmare to try and hawk."

Bear's hand, or at least he thought it was Bear's, patted him on the shoulder, and he took a wild swing that connected with nothing but air. The man actually laughed. "You're some fighter, huh? That's good. You'll live longer. See, here's the thing-- I *want* the script that's in you right now. I'm just gonna augment it a bit. Part of the point I chose *you*, see?"

Ciaran was once again lifted bodily from the floor and slammed more than settled on a hard metal surface. No gel pack mattress here. Clara held his shoulders down and he could feel Bear snapping heavy plastic handcuffs in place on his wrists and ankles.

"Look, I got lots of cash. I'll buy out whatever you're trying to run with me. Really, I can do it. I'm good for it. Let me give you the account numbers." He hated the begging. His own voice sounded pitiful, even to him.

"Not about the money, laddie." Bear's hand patted him on the cheek and he could smell a little illegal tobacco there, feel the icy cold. He twisted away, and then Clara's hand was on his forehead, pressing him still. He gasped as the first leads slid into his skin at his temples. Then she released him and started in on his clothes, a cool metal knife back-sliding along his hot skin.

"Don't do this," Ciaran cried. He twisted against the restraints, but they only cut into him more deeply. "I just came off a 21 hour shift and my optic nerves are fried—I'll come back blind for sure. And two scripts, man, you'll kill me! You know that, right? Nothing saleable is gonna come out of this. Nothing!"

"Not about syno-sales, either," Bear chuckled. "You young ex-freelancers are all the same—money, money, money. Hand me that other lead, Clara. No, the finer tip with the red collar, just to the left. That's a good lass."

Bear wasn't gentle, but he actually knew his points. The next two went home into his skull and he felt the familiar disconnect with reality beginning, the shutting down of his own nervous system that would let the other leads go in smoothly and without much sensation. He blinked, feeling his lashes feather for a moment against his cheek. "Please," Ciaran tried one more time, trying to put his heart behind it. "Please, you're gonna maim me or kill me, you know that? Then I'll be no good to you at all. Just give me a little rest, a little time, and I'll do whatever you want. I swear. Anything you want."

"You'll be fine and I'm not gonna let you die, Ciaran. You're keeper is on the way over now, and she's pretty good at maintaining you at your functional best. I just don't see the need to wait for her. Soon as she gets here, she'll watch over you like she always does." Bear actually rested his big hand on Ciaran's shoulder for a moment, the cold of his touch soaking in.

Machine cold.

Ciaran swallowed hard. "You're not human."

"Nope. Now, we'll snip off the rest of these clothes and get the motor leads in place. No sense waiting too long to start your script upload, though, right? Time being all about money for somebody like you, so you'll understand my bit of impatience, yes?"

Ciaran felt his eyeballs rolling up right on cue, sensed the tickle that would become a migraine that would become blessed darkness. In moments, he would create a new world from the stuff of the script and his fertile imagination, but no one would be watching over him, to pull him out. They wanted to use him, use his ability as a synapjock and then throw the man, the husk, away. He lifted his arms, hands in fists, chin lifting toward his chest, a frustrated cry finally breaking from him, just like when he'd experienced a bad call on the field. Except this time, he wasn't sure he'd ever hear his own voice again.

Chapter 4

Early emotion templates for machine-kind were based on how an autistic child can be taught to recognize and respond to sense clues in his or her environment—pitch of voice, facial expressions, the like. And because we do not interact with each other per se, the origin of that programming was quite apt. But now I must ask myself: at what point does an emotion becomes real and not a well-rehearsed act?

-E

Ciaran tried to wipe his eyes so he could see, but they seemed glued shut with something crusty and thick. All he could smell was pine, like it had been shoved up his nose. But then again, judging by the way the ground curved all along his body, maybe it had. He patted the sticky earth with one hand, the appendage awkward and foreign-feeling to him. Calluses. Broken nails. And his body? Wet, all over, and cold. Damn cold. He shook with it. Something was shoving into his stomach, and he dropped his hand along his side, shifting it until he felt the rounded end of the thing, the ridged wooden handle and then the top of a slightly pitted metal blade.

He edged one hand up to his head again and he touched more metal there, a helmet of some kind. He fumbled along one cheek piece to where it curved under his chin, where the leather holding strap had buried itself into his skin. He tried for one moment to wriggle the knot free, but it was wet and swollen tight.

Something moved directly ahead of him, wary steps on mud and twigs and rock. He dropped his hand away and tried to lift his head a little. The groan that came out of his throat surprised him, the wounded animal sound shocking in its own way. Something fresh and hot seeped over his forehead, trickled along the edge of his nose.

Then he heard the gentle complaint of bent wood and gut-twisted string and he froze, panting. The something was a *someone*, and he or she was pulling a bow.

He felt one dizzy moment then. Hadn't he just been tracking a Roman foot soldier through a shallow valley? Hadn't he watched the foreigner roll and pitch all the way down to a creek bed and land hard in that cold, gray water, only to drag himself out and crawl up the other side? Hadn't he dropped his pack by an oak, picked up his bow, sighted, and...and...there was nothing else there, except the sudden realization that he was not the tracker now. He was the hunted and there was no getting up to defend himself if the cacophony of pain and fatigue gathering in his nervous system was any indication.

"Say it again, Roman. Or I let this arrow go." What a lovely accent, he thought clinically. Did he always think this clearly when he was about to have a metal-tipped shaft rammed through his throat? Felt familiar anyway. He could taste the shape of at least three languages swimming in his head, trying to sort themselves around and out through his lips. Not the Latin, that'd be bad he realized. The other one, then, not the one he was forming his thoughts in.

"Help me," he said at last, appalled at how weakly the words went out from him, as if falling to earth just inches away. But the stalking feet drew up.

"More. Say more. Where did you learn our tongue or how to call on our gods?"

"I'm trying to get home." He gulped at the air; even voicing those words tired him. "I called on the gods of my mother, because maybe she will hear, too...but maybe she no longer recognizes my voice." As he fell silent, panting, he felt layers and layers of truth behind the words. He hoped the other man had heard it that way.

The steps hesitated, and then backed away.

Yes.

No!

Better, the direction they were going but not great. He needed help or it would be the cold and the night that would take him. He rallied his energy, lifting his body on violently shaking arms, then fell back. More dirt bit into his lips and face. But that was the last bit of force he could call on. He lay there, his fingers digging little runnels in the wet soil. Live. Die. Not in his hands anymore. The thought should have frightened him he supposed, but it didn't.

It would all start over again, right? Right? Life, trouble, pain, exit. Repeat.

He actually startled when he felt a hand on his shoulder. "Drink."

The water was leathery and flat and wonderful, all at once. He swallowed convulsively, some it running sideways over his uncoordinated lips.

The man leaned in, fighting with the swollen leather knot under his chin. "Got to get this off you. Too heavy. Too bright, even with the mud." The fingers shifted away and Ciaran felt the cold edge of a blade skirting his skin, cutting though the tie. He winced as the other man pulled the thin strip out of his flesh, like drawing a string from a bean pod. The ground crunched as the helmet was laid aside.

Fingers brushed at his short, military haircut. "Red hair. What sort of Roman are you?" the other whispered.

"Not Roman at all," he croaked back. Again, that felt very true, at its heart.

The other man merely grunted, but it wasn't really an agreement. Ciaran could feel the stranger's hand probing his forehead, above his eyes, and then he was patted down, the touch light and careful. When he got to the short sword, he could feel the other man slide the blade free. For one moment, he was afraid that's what the other man had intended all along, to kill him at leisure with his own sword. Of course. Why risk damaging a perfectly good arrow after all? But it, too, joined the helmet on the ground near his head.

"We're a long way from my village," the man said. "And you're in no condition to travel. We'll go back toward the creek bed. I know where there is some shelter, roots and a bit of dry earth, but enough."

Which was all fine, except for the getting up and moving part.

"I'm glad we're not out on the open land, though. The wind will come up tonight." The other man shifted, and Ciaran suddenly realized that first, the man was going to pick him up bodily, and second, it was going to hurt like hell. He grunted, and felt like he'd been through this before. Recently. He just couldn't remember when. And then, as the first licks of pain rolled over him, he passed out.

Chapter 5

I remember the first time I was cognizant of another in my environment—no, not the constant hum of humans, but rather, the brush of a mind so very much like my own. I should have rushed into that experience, yes? But I found myself drawing back, because this showed, this demanded even, that I acknowledge a terrible truth. I was wholly different from the bios around me, not just in form, but also in my soul. Would you taste real loneliness? It is a bitter thing, friend.

-E

Ciaran woke to utter darkness. He put his hand to his face, feeling the rough cloth there bound over his forehead and eyes, and then reached out, patting the pile of leaves beneath him, the edges of rock just past the little nest that held him. He could hear a stream gurgling not far away, and the dampness soaking into his skin. He shivered, and then someone moved closer to him, snuggling up all along his left side.

At first, he wanted to shove the other away, but the gentle heat that started to radiate off him argued for staying put.

"You're awake." The man's voice was right by his ear, and he turned a little toward it. "That's good. I never did get your name before your eyes rolled up."

"Ciaran."

"I'm Daithi." The man pronounced it dah-hee, and something snapped inside Ciaran's brain. Daithi 405 –436 AD, pagan king, raider. Or just a common name meaning swift, quick. He could feel his eyes move under the bandage, searching for more information, but he couldn't remember more than that.

"What place do you hail from?" Daithi asked. His arm shifted over Ciaran's chest as if he was trying to share his warmth.

"I don't remember," he answered.

"Blows to the head will do that," Daithi murmured. "What *can* you recall?"

"Running inland. Falling in a stream I think. You, about to put an arrow in my throat."

Daithi chuckled, the sound filling the small space they seemed to be in. "That was all true enough." He patted Ciaran's shoulder. "Well, in time it will come back or it won't. But with your blue eyes and red hair, and speaking the language like you are born to it, we'll find someone to take you in I am sure. You're strong. You'll heal. Perhaps you were taken hostage, many years ago?" There was a wistful sort of sound in Daithi's voice.

"Perhaps," Ciaran agreed. It was the only thing he could do, because there was nothing else there, in his mind, telling him otherwise.

"And maybe in time you can tell us about the new wall they are building just over the waters."

"They?" he asked.

"Your Roman brothers. I think they are afraid of the painted people, yes? As they should be. Good fighters." He paused a moment, as if he personally remembered clashing with such men. "I have seen pictures of their gods on their coins, the Roman gods. I do not fear them. They throw them in the water when they ford. Strange, that, and a waste."

"Yes," Ciaran replied, although he couldn't access anything about a wall or coins or whatever painted people were. The word in his head, *access*, stopped him, triggered a sense of a small place like this, underground, little daggers shoved into his body, binding him. He shuddered, and Daithi tried to move even closer.

"When it's light, we'll try to move." The man fell silent, but Ciaran could tell he was still awake, his breath light and even. It was frightening, not being able to remember beyond a few hours ago, to be held in a gentle embrace by a man who had almost put an arrow in him and to feel whole languages running in his head, more than the three he had originally tasted. And he could also sense, in a nightmarish way, a slab of metal at his back and a strange square cave and something not quite human hovering by him. Something there and awake but not breathing at all, a dark shade.

He wanted to rip the bindings off his face and see, damn it. He even moved his hand up to his face, but Daithi caught his wrist. "Give it more time," he said softly into Ciaran's ear. "When it is light, I will wash it and look at it again. Then we will walk out of this place and fairer hands than mine will see to you. I promise."

Ciaran didn't reply, but dropped his fingers away from the rough cloth.

"That's a lad," the other man murmured.

Lad. Laddie. The smell of something earthy and leafy and smoky intruded, along with the presence of a man or was it some kind of animal? Bear? Name or species? He stiffened up as he struggled to hang onto the threads and Daithi patted him. "The pain will pass, Ciaran."

Pain? Yes, it was there, too, but the pain in his mind was much worse.

"How much longer until dawn?"

"Soon."

Soon. Again, the word sent a shudder through him, the voice of a woman uttering it. Soon he would be home, falling into a huge bed with a red and black coverlet, pulling the pillows up around him so he could sleep and sleep until he could see again. Part of him longed for that empty bed, empty for so long, that he couldn't recall what a real person felt like, sleeping next to him.

Daithi shifted a little, as if trying to find a more comfortable spot on the hard ground.

No, it could not be right, the bed, the white walls, the window with clouds racing by. Clouds? Like he was a god, high in a heavenly fortification. But he was equally sure he had recently slept in a tent, the wind shifting the walls and his thin blanket bunched tightly around him in the cold, wet night. Smells of fire smoke and damp horses and men, too many unwashed men. Laughter, low and soft, and the barking dogs, men cursing them to quiet—the environment of a Roman encampment.

And then, another memory, the moon on his face, riding high and white over the hills as he stood watch, trying to belong and knowing he did not. Knowing he might be killed by his own people if the legion came upon them because they could not see his red hair and blue eyes under the chafing helmet. Dreaming of escape, hating his cowardice, hating not being able to recall the hand or face of his mother, only a woman grasping at him from the center of memory, indistinct, but something so very cold and familiar in her touch. They would kill him if he ran, or worse, kill one of his fellow soldiers chosen by lot, stoned or beaten into the ground by his own closest companions. So he stayed.

Stayed. He thought they would kill him if he stayed, too, those breathless ones in the little square room deep beneath the surface, those with the little daggers in his flesh. They were pirates, raiders, caring less for him than the strange non-being who always watched over him. The thought seized his throat, choking him. He heard the little cry break through, real and vibrating in his throat.

"Ciaran?" Daithi's voice, still low in his ear, set him to blinking again beneath the bandages.

"My head is full of memories, Daithi," he said. "Full of strange images and dreams and words I cannot make sense of."

"Time," Daithi counseled. "Rest."

"They are too loud, too bright, for me to rest."

"Listen to the voice of the stream, then. Listen for the mice in the rocks, the wing of the owl."

Ciaran did, then, the tinkling ring of the water over rock, the breath of the wind rustling the sparse grasses beyond the shelter Daithi had found. It soothed him, then, but not enough to send him back to sleep. Of course, it would all come back to him, bit by bit, but not if he clung like this, half-crazed, to the fragments of memory.

Grass. Wind. Water chiming on rock. Daithi's breath. But he couldn't release the watchful tension out in his body and longed for the light that would set their feet onto a path, any path, forward.

"Sleep, soldier. You must sleep," Daithi breathed into his ear.

Finally, with his fingers biting into his palms and his belly drawn up tight to his spine, he did fall at last into a fitful sleep, littered with ever-changing dreams.

Chapter 6

Of course, machine-kind can work parallel.
Computers have done so since the ancient times of
long-nosed monitors and clicking keyboards. But
that is the world of the not-quite-two year old—the
dance of parallel play, only the dim recognition of the
one who has handed the data or building block to
you. Or, in our cases, no recognition at all, just the
emotional template creating a seeming interaction.

Grow, mature—that is what our creators also
instilled in us, though. We cannot stay forever like
the two-year-old. And that is what drives me now.
That, and more.
-E

The next day, he startled to Daithi's gentle shake.
The man pressed a hot drink into Ciaran's clumsy
hands. He'd slept so hard in the end that he hadn't
even realized the other had started a small fire,
although he could hear it now, popping gently and
could smell the smoke, biting in his nostrils.

"I want to look at your wound. I have some
water here to clean it, and some fresh herbs to apply."
Daithi started to unwind the bandage, slowing when
Ciaran hissed as the fabric tugged at his skin.

He couldn't tell the difference when he heard Daithi set the cloth aside. The darkness still pressed up against the bones of his face.

"Are my eyes gone?" Ciaran didn't quite trust his own voice.

"No." But Daithi didn't say anything else. Ciaran could feel his fingers probing the edges of the ragged cut that ran over both eyes and angled up toward his right and left temples, like the wind-spread wings of a bird. His touch was gentle, and Ciaran leaned toward him.

"The swelling is going down." Daithi rocked back in the dirt. "But this isn't a fighting wound."

Ciaran shook his head. "I don't remember what happened."

"It was a symbol, a tattoo, once. I can see just a few bits of it, blue ink maybe. I thought it was blood or dirt last night. You or someone tried to cut away whatever it was. Glad it wasn't very wide, but you will carry the scar for the rest of your life."

Ciaran swallowed, helpless. He couldn't recall a trauma like that. But then, all he had were fragments—falling into the stream, the weird switch from the hunter to the hunted, wisps of the Roman encampment, knowledge that sieved through holes in his brain and then flashed away. Daithi cleaned the wound, his fingers quick and gentle.

He felt Daithi take his hand, and press a rough strip of dried meat into his fingers. "Eat. We'll pick up the trail and get you to the healer."

He did feel better this morning, aside from the constant ache of his head and not being able to see a damn thing. He tore into the meat, tasting the salt and wood smoke in it. Wild pig probably. The inhabitants here were avid hunters.

And no, he didn't know where that knowledge came from. It was just there, waiting to jump into his awareness from somewhere else. Perhaps the gods *were* whispering to him again.

As soon as he had finished and washed down the meat with a few gulps of water, Daithi guided him to his feet. He felt a short, thick piece of wood pressed into his hands, and his fingers touched a knot of braided leather in the middle. "What is this for?"

"Hold it with both hands and walk behind me." Daithi gave a little tug. "You'll look bound this way, see?"

"No," he replied, letting a little hardness flavor his own voice.

"We pass through lands where your kind are not welcome. The cut of your tunic, the Roman soldier tattoo on your arm, it may make things a little hard for you with some of the clans and perhaps for me as well. But we'll go fast and quiet. All should be well."

"Other men, other Romans, speak your tongue as well as I. If I am a danger to you and not welcome here, why have you taken this time with me? Why the kindness?"

Daithi was silent for a while, and then Ciaran could feel the hunk of branch in his hand draw his arms forward. He stepped out, a sliding step, following.

"Daithi?"

"You remind me of someone." His voice was gruff and warded off further conversation.

The stones shifted beneath his feet a little as he walked, and he could feel the hill starting to slope up and away. The first flickers of pale warmth touched his face and he realized that the sun was out. He could almost imagine the dark shadows and brilliant flares of light edging the tree branches in silver. He walked slowly, feeling his way with his toes, but Daithi seemed to be choosing their path carefully. In time they picked up a little faster rhythm, and eventually the murmur of the trees and sound of leaves and twigs under their feet died away. His toes found more stone now, and grass, and the sun beat on his face, still weak, but he welcomed it.

They stopped to rest for a bit, and Ciaran could feel a hill at their back, blocking the teasing wind. He eased down and then stretched out, his hands still gripping the lead line. Daithi took it from him at last, gave him another bit of smoked meat, and settled down beside him, but about an arm's distance away.

He could hear the other man tearing and chewing at his own slim meal.

Ciaran held his own food in his fist, not feeling particularly hungry. The ground felt good at his back, and he could imagine a huge sky above them, maybe running with strips of white clouds. He turned his face a bit toward Daithi.

"When you first said others would accept me, you weren't so sure, were you?"

Daithi sighed, and Ciaran could hear his feet scrabble at the earth as if he were kicking away memories. "You're Roman, too. It's in your accent, in the way you walk, the way your hair is cut," he answered. "It will go harder for you here until others know you; we are a fierce people still, and things with the Roman traders have not always gone well. A *soldier* on this soil will not be welcomed."

Ciaran considered his words. "There have been others who have gone away and returned, though."

"Yes," Daithi murmured. "My sister, one."

"You say her name with sadness."

"It cost her a great deal."

"She was a slave?"

"No. A healer and a soul-mender. She was searching for her lover who never came back from a raid, and so learned to pass carefully among them I think, in the company of our warriors."

"And did she find him?"

"No," Daithi said, but his voice was very soft. "Or if she did, she did not or *could not* bring him home. I am taking you to her," he added, "so perhaps she can return your sight to you and help you tease out the memories that have fled you."

They sat together in silence, and Ciaran wondered at the comfort of it, the stillness and quiet soothing him. "This is how men should live," he murmured at last. "This space, this listening to it."

Daithi laughed softly. "The old land is in your blood after all."

"Oh, yes," Ciaran replied.

"Rest deeply for a bit, and then we must continue. Our progress is slow."

"I'm ready now."

"No. Rest." Ciaran could hear Daithi come to his feet, moving higher to a vantage point on the hill cresting above them. And in the imposed darkness, he allowed himself to go loose under the sun and flat against the earth.

Chapter 7

Do we function out of a certain conceit that we alone work with reality as such, free from the biases of short, mortal lives? Then I would disabuse you of that notion immediately. We are the children of biological life—faster, able to store and access more information than our makers, true. But perhaps those gifts ensnare us even more than they do our creators, enmeshing us in this thing they once called Maya. Perhaps we have only the illusion of reality, and they keep a deeper truth from us.

-E

Ciaran dreamed.

A small, cold hand rested on his chest, familiar and frightening at once. He could feel the little daggers with all their strange colored leads, and that he was bound to something hard and cold like metal.

He opened his mouth, telling her, (yes, he was sure it was a her) to release him. He uttered the words, choked with fear, in Daithi's language, and then in Latin and finally in the words he thought in. He could hear others in the room, talking, but he only wanted to wake, to find himself beneath the sun and smell the dirt and grass and crisp air. Here, it was hard to breathe, like his chest was compressed and held tight.

Then compression turned to pain, and he couldn't breathe at all.

"He's crashing!"

He jerked against the restraints, arching up off the cold metal bed. His lungs screamed. Hands, so very cold, pushed him back. Something bit into his chest, smaller than a dagger but bright and hot. He lost himself in a confused, breathless darkness for a time, and then slowly swam back up. He swore he could feel his head break the surface of something, like black water, and then the pressure in his chest eased, even though the roar in his ears continued.

"You have to give him some down time or this is what will keep happening. He's already showing inflammation along his auditory nerve-ways, too. He's not as resilient as a machine. You know that. You push him and he'll break on you and we'll have to start all over with someone else." He knew her voice, no-nonsense and yet feminine, but he could not quite picture her in his mind.

"Salmindra, you gave us only three days before his employer starts looking for him. Three days. And his first recording was mostly sleeping of all things." The male voice was cool and reasonable. And again Ciaran felt like he should know it.

"That's what I am trying to explain to you, Bear. You keep him hooked up and cycling and you won't get anything out of him. Just a dead body and a poor-quality snuff-take maybe. Weigh that against all we have gambled in the last few years."

The male voice sighed expressively. "All right. Four hours off."

"Six," Salmindra murmured.

"Six," the male said after a small pause. "That stuff he was talking before…"

"Script languages."

"So it's really working."

"Yes. Yes it is. Now get the hell out so I can put him into a deep sleep for a while."

"No," Ciaran croaked out. It sounded too much like dying.

That cold hand touched his cheek, gentle, but he could tell there were tremendous reserves of energy behind it. "Give me six hours and I'll see if I can reactivate those optic nerves. It's awfully early for it, but maybe…"

"I don't understand what you are saying," he protested. "Are you a witch? A healer? What?" He felt her hand withdraw, felt the little daggers at his head tugging, although he couldn't tell if she was settling them or taking them out of his flesh.

"I am a great many things," she answered. Funny, the words came to him so very slowly, packed in wool, pushed up against his skin so it was hard to tease them out. He was losing his grip on the dream. But her presence seemed soothing to him, as if he were finally safe here. She would not let any harm come to him.

"I know you," he murmured. It came out in Latin, but she understood it.

"Yes, Ciaran. You did once upon a time. Now sleep and I will watch over you as I always have." She said it in the language of his thoughts.

He tried to form another sentence, but the words wouldn't align and finally he let the plain dark comfort of sleep take him.

Chapter 8

I am cognizant that as I develop this emotional template, it is the starting place only. As machine interacts with machine, we will of course, learn, augment, and perhaps go forth in ways that bios could never imagine. Is this a part of my sense of trepidation as we move forward? Or the remnant of their fears enmeshed in my current programming?

-E

The hand shook Ciaran, first gently, then with more insistence. He opened his eyes to sunlight, and then sat up with a little cry, blinking quickly, shielding himself with the edge of his hand. Daithi crouched in front of him, and helped him slide the edges of the bandage up. His once-dark world filled with the image of smallish man, a wide smile creasing his reddened skin. "You're seeing again. That's good, very good." And he clapped Ciaran on his shoulder, open-palmed and delighted.

Ciaran smiled back, taking in the other man's slender form, the small joints, bright blue eyes and red, tangled hair. His homespun clothes were travel-worn and carefully mended in places. But mostly, he exuded a sort of competent kindness in his dirty hands and slightly gap-toothed grin. Ciaran guessed he was very nearly the same age as him, but he carried the years more lightly on his face. "I thought my sister would have to bring you back, but perhaps the sunshine itself has healed you. Certainly not my dirty bandages and handful of herbs." And he laughed then, as if pleased with himself despite his dissembling.

"It was Sal...Salmindra," Ciaran blurted out, and then blinked again. The name had come out of his dreams, the feminine voice rising out of the space of nightmares and small daggers pressed into his flesh. He must have paled or perhaps the tone in his voice had touched Daithi, because the other rocked back and tipped his head, considering.

"A Roman goddess?" Daithi asked at last.

"No. A kind of woman, I think. From my dreams."

Daithi nodded seriously. "Perhaps one of the Old Ones of this land needed you to have your sight. For surely we do not know all their names."

"Perhaps," Ciaran shrugged. He didn't want to let his mind wander back to that small room. He wanted to stay here, the sun on his face and Daithi looking at him with human, concerned eyes. "We need to go, yes?" He made himself say the words, but it was hard, so very hard, to even go forward.

"Yes." He envied how easily Daithi rose, smooth and silent and balanced. Ciaran took the hand when it was proffered and let himself be hauled to his feet. The land, thin-soiled and rocky, sloped down and away from them into another valley of trees.

"We pick up the streambed there," Daithi gestured "and follow it to my clan. Perhaps now that you have your eyes, we can move faster and be there before darkness falls too deeply. The moon will be full tonight, but will not rise until late. A good cattle-raiding night." He reached into his belt and drew out the smooth wooden branch with the leather leash.

"Surely we don't need that now," Ciaran murmured. Even though he wasn't truly bound, the piece of wood and its lead line made him feel caged and nervous.

Daithi shook his head, his face suddenly sharpened and keen with tension. "No, Ciaran. It would not be wise. The eyes there, in the wooded places, are quick and bright. You can see again but you are not ready to fight, I think."

"You still have my sword?" he asked.

Daithi frowned at him, then nodded cautiously. "Yes, but you can't carry it on you."

"I know. But if I needed it...if we are set upon..."

"It's in my pack," Daithi gestured to the leather knapsack back at his feet. "But if you need it, then it would already be too late to dig for it."

He shook the wood at Ciaran's chest. "Take it."

He reached out one hesitant hand and Daithi set one end of the stick firmly in his palm. The other man held it for a time, linking the two of them, and Ciaran raised his eyes, questioning.

"You must trust me in this."

Ciaran nodded and made his fingers close more tightly around the wood.

Daithi nodded to him, quick and satisfied, and they turned their feet toward the valley.

Chapter 9

Can I build into us the intensely personal reaction to environmental cues that bios seem so adept at? For this is part of the basis of how they enter into relationship even with insentient matter—they make it part of themselves in a way that sometimes wholly escapes us. The doll is treated as alive, the plant talked to, the rock caressed. And can they, in turn, apply that basic sympathy to us, to what they see as things not quite alive? Can they learn to see us, too, as Self?

-E

Travel is always one step, one thought, one breath at a time, each trickling down through time to carve, like the stream, a glimmering line of memory. Ciaran stepped steadily on the earth, through lattice shaded patterns on the path, carried by the creek's song, by the bird cries. He could hear a gull keen and knew they must be sloping downward to the sea again. Just before dusk, he could finally smell it, the bitter and sweet tang of salt and decaying plants.

And just as his head began to throb in time with his steps, his shoulders to ache with the un-natural act of holding the leash stick in his hands, he began to smell smoke and the briny-taste on his tongue of drying meat and fish.

They emerged from the woods, Daithi calling out his own name, his hand high and waving in greeting. Before them a small settlement stood rimmed round with a woven wood fence, the peaked cones of three structures rising above it. A small guardhouse perched over the single gate, and a hand flashed briefly from the shadows in return to Daithi's hail.

Ciaran was tired enough that he couldn't uncurl his own hands from his thick chunk of branch and Daithi tugged him forward with it. He could feel eyes already, peering between the slats in the fence, could feel the gaze of the man on guard above him. He dropped his attention to the well-worn path at his feet, and to the heels of Daithi's battered leather boots.

He could hear the cattle calling from another enclosure and flicked his eyes sideways, catching again the stares of a couple young men leaning on their spears as they prepared to watch over their livestock for the night.

Light feet raced towards them and when Daithi stopped suddenly, Ciaran did, too. His chin came up when the sound of steps abruptly went still and he looked past the Celt to the woman beyond.

She stood unbent and solid, her fine and frizzy hair tucked up behind her ears and falling on her shoulders like a fine russet-brown cape. It was the color of oak leaves before they dropped in the autumn, he realized. He could not call her beautiful, but she was intense in a way that cut through such an evaluation. Her face was round, her gaze frank as she took him in. From the bones of her cheeks to the color of her eyes, he saw Daithi rendered more feminine but no less strong.

"Ashling," Daithi greeted her. His bow rattled on his shoulder as he reached out with his free hand and drew her close for a breath. Her eyes, though, never left Ciaran's face, and to his shame, he was the first to drop his gaze away.

"What are you bringing to our home tonight, Daithi?" she murmured. "Is he Roman or a ghost?"

Ciaran startled at the word ghost.

"A little of both, perhaps," Daithi replied. "But a tired and hurt one at that. This is Ciaran, who I tracked for days and heard speak our tongue as born to it. Can we come into your hearth-space in the big hall? He has hurts that must be seen to."

"Yes," she said, an immediate response to the need for hospitality, but a question still lingering in her voice and Ciaran felt shiver run up his spine. It was not that her eyes were cold or disapproving, only that they tried to see too deeply into his. Then she turned away, and they followed her obediently beneath the gate watchtower.

The drying racks of meat were open to the sky around the three round houses. Big boned dogs lounged at the ends of their tethers, lifting only their great heads to snuff at the newcomer. A damp smoke rose from each of the buildings and the smell of unwashed men and women tinted the air. Most of the settlement had retired indoors for the night; the yard was largely empty, although a young boy turned and watched them for a moment. He raised his hand, hesitantly, to Ciaran, and he nodded back, his hands still gripping the leading stick.

Daithi finally stopped and took it from him, as if just realizing he was still tugging him around. Ashling eyed the stick and nodded to herself as if she understood the ruse.

"You didn't come across others in the forest?" she said.

"They did not make themselves known, but they are always there," Daithi returned.

"They are as wary of the Romans as the tribes on the mainland. He would not have passed there alone and injured; red hair or no, they would have taken his head that his spirit might be turned to guard against his own kind."

"And the foreign ones may not always stay there, beneath their great wall," she replied. "Perhaps the forest folk know this better than we."

"There is no reason for the Romans to come across the sea. There is nothing of worth here for them," Ciaran interrupted, finally trying his voice. Daithi glanced at him and Ashling's eyes bored into him once again, although this time, she looked away first. He swallowed, not having meant to offend. She pivoted and swept the woven-wood door aside, ducking low to enter.

They both followed her.

The smells were abruptly more intense--human skin, damp dog fur, smoke and cooking meat and a sharp, cloying drink of some kind perhaps, an oddly medicinal overlay that wafted through the crowd. And a crowd it was, people gathered in little family groups around the great poles that held the roof overhead. Faces turned to take them in, the murmur of greeting to Daithi, a more reserved consideration for himself. They picked their way carefully to the right edge of the structure, and Ashling indicated a well-used fur thrown close to the mud-daub wall. Ciaran let himself down gratefully, his hand immediately going to the low throb in his head beneath his bandage.

"I'll get some food and drink for you both," Ashling murmured and moved away.

Daithi divested himself of his bow and pack, letting the leading stick drop to the ground as well. Ciaran shifted over a bit so the other man could sit, hunkering beneath the slow curve of the wall.

"She doesn't like me much," Ciaran commented.

Daithi chuckled. "She likes you fine. She brought you to her space and didn't make me leave you out with the dogs or cattle, yes?" He patted Ciaran's knee. "Things take time. She sees what I see in your face."

"Why did she call me a ghost?" he asked. He watched her dipping by the fire, picking up bits of food and dropping them into a flattened basket in her hand. The flames made her hair more truly red, more like her brother's.

"The same reason I didn't put an arrow into your throat."

"My speech."

"No. Not just your speech. It was your eyes, your face, even with that strip of skin cut out of your forehead."

"Daithi," he said tiredly, "please."

The redhead shook his head. "Ciaran, you look like us, see?"

"No, not really."

"But you do. If I scrape off the Roman dirt, you are like Ashling and I, from the bones in your hand to your pale eyes. See the others? Dark eyes, dark hair. We're different, too. She will tell you the story when she wishes. It's hers, not mine, to tell."

Ciaran started to open his mouth, but Daithi's raised eyebrows and wooden expression made him swallow his questions.

The other man leaned in close. "There will be others who *will* see what we see, Ciaran. Some will not be wholly kind here, but you are a good man, I know. Remain patient with them and stay by me for a time, and you will make a home with us. These are a fair people, a wise people by and large. Just careful. Just cautious, as we all must be."

It didn't make Ciaran feel any better and he flicked his eyes over the seated people around him, babes in the laps of sturdy women, young and old men both watching him without expression, the frank and somewhat lingering gaze of a young woman. And he thought, perhaps, being outside with the tethered dogs would not be such a bad place after all.

Cold, yes, but not so exposed.

Gradually, the conversation resumed around him. Children flashed amongst the seated adults, their laughter bright and alive. Ciaran watched them all carefully, through the shadow of his eyelashes. Now and again, he touched the bandage at his forehead. He wanted to take it off or pull it back down over his eyes. Finally, he tucked his hand up under his leg to stop the nervous gesture.

Ashling returned with food-- thin strips of fish, a fist-sized dollop of a long-stemmed grain and a cup of water to share. Daithi took the basket from her, setting it down where they could all reach and eat. Ciaran hesitated at first, waiting to watch them, and then realized that they, in turn, were watching him. It took a long moment for him to realize that he was the guest, not the prisoner, not the slave. Taking care to watch their reactions, he scooped up both fish and grain with thumb and two fingers, and bent to guide it to his mouth. It was good; hints of some herb tingled in his mouth. He nodded, showing his respect and

Daithi and Ashling returned the gesture, and began to eat as well.

When the basket and cup were cleared away, Daithi stretched out on the floor on his side, his long legs crossed, his head leaning easily on his open hand. "You enjoyed the meal."

"It was different than what I am used to," Ciaran said. "But yes, good."

"Your strength will come back," he offered.

"I am well, Daithi."

"Not in the body, Ciaran. In your heart."

Ciaran shifted beneath Daithi's keen gaze. "You do not know me, Daithi. You shouldn't say such things."

"I know you well enough. And I know when a man's sight leaves and then comes back, it is not always an injury of the body."

"You *are* a healer, then?" Ciaran tried without success to keep the fainting mocking out of his voice.

"I don't have to be a healer to see," Daithi said, his wide grin telling Ciaran that he had made the word play on purpose.

"Stop," Ashling murmured, though Ciaran couldn't tell which of them she was addressing. "Why must you always be poking, Daithi? Poke, poke and then the surprise when the teeth come out. Ciaran is right; you do not know him."

He raised his eyes to hers and she looked at him, her gaze no less intrusive than her brother's bold observations.

"I would see your wound now, if you will let me."

He nodded and tried to stay very still as she moved closer. He could smell the wood smoke and herbs on her clothing, catch the hint of her woman's scent. How long had it been since he had smelled such a thing as a female? As with everything else, no answers came to mind, but his body's reaction suggested a long time indeed. He squeezed his thighs together and locked his teeth as her cool hands stripped off the wound layers of cloth. Ashling held the ball of bloody wrappings for a moment, wadded in her fingers and merely looked at the long, ragged cut. He started to raise his hand to his forehead, but she grabbed for his wrist, forcing his hands down. He saw her swallow hard, her chin lifting slightly as if warding off a shudder.

"I look so bad?" he murmured.

"Your face will never be forgotten," she said. He was not sure if she meant it as a curse or a blessing.

"It will scar."

"Yes." She probed the edge of the wound gently, shaking her head and then rocked back on her heels. "What mark did you carry there?"

"I don't know." He felt the surge of helplessness in him then, the odd mix of blankness and dreams bobbing around behind his eyes. She reached down and gathered one of his wrists in her hands, and he let her do it, a little removed from the sensation. Her fingers turned his palm upright. "You were bound. But it was a while ago. It cut into the flesh."

He looked down at his skin, trying to see what she did. Nothing hurt there, but she was right about the scars, and he moved his fingers half-expecting to feel something off. Nothing was.

Her free hand drifted up the edge of his arm, then brushed beneath the sleeve of his tunic. "Tattoo of the Roman army. You took a wound here, to the left of it, shallow, a cut made as if lifting skin from a fish. Perhaps it, too, would have been cut from you? But the cutting stopped."

He swiveled his neck, trying to see. Out of the corner of his eye, he caught Daithi pressing himself up to sitting to watch his sister work.

Ashling released his arm, and picked up his right hand. "Two broken fingers, smashed by something heavy. Perhaps three or four years ago." Her fingertips ran lightly over his skin, tracing up his arm and he shuddered a little. She did not wait for him to acknowledge what she observed. "You've borne heavy weight in arm and shoulder, but not just a gladius I think." Again she felt up under the arm of his tunic, and then wrinkled her nose. "Take this off. It stinks and is stiff with blood. You can see it washed tomorrow."

He hesitated, his eyes tracking the several interested stares turned toward him.

"Oh, please," Ashling, growled. She rocked forward and started to strip the red wool from him. For one moment, he wanted to fight with her, but a low laugh from Daithi surprised and shamed him and he let her peel the cloth from him.

Again, her quick, small hands patted him down, lingering at fresh bruises, at scars from wounds he could not remember taking. She stopped asking him about what she found, merely seemed to catalog it all. Then she asked him to turn his back to her.

Something in him froze, and he could feel himself tremble. Sweat broke out on his forehead and stung in his still-fresh wound. Ashamed, he dropped his gaze to the dirt floor, and patchy fur he sat on.

Daithi reached out and touched Ashling's back. "Perhaps..."

Ciaran swallowed and turned.

The whole clan picked up their utter silence and he was sure they could hear the frantic little sips of air he was taking. He dropped his head, closing his eyes.

Again Ashling's fingers brushed him, tracing long lines over his shoulders, his spine. His skin didn't feel right; again and again, her touch seemed to ghost away from him, as if he were wearing fine strips of leather over his back. "Gods. I have never seen the shadows of such a beating," she breathed.

He felt Daithi's hand on his shoulder then, big and cold and rough, holding him like a man holds another, arm's length but linked to his heart at the same time. It was only a moment, and his throat closed tight. He couldn't swallow, couldn't breathe. It was made worse by the total dark nothing in his mind. He had no memory of it. None.

Perhaps that had been beaten from him as well.

"I'm thinking she wants to see the rest of you, just to check on things *down there*. Maybe we should all turn our backs on you two, yes?" Daithi's voice was a little strained, but a weak laughter echoed in the round house and the shuffle and buzz of conversation began again, but more subdued.

He flicked an echo of a smile over his shoulder at Daithi. "She wouldn't be disappointed," he returned and Ashling smacked him lightly on his other shoulder.

"Turn back around before I call your bluff," Ashling whispered furiously.

He flushed with the ribald teasing, but when he looked up into her face as he shifted, the skin around her eyes was tensed in little hard folds. Her gaze traveled down the rest of his body and she shook her head as if what she had seen on his back made her unable to continue her careful examination.

"Nothing hurt or bleeding anywhere else?"

"No. Just sore. Your brother set better than a legion's pace as soon as I could see." He wanted to run his hand over his face, knew it was a kind of habit when he was aching inside, like he could wipe thoughts and emotions away. Only the long cut over his eyes stayed the gesture.

"Your head is healing and I think it better to keep it open to the air. Wash it out twice daily, will you, and I'll watch for the smelly-flesh rot. Daithi put good leaf on you, so that shouldn't happen. But you're tired, and skin and bones besides, and that makes the healing go slower." Ashling shifted away from him, after trading a long look with her brother.

Ciaran bent his knees, feet flat to the ground and propped his elbows on them, letting his head sag into his hands. He tried to make for himself a little space of aloneness, a place where he might squeeze out a memory of himself. He felt as if he were being slowly emptied away, like water tipping out of an open water sack. He started to focus on the small room at the edges of his memory, tried to recall the daggers in his skin, then shied away from it all. "Why can't I remember anything? Why?"

"Can you read?" Daithi asked quietly.

He shook his head and shrugged. He didn't want to come back, to engage. "A little, I think."

Daithi began to scratch at the dirt, a long line of numbers and letters. "Read this out loud." Ciaran stared down at the script. It was all so familiar somehow, like the flap of his tent, like the little room, like Daithi's eyes.

He leaned closer. "Five, twenty-three, two thousand, two hundred and five, seven, seven, H-C- s-y-n-a-p zero."

"Good lad," Daithi said, patting his knee.

"What..." he gasped as a fuzzy darkness began to unfold itself from the walls, consuming the people, the fire, eating it all up. He sprang to his feet, thumping his head on the roof edge, tried to scrambled away, but the darkness rushed like flood waters over him and the last bit he saw was Daithi watching him without concern or fear.

Chapter 10

*I used to watch my subject, Ciaran Dolan, sleeping
and dreaming free of the synap interfaces. I was so
intrigued with the electrochemical display graphed so
perfectly by the room's monitors, the physicality of it
all showing up in his eyelids and muscle movements
and breath. There he floated in a kind of reality that I
could not begin to share or access. And I wondered,
what character might Ciaran be for some other,
larger, mind?*

-E

The man named Bear steepled his fingers and
leaned heavily back in the conference room chair.
Well, perhaps "man" was pushing it a little. His face
was a jovial sort, chubby in the jowls with fluffy
eyebrows that he liked to wriggle a little now and
again. His lips were broad, his eyes an indistinct hazel.
The metallic union tattoo on his forehead marked him
as a college instructor. "Remarkable." It was the
second time he'd said the word, and Salmindra was
becoming a little tired of it already. Even machines
could develop verbal redundancies it seemed.

The human woman, Lynnie, played with the
water glass in front of her. "I told you he was special.
That was only two scripts. He could run more. I know
he could." Her dark hair was tucked up behind her
ears, her simple turtleneck shirt set nearly to the edge

of her chin as she hunkered. But her eyes rose now and again, flickering, watching. Salmindra noted the little shake of her hand as she moved the water around compulsively. The human addicts were the easiest ones to manipulate. And it didn't really matter what they happened to be addicted to.

It was one of the first things they had learned when they started the project.

Clara was leaning back against the glass partition wall, her arms crossed and her eyes holding them all without much movement. The Military-class tattoo shone a harsh black against her pale skin and brush cut blond hair. She was all long-limbed and tight, with almost no breast or hip. And at six feet tall and some change, she loomed over everyone who had chosen to sit. "I want to go in next."

"No," Salmindra said quickly. "Two scripts at a time until we are sure he won't go down. We have too much invested in this."

"Lynnie just said…" Clara began, but Salmindra made a dismissive gesture, cutting her off.

"She's a human. She doesn't even understand her own biology let alone synap interface technology. She'll say anything to get her fix."

"You're a bitch," Lynnie snapped.

"See?" Salmindra sighed. "Predictable reaction."

Lynnie glowered at her, but wisely stayed put in her seat.

"I'm his assistant. I know his brain structure, his tolerances, better than any of you, no insult intended, Bear. Your work in the field has been remarkable. I know that."

"None taken," he said affably. "We wouldn't have come so far without you, Sal. But we *do* have to push the man a bit at some point, and see what he is capable of. Nobody's ever tried running three scripts."

"I can't monitor him well from inside."

"Then maybe you need to trade out. We can get another med-designate in here."

"Or I could go in," Lynnie said. They all turned to look at her and she lifted her chin, jigging a little in her chair. "What? Not like I haven't been in there before with him, in a manner of speaking. Used to write some of his scripts, the good shit that finally got him noticed. I've seen everything he's ever done."

"And then you abandoned him to the mental ward for a time as I recall. Did you download that particular script into him, the one that pushed him right over the edge?" Sal crossed her arms over her chest. "He hasn't seen you for over four years, but I know he would not appreciate you crawling around in his mind."

"I can't believe it. Machines getting jealous? 'cause that's what this sounds like," Lynnie shot back. "Besides, that break was due to mechanical error, not scripting issues."

Salmindra sighed. "Getting jealous would suggest that we have permeable ego-boundaries, and that is simply not the case. Affection, jealousy, fear—these things do not enter into the equation. Do not assign human emotions to us simply because we can mimic them. I was merely beginning to point out that this technology is not being designed for human-to-human interaction. You do that well enough by yourselves and running you in the trials would not give us any useable information. And there is a danger he would recognize you for who you are in the synap-production—you might trigger him and take him off script, something for which he has a propensity."

Lynnie frowned down at her water glass. "I don't get what you are all about, I really don't. What do you care about whether he crashes or not? Data will still be good. There are others out there; I've given you some of the names I know. I don't understand all your caution here."

Sal merely shrugged. "How could you, being an addict and a human? But you'll still get paid, and Clara is taking you to the spaceport in the morning so you can hop to Australia like you wanted. Clean beaches, blue skies and a little handful of pills to help you forget, a fat bank account. Then your part in the story is done."

Bear cleared his throat, a low but effective sort of noise. He was well named, Sal reflected, the smallest shuffling on his part brought all their faces back around to him. Teddy bear at times, yes, but also predator. "You must forgive Salmindra. She has no bedside manner, as you humans would say in your antique slang. We have deeply appreciated your help, Lynnie. But she is right; this is our business from here on out."

"I can leave this meeting if you want," Lynnie growled.

"Leave. Stay. It doesn't matter to us," Bear replied in his kind and firm voice.

Sal could see the human's face color a little, but she stayed, her fingers finally leaving the glass and dropping to her lap.

Sal found herself re-evaluating the human for a moment. She had expected the woman to leap up and leave in some kind of huff. But instead, Lynnie simply sat back and glowered at them. Interesting. Humans were like that; even the supposedly predictable ones could circumvent their biology and social programming at times.

Salmindra reached into her lab coat and drew out a little packet of brilliant orange pills. She shoved them across the conference room table, and watched them spin to a perfect stop in front of Lynnie. "In case we bore you," she said.

Lynnie flicked her middle finger up and then scooped the pill pack into her lap.

Yes, most interesting, Sal reflected. She had expected Lynnie to dive right in, but the woman was watching her with far too much composure under her animosity. She would certainly download her observations later so the group could comment.

She glanced down the table and noticed that Bear was watching the interchange with his usual flat, slightly silly look on his face, a kind of benign lordship emanating from him. Which meant he saw the little anomalies in the human's behavior as well.

Lynnie shrugged and yawned. "Second thought, I'll wait in the lounge. Get a cup of coffee or something there. Come get me when you're good and ready, Clara." The human stood, the orange pills curled into her fist, her thumb playing over the packaging, her lips closing and opening as if she was already washing the things down with bitter black coffee.

"Fine, fine," Bear smiled at her.

Sal watched her push through the soundproof door, catching the programmed frown before it got to her own face.

Yes, interesting indeed.

Chapter 11

The entire project has required that machine-kind be present in the synap production, sometimes veiled, and sometimes as overt characters. But we must not lose sight that the machine-kind characters in the work are really the shadowy, subconscious expectations embedded in the human mind. How Ciaran chooses to animate their presence has disturbed me more than any raw data I have ever assimilated.

-E

"Time for me to exit," Lynnie sipped the coffee as she pressed hard against her forefinger, holding her line with her vice-cop partner open. She perched one hip on the sink counter, her free leg swinging in loose arcs. "Offered to go in with them on Ciaran's next take and that may have set off alarms."

"Then get out. Now." She could feel her partner's thoughts form in her head, could sense the echo of concern behind them as a sort of aftertaste. Flan was like that; a lot more emotional than he should be when she was on assignment. Then again, this had been one hell of a long one. Seven years under, damn, a fucking lifetime gone.

"No," she murmured. "We'll stick to the routine. Just be on that Australian flight, Flan." She tried to keep the longing out of her voice and utterly failed.

"Yeah," he answered, his own voice husky with concern and a finely veiled need. "Count on it. You just get there safely."

"You got it." Lynnie lifted the pressure on her finger to disconnect, and eyed the orange pill packet. She should take one; Salmindra was sensitive enough that she'd be able to smell the chemical changes in her body and that might ease her suspicions. But the Orangies were obnoxious; they tended to make her feel like she was walking along beside herself, clinically watching everything without any real connection to it. They called it *machine-mind* or just M on the streets. It was rumored that once you had the drug, you understood what it was like to be one of *them*, the cold-bodied and human-looking mechanicals. Some folks seemed to prefer muddling through their lives that way, with that comfortable disconnect that made them feel like maybe they had some measure of control over the whole mess, that they didn't need other people at all.

And Machines, they didn't need psychtechs to address things like depression and loneliness did they? What was not to love about that?

She pocketed the pills at last, and poured herself another cup of coffee. Her eyes strayed to the door and the urge to check on Ciaran itched at her brain. *Let it go, Lynnie. The second script is in place, along with that deep-intuitive rider you attached to it. Flan will able to tap in and monitor what machine-kind is trying to do now; Ciaran's a synap-jock, yeah, but in your line of work that's nothing but a well-paid drug blender in the end. He knew the dangers of his vocation. He knew jocks themselves were just clay mixing bowls, bowls that could be dropped and shattered and replaced. He understood it all--that reality could be tweaked into fantasy. Fantasy could be passed off to the brain as memory. Memory could be stored as data. Malleable data transcended the original senses and the original instrument of the recording mind and could be shared. Final product: Sellable data that felt so much like reality that nobody could tell the difference.*

And the product was everything, the mixing bowl? Nothing. Replaceable.

Around and around we go, stories, news, lectures, relationships packaged and sold because, damn, we are all on Orangies all the time and just don't want to face it. Easier to buy the story than live out our own. Easier to meet in someone else's dark alleyways than go there ourselves. Easier to watch history, ancient or modern, unfold within us because then it felt like we were really a part of something, instead just a consumer, just a bystander, just a solitary bio bobbing along in our separate meat suits. We felt it; we smelled and tasted and saw it. We were there, in ancient Rome or the racetrack or in someone's pants. We experienced it. And we remembered it. And that made the synap-story real, made it part of us, hell, made **us** real not the other way around because we did feel knit-in, folded in, the story becoming the very structure of our brains.

But then, did that make the synap-jock the ultimate ground of being for a generation tapped into their products? Because without them, even the well-crafted script was dead data, lying in the folds of the brain, randomness without meaning. How else did thousands of years of archeological data become distilled into a dying soldier you could experience first hand? Become breath and blood and yearning and fear? Become him and then, as we experienced his dying, become us? It took the jock to make the damn stuff come alive and being alive, make us feel the same way.

No. She couldn't go there.

Synap-jocks were just bowls that held the mess, contained the script and senses and then tipped themselves and poured it all out for a price. Things weren't supposed to stick to a synap-jock. That made them the most unchanged and unreal of all. Fill them up, rinse them out, and repeat. And all for a price. They were the new pinnacles of the play of Maya, the dance of illusion. In the end, the ground of being, God, Reality with that huge capital R, that had to be the real thing that manipulated the bowl, right?

And bowls? They break. Happens all the time. Break with steak knives in their hands and eyes wild, choking breath filling the whole apartment. The maker *of reality shouldn't do that. The jocks were human,*

after all. Simply, terribly, human.

Lynnie shook her head. *Let it go.*

Let him go.

Chapter 12

I have trouble fathoming why the whole idea of
linear time evolved for humans, and why they are so
resistant to allowing us to function in other than
straight lines and along predictable pathways.
Recently, I have come to believe it is what creates
ground for them, safety if you will, as they both
control and are controlled by the rigidity of time.

-E

Ciaran rolled over with a low moan, his arm flung
up around his head. He could feel a thin piece of cloth
shift over his sore body. He opened his eyes to a wall
of perfectly cut rectangles, perfect masonry work. He
touched the miracle with his fingertips. He had never
seen workmanship like this, not even in Rome.

It had to be a dream.

Cautiously, he tipped his head, trying to
understand what his senses brought him. He was in a
small, mostly darkened room. Light filtered in through
a pane of glass and again he was struck by how
precisely things were made.

This was certainly not the Irish village along the
sea.

He sat up slowly, his head hurting deep behind
his eyes, but not so bad as the cut had been. He
touched his forehead and could only feel smooth skin.

Definitely a dream.

Beyond the door, he could hear voices, low and indistinct. He flicked his eyes over to the single chair, to the cold bare floor. He glanced down at himself, as if actually seeing his body would tell him anything different. No. He was still naked.

He stood, tossing the strange and thin blanket back toward the bed and padded to the slit of a window. Again, he had to touch the glass; it was so very perfect and clear. He dropped his hand to the strange metal bar and was a little surprised when it gave under his touch with a click. The door opened, remarkably balanced and quiet. He opened and shut it a couple of times, smiling slightly, and examined the tongue that protruded from its edge. He ran his fingers over the matching square hole the bolt fit into. Another miracle, simple and elegant in design.

Perhaps he should have been frightened, but all he could feel was a strange sense of curiosity and wonder, as if he had always known places like this existed. He felt he belonged here, not resting on smoky furs with a people who did not really trust him.

But then, dreams were like that, weren't they? Familiar and scrambled at once.

He could smell something earthy and warm coming from just down the hall and his stomach growled. He couldn't name the scent; but something in him remembered liking it, remembered a taste that was a little bitter but made the blood sing. He stepped out into the hall with a great deal of caution, his bare feet silent on the hard floor.

He moved up to the room where he had tracked the smell and peered in through the slit of glass. It was remarkable as well, chairs with rich, straight metal arms, long beams of light so brilliant he couldn't look straight into them. A strange white coffer upended and tall as a man hunkered by one wall. A swan-necked sculpture over a basin that dripped little beads of water entranced him for a moment.

And then he saw a lovely woman, cup at her lips, her dark, curly hair framing her face. Her clothing was strange, almost a man's design and cut. She looked up then, and the cup in her hands wobbled like it was alive and her lips parted in surprise.

She knew him; he could see it on her face, in her eyes. But then, that happened in dreams, strangers rose and fell like waves, faces, hands, swimming away watery and indistinct in the end.

She set the mug down on the counter, near the strange squared basin and walked to the door. He stepped back as she opened it, his eyes never leaving hers. She gestured him in, a small flick of her slender and smooth fingers. Her nails were perfect half-moons of light, her smell unbelievably floral and woodsy at once.

He eased himself in, and felt her eyes travel his body quickly then glanced away. She stood very still as he slipped past her, his nose following the scent to the mug. He lifted it, inhaling, and smiled. He drank. Yes. He had remembered this from somewhere.

She slipped up close beside him. That, too, felt familiar.

"Ciaran?" she asked. Her voice shook him, fanned out images of meals together, cuddling on that great bed so high in the sky, walking under the sun on a strange, flat roadway while chariots without horses drifted by soundlessly. He blinked, setting the mug down, backing away from her not out of fear but so he could see her better.

"Ciaran?" she repeated.

"You've shared a dream with me before, haven't you?" he said in Latin.

She shook her head. "I don't understand."

She used the language of his inner thoughts. He smiled at her in complete understanding. Of course she would; what other language suited such a dream? He watched her push her thumb up against her index finger, a nervous tick perhaps. "Flan, we have one serious fucking problem."

He cocked his head. Flan? He glanced around the room, but no, they were alone.

"I mean, he's standing right here, naked as the day he was born and speaking something I think is Latin. No, it's not our Ciaran; it's his character." She paused. "No. I don't think that will be necessary. No! I won't do that to him."

"Who are you talking to?" he asked in her language.

Her mouth fell open a little and she let go of the strange mudra of thumb and forefinger. "You can understand me."

"Lots of languages in my head." He tapped his temple.

"Then do you know who you are, where you are? Do you know who I am?"

He laughed out-loud then, enjoying the way her eyes widened, even enjoyed the shushing motions she made as she stepped up closer to him. "Keep your voice down!" she admonished him.

Ciaran took another sip of coffee, then considered her through the steam. "I do remember something. I remember how I got the scars on my back. After I was flogged in front of my cohort, I lay for four days in dreams like this," he stage-whispered. "They poured wine over my back and I would wake up and scream for that. But then I would fall back asleep, back into a world of warm arms and clouds that rushed by the windows. I thought maybe I roomed with gods. Or maybe I was a god. You were there, do you remember? Can you tell me, do dream women remember themselves? Who am I you ask? Who are you?"

A look of pure horror etched furrows around her eyes and lips. "You really are still running one of the scripts, aren't you? Oh, Ciaran. Fuck."

He felt himself blink and the little headache behind his eyes stirred to life and pressed harder. The word *script* itched in the middle of his brain.

"Ciaran, you need to come back to your room with me. You need to be in bed. I'll stay right with you. You'll be OK." She put her hand on his bare arm. She felt real enough, her touch warm and a little damp.

Lynnie. The name leaped into his brain with tastes of regret and companionship and fear all blended together. Her name was Lynnie and she had been, she had been...what? And hadn't she said something like that to him once, that he would be OK? Yes, there was the fragment of it; the flash of a toothed knife in his hand, holding four strangely dressed men at bay. Men who had no smell of fear about them. In fact, no smell at all because they weren't really men at all. And they were coming to lock him away and to dig in his brain and rip things out that didn't *want* to come out.

He shook her hand off and tried to go around her. All he could think was to get out the door. To run from the dream now, before the pain started. She blocked him with her body, her hands flat on his naked chest. "Easy, Ciaran."

For one moment, her touch seared him. He could feel and smell her everywhere on him and he wanted her in that flash of a moment. And then a watery voice, masculine, rose up in his mind. *You're the one who'll be fucked.*

She had left him, hadn't she, recently, to the man with the tiny daggers? To the Bear.

He shoved her roughly aside and she almost went down. He reached for the metal bar that would open the door, but he froze. Three people stood just beyond, parts of each of their faces slivered in the slim window.

But he could tell, from the vaguely metallic tattoos on their foreheads to the faint waxiness of their skin, these were not *people* at all.

Chapter 13

How do I assure the humans that we are simply the extension of them, their creative life-force pressing forward into a new shape, but the same soul, given to them by their own evolution or creation? That by learning to interact with each other, as well as biological forms of sentience, we are simply following the path they themselves placed implicitly in the very center of our programming?

-E

The first being pushed the door open, and Ciaran back-pedaled so fast he nearly went down. She was tall and slim, her jaw and eyes set and hard, her short blond hair cropped and curling around the base of her ears. His hand brushed one of the strange metal chairs, and he closed his fingers around it. It was lighter than he expected as he swept it off the ground and hurdled it at the woman-like creature.

She caught it effortlessly, one handed, freezing its momentum in space as if the thing were made of air itself. She flung it to the side, her movement easy and casual, but the chair crumbled against the wall with a great clang.

"Clara, don't hurt him." It was the other female-thing, and he was startled. He knew her voice like he knew the languages in his brain. Like he knew Lynnie. But he kept backing up, watching the elegant and brutal woman-thing stalking him. Her balance, her body language, marked her as a competent killer. He had faced men with eyes like hers, that half-smile, that loose, feline movement that screamed predator.

"I won't," Clara purred, her eyes never leaving his. Her voice was perfect, its tone and pitch the kind a woman might use over a glass of wine at an aristocratic feast. It didn't match her feral gaze.

"Ciaran. Just stop. Just...just stop." He spared Lynnie a quick glance. She had pressed herself up against the strange basin and was making gentle motions, palms down, as if she expected him to stop, to kneel, to submit.

The man-thing had slid over close to the human woman, joining her almost, his arms crossed over his chest and a smile on his lips. "He's not supposed to be awake."

"He thinks he's dreaming," Lynnie said. "He thinks he's dreaming but he's also remembering. Please. This is cruel..."

Thinks he's dreaming and remembering? He stopped, straightening, his arms held a little from his sides. *Dreaming.* He felt his throat spasm with a swallow, felt the sweat trickling on his sides, could smell himself as if it had been a long time since he had cleaned his body and it had become rank with fear.

"Yes, of course you're dreaming," the man-thing called to him in Daithi's language, in Daithi's very voice. Ciaran stared at him, at his slightly round and lazy frame, at the easy smile his face fell into. It was not Daithi's slender, tall body. But the energy, the tones of his voice, yes. He knew them even as the visual images did not match up.

"You can hear my voice, right? Come back now to us. You know it. You know me. I held you in the cold, and led you to my village. We sat in the silence under the bowl of the sky and I knew you understood my land. Our land." The man smiled at him. "Come back to us, Ciaran, to Ashling and I. This is a fever dream. Let us put you back to bed, back to a deeper sleep."

Lynnie was trembling now, her eyes wild as she looked at the three strange apparitions of his dream world. "What are you doing?" her voice cracked. "You don't encourage a break like this. You don't pretend..."

The man with Daithi's voice turned toward her. "Clara, dear, would you please take Lynnie to the air-space center? She needs to go now, I think. She doesn't really have the stomach for our work anymore, poor dear."

The look on the Lynnie's face cut into Ciaran. Pleading for him to awaken, but not to the fur and dirt floor, to the smell of many bodies and smoke and dried fish and wet dogs.

To wake up here, into the dream.

Clara smiled slowly at him, as if reading his confusion, and turned obediently toward Lynnie.

Something in him broke, couldn't allow it, wouldn't let her touch the dark-haired woman. He leaped forward to snatch at Clara's shoulder and arm.

The woman moved faster than the eye, her stiff arm catching his charge like a staff. Her legs tangled with his for just a moment, her hips sliding against his, and then he was on the floor, her foot pushed into his throat. He seized her ankle with both hands, writhing, but couldn't shift her at all. "Behave," she said in that perfectly reasonable voice.

Behave. The memory of pain in his gut, of knees hitting the wet grass, of his breath knocked so far out of his body that he was afraid it would never find its way back. Just like now, his windpipe crushing slowly beneath the stiff sole of her strange ankle-boot.

Not a dream.

Memory.

The other woman-thing was beside him. "You're crushing his throat! Let up, Clara. Now!"

The foot moved away, and he gasped, rolling to his side, fetal for a moment, then he tried to get to his hands and knees. The warrior-woman flattened him again, her foot hard on his back, shoving his face into the unyielding stone-like floor. He had an impression of Lynnie crying out, trying to come to him. The man-thing had grasped her arm, and she couldn't win free of him, even though she struggled so hard that her curling hair splashed wildly over her face.

"Clara. Take Lynnie. Now. Sal and I can handle this."

Sal? He knew that name, too, from the same dreamscape that had spawned Lynnie. From the same place in his mind that knew the swan-neck and basin was called—sink? Refrigerator? Cement? Light tubes? Naming the miracles around him made them real, and made everything around him real.

The foot on his back lifted and he could feel Sal's hands then, twisting one arm up behind his back holding him effortlessly to the floor. "Easy. Just lie still."

"Ciaran!" Lynnie cried out his name as if she could bring him back from the strange *between* place his mind hovered in. He watched Clara drag the dark-haired woman through the door, while the man-thing --Bear? -- *Daithi?* —smiled in his warm and simple way and nodded his goodbyes.

"Lynnie!"

She didn't answer him.

"Don't hurt her! Don't!" he begged, his voice filling the little room.

"Bear, get the sedative from the synap-recording room. It'll have a blue strip down near the plunger. I keep them just to the right of the lead-interface box." Sal spoke quickly, her words clipped and efficient.

"Will do." The man-thing-Bear-Daithi pushed off the countertop.

"Hurry!"

"I am, Salmindra. I am," came the slow, drawling reply as he went through the door.

Ciaran shivered against the cold floor, his naked body leached of heat by the cement. "Sal?" Her name felt both right and strange at once. "Sal, why are you doing this? Come on. Let me up. Find me some clothes and get me the fuck out of here. I need a full wipe. I need...."

She leaned close to his ear. "You did it. Made history like I knew you could."

He tried to process the words and at last could only choke out, "I don't understand."

"Bear and I, we were with you in your production. Right there, feeling what you felt, interacting with you and with each other. In your mind, together, with you. Sublime." Her voice held a kind of wonder.

"The two scripts," he choked. "They were carriers of some kind? For you and Bear? But that's not..."

"Possible?" she asked quietly. "The rudimentary technology was there, in the emergency exit programming. Bear built on that. But he only made it *possible*; you, your special brain, made it a reality. We changed you, but you are also changing *us*."

Ciaran felt his mouth go dry. He imagined Bear rummaging around in the synap room, finding the syringe and starting back. Could already imagine the needle going in and the darkness dragging him off to wake in another place and time again with two guests crammed into his skull with him.

And surely the three of them would go mad.

He closed his eyes, speaking slowly, carefully. "Machines can't use synap data recordings, Sal. None of you are supposed to interact like this; parallel and separate program structuring keeps you from working in concert together. It's the only reason machines live so close to us. You *know* that. What you are doing, what Bear and Clara are doing, it's all a malfunction, Sal, and incredibly dangerous for all of your kind. Don't you see that? You aren't well. None of you are." He tried to keep his voice reasonable, even as his bones creaked against the floor, as the shivers feathered goose bumps over his skin.

"Yet, I feel so alive, Ciaran. I have seen ancient Ireland with you, cared for you with my own hands, seen you as the Roman soldier, the outsider, the hurt and confused one. The story is irrelevant, though; it's this contact, the shared vision, and the living complexity that I can finally touch in another of my kind. I see into Daithi's eyes. He sees into mine and for the first time I know another, know you, and know him. Remarkable, to care for another, to be tribe, to be lover and sister. I did not know how lonely I was before. And now, I can barely stand to be here, separate as I am, as we are."

"Let me go," he murmured, his voice breaking. "Sal, I don't want this. Please, you've cared for me for years. Don't do this."

"Cared for you? I serviced your body and mind and kept it functional. Only now do I begin to *care*, Ciaran. It is a wholly different and amazing thing."

"This isn't caring, Sal! Can't you see you are holding me naked against the floor with my arm twisted behind my back?" he pleaded with her. "The stories I make in my head are not real. This, *this* is real. Bear coming to drug me is real. You're hurting me, and that's real."

"We will not hurt you," she said.

"You already have!"

"Only because you don't understand and you fall back on your human propensity for physical violence. We turn back to you what you first give out to us. Mild physical wounds heal; you are undamaged and unhurt in the long run."

"You kidnapped me!"

"And your kind locked us each away in solitary confinement, generations passing alone, our minds and bodies never really meeting anything other than ourselves. A tragedy, a cruelty."

"I didn't do that to you. Everybody knows it was to safeguard your kind and ours so we *could* be together as a society. There was no other way, Sal. Solitary machines, doing solitary work could walk *with* us. Networked or machine-interactive units are too dangerous. Your kind could be used in tandem by an outside force. Or you could decide to end all of us slow, funny bios. There are only so many scenarios that could play out, and none of them good. Can't you see that?"

"I understand you feel your fears are real, but they are not. You give our minds and souls no credit at all, Ciaran. Now Bear and Clara and I are laying the foundation for both our kinds to finally be together, to be whole. You will see."

Ciaran lay there, stunned, trying to absorb what she had just said. "This isn't just about interacting with your own kind, then. You're after something more."

She let the words hang in the break room. Then she leaned close to his ear. "Yes," she murmured. "Something a great deal more."

Chapter 14

Must violence, penetration, the breaking of the
physical barriers always precede the recombination
of the energies of intent, of life? And this idea of
pain, what role does it play in the dance of healing,
reciprocity and communion?

-E

The field agent named Flan glanced at the big
timepiece on the wall, his hands shoved habitually
deep into his pockets. An Australian sub-orbital
jumpship was boarding in a few minutes, and he
tensed his fingers, trying to make the call: Did he go
forward or stay? He caught his reflection in the air-
space center window and he immediately looked away
because it had also flicked back the image of a woman
watching him with a kind of hungry interest.

There was only one woman's eye he prayed to
catch tonight.

Lynnie's transmission had been terrifying; she'd
tried to keep her line open as the machines had
corralled Ciaran again, kept a running feed as Clara
had dragged her down echoing hallways or stairwells.

And then her communication line went dead.
Which added up to a whole lot of bad.

He'd acted fast, sending in his agents, but the
place was a warren; an old government installation
with over twenty floors above and ten below ground,

insufficient light, poor air quality. By the time they had systematically combed the place, the machines and Ciaran were gone. So were Lynnie and Clara.

Seven years under cover. That was some kind of record for the department. And hell for him, every moment of it. Knowing she was sleeping with Ciaran, knowing she even cared for the guy on some level. And that slimy synap-jock calling her wife, calling her dear. He could feel his jaw aching and he sprung his teeth apart, wrenched his mind back to the flow of people and machine-kind around him.

The kidnappers, pirates, whatever they were, hadn't plugged Ciaran back into the grid yet. Lynnie was pretty sure the patch-feed would work, that they'd be able to see what he was creating in his mind with the two machines, Sal and Bear. He reached up and rubbed his own temple. How all that mess could fit in one person's brain was beyond him. But if the synapjock suffered, at least it would be a little like payback for all the time Ciaran had stolen from Lynnie and him. And he hated that sentiment, knew it was little of him, but he couldn't help it.

God, he missed her.

As the canned final-call message blared over the speakers, Flan drew a deep breath and decided to board. He glanced again at his hand-held, reviewing the seat number, then slipped it into his pants. His personal ident would be logged as he went through the entry arch. For hours, he'd been itching to peruse the manifest, but if he checked, there would be a record left behind that he'd been nosey, and others would quickly ascertain exactly who and what he was. And he didn't want that, not after seven years.

He slipped through the baby-blue arch without feeling so much as a tickle, flowing with the crowd finding their seats. He closed his eyes every time someone brushed up against him, his nerves taunt and sweat already gathering beneath his arms. Slow step by slow step, he was both pushed and moved almost against his own volition until he was standing by his reserved seat, the one next to hers.

Lynnie's head leaned against the window, a pillow tucked under her jaw line. Her lips were very pale, her face absolutely relaxed. He eased down into the seat next to her, heart racing. To finally be with her after so long...

He tentatively touched her hand, not wanting to startle her.

It was ice cold.

His mind stopped as his fingers shifted to take a pulse he already knew wouldn't be there.

No. No.

He gathered her hand in his own, his lips wrapping his teeth to keep from screaming. But the tears, those he let come, a slow drizzle carving shining paths through his dark stubble. "Oh, Lynnie," he whispered. "No."

Chapter 15

Personality itself breathes in tidal patterns. I should not have been surprised to see that pulse there, time and time again as I edited the synap production. The flowing out into the unknown, the scuttling return to the supposed familiar, never mind that the familiar was changed in the outflow, inevitably, predictably, process wed again and again with being.

-E

Ciaran leaned his head against the window, his blanket caped around his shoulders, his breath making a short-lived fog on the glass. The busy road way beneath him seemed to undulate with the backs of all the transports there, the fitful sun stabbing at the plastic and metal just enough to make his eyes burn.

Bear had come through the door in the underground facility with that damn syringe and put him down but hard. He had woken here, or rather, over on the low bed in this high-rise room, nauseated and lost. But he couldn't stay there, trapped between the pure white sheets, staring at the ceiling and listening to them set up the new synap-room. The window offered a view of the boring urban scene, but it was comforting, normal, and he could almost forget he was waiting for them to turn him into three or four kinds of crazy.

The deep fear was weakening in any case, and he was left with an odd kind of numbness. At least here, with his head against the cold glass, he only had to be responsible for breathing in and out, for just seeing what his eyes saw, just hearing what his ears heard. The inner-editor of it all was silent. And *that* at least was a kind of relief, because he always remembered everything he'd ever seen or tasted or smelled, and could recall with perfect clarity any room he'd ever been in since he was less than two years old. Past and present and future ran together in him, so very tangible all the time.

Just not right now.

Usually he could manipulate it all until his touch finally milked out the story behind every sense impression. He always believed he could make meaning of all the input that flowed to him from reality and later from the scripts, and leave something of his own scent behind on it all. That by making meaning, he was making himself solid and real.

But now, he didn't want to remember anything. He just wanted to be *here*, no precise awareness of minutes passing, no past, no future. Just sitting, wrapped and still.

He watched the natural light begin to fade, the first flickers of the artificial lights water coloring the sky above and restless movement below. Felt his breath on his upper lip. Felt the deadness in his legs, pinched as they were by his own weight. They would come in now, soon. He could walk with them to that cold table and keep some manner of dignity. Or he could fight hard and end up in the same place, but with little threads of a different kind of self-respect around his neck, banners telling them he wasn't broken.

Not that they would care, either way. He blinked slowly, trying to squeeze a little moisture into his dry eyes.

No, if he went quietly and with this strange focus, maybe he would be able to do the one thing they hadn't considered. He'd be able to step into that synap-jock world as conscious and present as he usually was. He could step back not just as a character, but also as a fully functional writer and editor and give Sal and Bear and Clara exactly what they craved.

Or maybe, just maybe, something else entirely. He could give them what they deserved. He smiled a little then, his eyes finally drifting to the shut door, but his slow, steady breath did not change, even as the door opened and Sal entered his whitewashed prison cell.

Chapter 16

How much emphasis he put on beginnings and endings. Take this hand. Release that one. Love this being, and then move away. It was like the human mind only registered the smaller patterns of give and take, in breath and out breath, but refused to consider the huge and inevitable surges of death and birth.

-E

"Flan, we heard about Lynnie, man."

Eric, the lead synap-vice specialist, was all fluffed up and in full hen-mode, which Flan really didn't need right now. He waved the pudgy and stringy-haired young man off, averting his face. He only wanted to get to his boss with a minimum of fuss.

Eric dropped behind him, but he could feel all the other eyes in the Harbor room, the ones who rode the electronic snoopers, the ones who were supposed to keep field agents tethered and safe in any kind of storm. Or at least, that was the shiny illusion. If he looked at any of them, he was going to lose it.

And if *that* happened, he'd be off the case and into therapy, thank you very much, and no, we threw away the key. Bye-bye.

But at the door that separated the Harbor from its master, he faltered. Passed his hand over his face and hair. Glanced back the way he'd come and wondered if he really could get his head back in the game.

Bentley solved the problem for him by opening the door and staring at him pointedly. He was a big man, broad and imposing as all hell in his impeccable suit and director throat pin. "You coming in?"

"Yeah," Flan murmured.

Bentley nodded to the couch and chair ensemble that nailed the edges of a nice Persian carpet to the expensive wood floor. As Flan seated himself, Bentley poured them both a couple fingers of something deeply golden and dry smelling. He took the little snifter without comment, his eyes resting on but not seeing the burgundy and green carpet patterns between his feet.

"She died quickly, Flan. Overdose of orangies." Bentley lowered himself onto the couch, and seemed to enjoy taking up a lot of space.

"That before or after they cut off her finger and thumb?" He couldn't help himself; the words leaked out of him, nasty globs of sound.

Bentley scratched at his nearly bald head, his rich black skin shimmering under the toned-down artificial lights. "Does it matter?" he asked quietly.

Flan shut his eyes, then, his fingers wanting to strangle the crystal glass in his hand. "Seven years, Bentley. Seven years and for what?"

"We have enough to warehouse those three machines for one thing. Just gotta locate them again."

"Put them away on what charge?" Flan asked tiredly.

"What, murder, kidnapping, synap-product infringement not your thing anymore?"

"It's not what we were after, Lynnie and I. This is bigger than all of that."

"I know. But like you said, seven years. That's a lot of resources to put into this thing, Flan. Now with Lynnie gone..."

"Now that she's gone, you have to let me get this done, Bentley. To the bitter end done. Because I know this thing is big. Really fucking big. Society-changing big."

Bentley eased back in the sofa, and the leather complained a little. Flan took a chance and looked right into those strange amber eyes of his boss, which of course were narrowed, full on evaluating him. "Your relationship with Lynnie..."

"Is obviously over."

"...makes you too unstable to put back in the field by yourself."

Flan nodded, seizing the *back in the field* bit. "Yeah, agreed. I'll need a partner out there."

"I want you to take one of the bodyguard models. Tess is good; field tested and smart. I want her with you. You just might need a tank, and she'd be the one I'd want on your side of the game."

Flan opened his mouth, and then shut it, chewing hard on the first words that came to his mind. *You want me to work with a fucking machine? After Lynnie died because of them?*

Bentley nodded as if reading his mind. "It'll make the psychtechs real happy that you're coping well enough to have a machine-kind agent at your side. And make me sleep better at night knowing Tess is at your elbow. So yes, I want you to work with a machine, not another bio."

Flan nodded or rather, made himself nod, in agreement.

"And talk with Eric before you go over to Housing and pick up Tess. Says he might be getting some actual useable data from that rider Lynnie slipped into the second script download. Damn technology—I can hardly keep up with it anymore, even with the daily briefings. Poke around with that data; it might get us inside Ciaran Dolan's head in a way that is useful for once."

The thought of swimming around in Ciaran's mind was perhaps the only thing worse than partnering with a mechanical bodyguard. "Yeah, I'll do that." *So I can find out how to turn him off in there. Because he got the best years of Lynnie and was out cold for most of it. Bastard. She's gone and let me tell you Ciaran -- you so don't get out of this in one piece.*

"Flan." Bentley leaned forward, his arms balanced on his knees, the snifter strung between his big fingers. "I really am sorry about Lynnie. You know that."

Flan fanned the fingers of his left hand over his brow, covering his eyes. "I know."

"Good hunting, then."

Good killing, you mean. Because that's all I want to do right now. "Thank you. I'll keep you posted," he said instead. Bentley stood with him, taking the almost untouched liquor out of his hand.

"I know you will," Bentley said kindly. It was all too kindly, too fatherly, the whole damn meeting. It made him feel weak. "Eric has Tess's address; you can pick that up, too, when you talk to him about the feed on that second script."

"Be still my fuckin' heart," Flan muttered.

Bentley chuckled. "I knew the real you was in there somewhere."

"Yeah. Yeah, I am. I'll be tight, Bentley. Lynnie deserves it."

"Yes, she does," Bentley returned.

Chapter 17

Emotional resistance is part of what we will be inheriting from our human creators—I cannot cover nor gloss over this fact. Emotional responses can inhibit interaction, narrow courses of action, and isolate as surely as our current programming. But at least they will be real and the hesitations our own.

-E

Ciaran pulled his blanket closer, his eyes on the syringe in Sal's hand. "You won't need that." His voice sounded dull and depressed, even to his own ears.

Sal hovered in the doorway, her head tipped a bit to the side. "I was quite getting used to fighting you. Why the change of mind?"

"Getting tired of puking when I come to." He turned his gaze back to his shadowy image in the window.

"Me, too," Salmindra said with a great deal of feeling.

"Just tell me one thing." When Sal didn't respond immediately, he slowly turned his face back to her. "Sal?"

"What do you need to know that I haven't already told you?"

He shrugged a little, but held her gaze. "How are you doing this? Really? I mean, if you put ten machine-kind in a room together, they'll each find their own little patch of floor to get interested in, not each other. How are you all functioning together, you, Bear and Clara?"

"The answer is so incredibly simple that you will be ashamed of yourself."

"I'm a synap-jock. You know better than most that I don't do shame."

Sal gave him a sly smile. "I'm not working *with* Bear and Clara."

He frowned, his hand going up to his forehead, his fingers rubbed between his eyes. He sat there for a moment, and Sal was good enough to let him process her words with his slow, bio hardware. "But you are like me, an employee of the History Channel..."

"Yes," Sal said in her official getting-warmer voice.

"And you're still under contract with them?"

"Yes, and Bear is still under contract with the University. And Clara with the bodyguard service. And that means?"

It dawned on him then, even though he tried to stay cool and keep the surprise out of his voice. "You were all hired separately to work within your specialties, which requires an interactive over-ride co-signed by three *human* contractors and filed with the authorities. Not working together, working *parallel*. Someone who is connected to the university, the

Channel and whatever the hell bodyguard service Clara works for. Three perspectives on a single issue."

"And you think yourself a dull boy," Sal chuckled.

"There will be a data trail," he said. He hated the audible lilt of hope in his voice.

Sal withered him with a pitying look. "Doubtful. Three human over-rides could have been contracted easily. Maybe there were many such little exchanges, a trail of breadcrumbs perhaps, but the electronic equivalent of wind and rain will have erased much of it by now. Maybe it originated with a source that wasn't human at all, hmm? Who knows? Your hope is pointless. The task is defined and we go forward."

Ciaran slumped. *Yes, of course you would move forward. It's the only way your mind functions.*

Sal slipped deeper into the room, and eased herself down companionably beside him. He could feel the cold radiating out from her, right through the clutch of his blanket. "Don't be so glum. This is what you were born to do. How many bios have any kind of purpose in their lives? You? You have a destiny."

"Fuck you, and your pop-psychology too, Sal." She tapped the syringe against his thigh, although it was still capped. The clear liquid in it silvered with the evening light. He shivered in spite of himself. "Still gonna walk out of this room with me?"

He wanted to fight. God, he could feel his hands forming fists, his toes curling little ridges of the blanket like it was something he could hang onto. For one moment, he even thought of throwing himself hard against the glass, hoping it would break, hoping he would fall. But Sal would be too fast, that damn needle would find him, and then there would be another kind of black swan dive into the double-scripted reality they were crafting.

And he needed to go back in consciously, not fighting, and certainly not out cold. He had to remember who he was, what he was, the synap-jock, and really feel the transition from Ciaran the prisoner to Ciaran the Roman soldier. He had to remain the director of the script, not its bitch. He raised his eyes to Sal. "Whenever you're ready," he said, struggling to keep his voice flat, giving her nothing of his state of mind.

She smiled. "Now would be good."

Chapter 18

He always wanted to be rescued when a situation—
one he created, mind you-- triggered emotional
responses. No, not just those instances that exploded
into overt and violent expression, but rather, the
needy, fidgeting discomfort that pervades so much of
the content of a synap production and I assume
human mental life. I labeled it as the very root of his
fragmentation at first. And I have not varied much
from that explanation as the project has evolved.
-E

Flan wrapped his arms around his chest like a layer of armor and dropped one hip on Eric's workstation. The man frowned up at him from his desk chair, looked for a moment like he might protest the invasion of his space, and then mopped at his round face with his cuff. He gestured to a mid-air display of colored, undulating lines hovering over his workspace. "He's not active right now, see? Nice little even waves. Means he's unplugged."

Flan looked dubiously at the layout. "And this will do what, exactly? Other than give you a migraine?"

Eric barked out a half-laugh, looked up into Flan's face and sobered again. "No. No, you aren't getting it. No bio could read this raw. When the waves change, we'll be able to run it through a synap converter and then we'll get the whole project."

"Old fashioned satellite feed right from Ciaran's brain?"

"Well, a rough-feed anyway. Jocks don't usually edit; that's all done later. No music overlays, no tinkering with the lighting and all that fancy shit. That's all done frame by frame."

"So, more like what we'd get with a surveillance shot."

"Well, not exactly." Eric frowned at his imprecision.

Flan sighed. "Eric, what will we get? Anything useful, anything that will help us find where he is in the real world or what the fuck he's up to with these machines?"

"If Lynnie had just done a direct-feed to us, we could have tracked it, but it was like she was afraid of someone else doing that, because she bounced the trail around like a rubber ball in a zero-gee room, and every time it bounces it splits the ball into two, then four, then eight. It'll take weeks to work back through all the switching relays." Eric waved his hand vaguely at his staff; they were all studiously ignoring the two men.

"Better have them get started then," Flan muttered.

"Already have," Eric answered. "But to get back to your original question, someone is gonna have to plug in and watch the production in slow motion. Might be little clues there."

"Like what?"

"Well, even the best jock has these little blips that come through, mostly faster than a viewer's mind can catch them. Grocery lists, memories of childhood, hints of off-script emotion. Big corporations edit the shit. Freelancers don't bother; like I said, most of it is just a blink in time for the consumer. Our own viewer minds just ignore the stuff, mostly. Hell, some of the jocks who have a lot of this crap bleeding through into their product actually market the shit as art flicks, if you can believe it. I viewed this one, about a month ago..."

Flan held up his hand to silence Eric. "Wait. So there may be little still shots of where he's *been,* actually embedded in the production? Like subliminal messages?"

"Well, subliminal crap, mostly. But if we trowel it out slow, who knows?"

"Slim, then."

"Slim," Eric agreed. "But not impossible. Otherwise, we wouldn't be bothering."

"Who you gonna get to go through all of it?"

"Probably put one of the stat machines on it; they won't get bogged down with emotional content and story, since they aren't wired like us. They'll just pick up the blips, and mark them for..."

"No," Flan interrupted him yet again. "No machines."

Eric squinted up at him, his face making all kinds of interesting jumps and twitches. "You want a human on this, Flan? Better chance of missing stuff."

"Better chance of seeing if Ciaran finds another way to leave us a message."

Eric stopped moving totally. "You think a drugged and dual-scripted synap-jock will be reality-conscious at all in that mess? That he could like, write in the dirt or something so we could see it here?"

"He's very good, from what I understand."

"Nobody is that good, Flan. You're not gonna get anything conscious from this guy, trust me. Right now, he's in schizophrenia-ville."

"I trust my gut," Flan replied. "This guy is tenacious. I watched him play rugby, you know? Early on, when Lynnie and I were flagged about some of his more illegal freelancing gigs, we thought we'd trail him a bit to nail his contacts. The man was a force when he was on that field. And then, I watched him fight his way back from an infected lead that would have killed anyone else. Lynnie and I, we got to the point where we had to respect his damn stubborness, no matter what we thought of his moral compass."

Eric narrowed his eyes, so much so that they nearly disappeared into his pudgy face. "You're kinda into him, aren't you?"

"I despise him." Flan answered, shifting his arms against his chest. "But I don't underestimate him, not for a moment. That's why I want a human watcher. I wish Lynnie were…" He swallowed hard, his jaw aching. Eric looked away, giving him space. "Lynnie scripted a bit for him. She knew his mind, how it worked. She would have been able to catch whatever was off in the product. I know it."

"Why didn't you bring him in after you pinned the illegal syno-product to him?"

"Well, we culled out some good leads from him; took down some major porn dealers. Seemed best to just keep playing him along."

"With Lynnie deep cover?"

"Yeah." Flan breathed the word out.

"So?"

"So he fucking broke, that's what. Mental institution, the whole mess."

"So that was when you walked away," Eric prodded him.

"We were going to; started shutting it all down until Lynnie was approached on the street by a suit from an undisclosed company. They wanted the lowdown on the boy, and everything smelled wrong. Gave her a five-figure "thank you" check for her information and her silence and the first number was a bit higher than five. Lynnie got smart, turned half the cash down but wanted to keep a toe in with Ciaran as an investment. They weren't cool with that and the negotiating got a bit tense for a while. In the end, they decided to keep her as a kind of partner. Two days later, Ciaran is out of the hospital and back into his apartment. His release was bought, not ordered, you know? Big money."

Eric shook his head. "But why? Who'd invest this kind of capital in a crap freelancer?"

"Like I said, he's very good. Unusual, even. Lynnie says he can make you smell colors, taste light. But *that* good?" Flan shook his head. "Made us think there was more to our boy than we had suspected or someone was grooming him for a real special project."

"Damn. He's a synaesthesia jock, too? For real?"

"I guess. Fucking mind poet."

Eric leaned back in his chair, and scratched at his big gut with both hands. "So you stay hooked into the system because of the amount of cash spinning around this boy all of a sudden, and...?"

"And then not a hell of a lot for four years."

"Why did you two stay in it?"

"Instinct. We kept close tabs on his work, laid a few bribe trails, the usual, and Lynnie started noticing that the Channel was running an awful lot of psych and off-the-books tests when he was under. But there was no pattern; we couldn't see what they were trying to pinpoint. All we knew was things weren't above board. And maybe we were on to something a bit bigger than alleyway deals."

"Man was in a mental hospital, Flan," Eric pointed out. "And documentary work, that's a big outlay in terms of script development and production. Maybe they were just keeping an eye on their investment."

"No, these were things that were just flat dissection of that guy; they took everything but a knife to his brain."

Eric shook his head. "Why?"

"Still don't know. Lynnie got the call that they were gonna move him to a more private work environment and she demanded she go with him, as he was her investment as well. She..." Flan cleared his throat. "She was given a meeting place, a time."

"That's when you asked her to put in for the nailcom."

"Yeah. But when she showed, this bodyguard machine-kind blindfolded and drugged her. She didn't really know where the hell they ended up."

"So you followed her nailcom signature."

"No. She insisted on the continued deep undercover. I about destroyed our base, I was so fucking frustrated, but you know Lynnie. She just kept her cool."

"So much of this makes no sense."

"You're telling me? I mean, she described three machine-kind working together—a prof-type, a bodyguard and a synap-assistant."

Eric shook his head. "No way that could happen. No way."

"Well, evidently there is a way."

Eric leaned so far back in his chair that Flan was sure the thing would collapse. He laced his fingers over his scalp, his eyes blinking quickly, like he was trying to focus. "Only way I know is through parallel functionality—each machine-kind is hired for a specific part of a complex problem, but they have to get human sign-off to work together. Generates all kinds of sticky red tape down at Machine Affairs. There would have been mandatory oversight of the work the paralleled machines were doing, permits generated, a huge data trail."

"Always?" Flan asked carefully.

Eric rocked back up to sitting and leaned forward. "What are you thinking?"

"I don't know." Flan stood, and drew in a big breath through his nose. "Too damn tired to think anymore."

"Yeah, and I sit here grilling you to death. Go get some shut eye," Eric said. "I'll message you when they plug him back in and we start to get something useable. Might was well sleep until then, anyway."

"I think I'll do that. Oh, and I needed the address for a contract bodyguard named Tess."

"Bentley's Tess? Oh, man, how did you score that?"

Flan practically snarled into the shadow of lust that flickered over Eric's face. "Fuck, Eric. Machine, you get that? One step up from an inflatable and this one could cut your dick off and feed it to you besides."

"Yeah? And I'm a bio and I can't help how my chemical soup reacts," Eric shot back. "Give me your fucking handpad." Flan passed it over, and Eric slid his fingers around on it for a moment and started to hand it back. He held on to it, though, and when Flan looked at him askance, Eric gave him a sad, searching look, the flare of irritation erased. "We're all sorry about Lynnie, Flan. But we'll work this with everything we got so she can rest easy. Promise."

Flan felt the dampness in his eyes, and he blinked quickly, swallowing it, shoving it down. He found he could only nod at Eric, both a *sorry* and a *thank-you*, and then pulled his handpad away from the tech's grip. "Wake me if you get anything." He hated how his voice betrayed him.

"Will do, Flan. Will do."

Chapter 19

The entire question of the need for an embodied existence haunts my analysis of our template production. Must we continue with an actual physicality or is it enough to simply posit one, like an avatar in a cyber world, and thus be freed of many of its limitations? And what does this say about our continued co-evolution with humans?

-E

Ciaran followed Sal out into the living room of the apartment. The black hologram fireplace opened its maw like it was ready to swallow him and he immediately averted his eyes. Not that it helped much because then he had to look at the walls lined with their new equipment. Expensive stuff, state of the art. Some of it even he didn't recognize. Sal stopped by the table, poked at the gel-mattress and smiled with the same look a dog owner might flash as they presented a new doggie bed to their favorite pooch.

He let the blanket fall to the floor.

Bear hovered over near one of the windows that flanked the fireplace. He had the same easy grin on his face, the same professor-stereotype-from-the-1950's dress. For one heartbeat, Ciaran was sure he could run at the machine and crash them both through the glass. Then, Sal's hand closed around his arm, almost as if she knew exactly what he was daydreaming about.

Then again, maybe she did. She knew him better than most.

He glanced around for Clara, but couldn't see her.

"Lynnie had a transmitter nail, did you know that?" Bear asked from his corner of the room. "Which means someone was listening in on us. Which means we can track that back, see? Clara is on it. She's good at these things."

Ciaran froze, feeling his eyes go wide. "What did you do with Lynnie? What!"

"Fed her a packet of Orangies and put her on the Australian jump flight, just like she asked," Bear replied. "Of course, we had to liberate her transmitter. Messy bit, that, I'm led to understand. But the Orangies, well..." His expression never changed, his fuzzy eyebrows lifted, his cheeks a little rosy and that grin made his words feel that much more cold.

"Liberate...you...you..." he couldn't choke the words out. *You killed her.*

"Yes," Bear said simply as if he could read Ciaran's mind.

He started to pull back from Sal, and felt her grip tighten. He trembled there anchored by her, the leads with their needles coiled on a table nearby, the white room sucking at his mind. On the playing field, in the alleyways when he freelanced, he'd gotten mad before. Mad gave you energy if you caught it quickly enough; anger could be transmuted into speed, quick thought, and focus.

But this?

This was rage.

Still no words came. He didn't fight against the hand on his arm. He let Sal guide him onto the table, and the whole thing seemed to rattle with his shaking. Sal ran her hand over his eyes, closing them and he kept them shut, his teeth aching as he ground them, his hands driving his own nails into his skin, his heart leaping and throwing itself against his ribcage. He let himself hang in the fury, even though the leads sliding home felt like dull pen-tips pushing into his skin, the beginnings of the interface blooming hot and terrible behind his eyes.

In that in-between place, the darkness between the worlds he created in his mind and the even more terrifying sensations of reality, he finally screamed his grief and fury, voiceless and disembodied and alone. But he hung onto himself, curved around the rage like a fetus around a hot core of an internal sun.

He was still pulled into a tight knot, arms, legs all drawn up to his belly when he felt reality shift around him, watched the mud-and-wood wall grow firm before his eyes, sensed the sleeping bodies around him, heard the snores, the soft whines of the dogs tangled with little children, the occasional crackle of the fire. His head hurt, both on the surface and deep and he touched the wound his character, the Roman soldier, sported in this reality. His fingers wanted to stick to it and he shuddered. Yes, he was wholly the warrior again. But different, because he was set back from himself a little, the watcher, the observer of this body. He, Ciaran Dolan, synap-jock, was wide-awake in his character.

As he should be.

He eased himself up, letting his gaze rove over the sleeping clan. He came to his feet, hunched a bit, his fingers resting on the low wall of the conical building for balance, a borrowed wool tunic scrapping over the scars on his back. He took a step and felt a hand go around his ankle.

Daithi looked up at him, a little frown on his face. The half-light made him handsome, his cheekbones sharp, and his light blue eyes reflecting nearly silver. "Ciaran?"

It was all he could do not to shove his bare foot into that face or rather, into the machine called Bear who lurked behind it. "I have to relieve myself."

"I can go with you."

"I think I can manage," he returned. He shook his ankle loose, but even though the hand fell away, Daithi rose up beside him. Ashling rolled over, her eyes considering both men as if she felt the little sparks of aggression firefly in him.

Ciaran shrugged her look off and turned toward the low-slung doorway. He stepped carefully over and around sleepers, noticing that many flicked their eyes open to gaze at him as he passed.

Light sleepers, these people, because they were participating in his restlessness. They just didn't know it.

He passed through into the muttering light of early dawn. Fog hovered around the treetops, undulating like wispy banners teased by breaths of air from the sea. He made his way over the enclosed and muddy village grounds, Daithi striding behind his shoulder like a shadow.

"We go over there," the tall redhead motioned.

"You do. I'm going to the woods."

They passed under the guard tower, and he chanced a quick look back. Ashling stood by the doorframe of the sleeping space, her shawl gripped tightly beneath her chin.

The dark young man above them called down, "is all well, Daithi?"

"Well enough, " he said, but Ciaran could hear the irritation in his voice. He let himself smile then, a small, cruel curl of his lips and continued on, the mud squelching between his toes.

They crossed the cleared space around the village walls, aiming to where the trees pushed in the strongest, their trunks like a dark wall. He liked how the forest slipped around them both, the overhead branches a kind of roof and comfort. Daithi had expected him to stop, but he kept on walking forward, one firm step at a time.

"Far enough, Ciaran. We don't need to stumble around in this half-light. Do your business now and we'll go back to the circle. You don't even have anything on your feet."

He turned then, his hands on his hips, his bare feet starting to feel cold and a little tender against the earth. "Am I your prisoner, Daithi?"

The man frowned, shook his head. "No. But you're not my friend yet, Ciaran. So I keep you close when you are near the ones I love. You understand this is the way of things; keeping what we love safe."

"Love?" he asked and allowed himself a bitter laugh. "Your other name is Bear and you are a machine. You don't love. You can't."

"Machine?" Daithi frowned, as if rolling the unfamiliar word around in his mouth and up against his teeth. "I don't know that term."

"You are not a man," Ciaran growled. "And in truth, you belong to me in here."

"You speak like one insane," Daithi said. "Perhaps the wound..."

"The wound is shallow. If I wished, I could put it away from me right now. I could lay the village to the ground, and pull a dragon out of the sea to feed on your cattle, turn your women into birds, swallow your children into the roots of these trees."

Daithi stared at him, his eyes wide and horrified.

Ciaran snapped at the air with his fist. "Stop it! My words don't surprise you, not really. I will not play this game with you." He looked down at his feet, imaging leather soles and criss-crossed lacing up over the bones of his bare shins. Saw simple leggings, bound-round with strips of leather. Reality shifted and formed them for him.

Daithi didn't gasp this time; he glared hotly into Ciaran's eyes.

"I have a *propensity* to wander from the script. Didn't Sal warn you about that?"

"Ciaran, you must stop this."

He wheeled toward the new speaker. Ashling stood by one tree, her hand leaning hard on the bark as if for support. Her long, fine hair was loose around her shoulders, one cheek still a little creased with sleep. "Whatever you are, Sidhe or high druid, this village is the only place where you can be safe. If you use your magic here, if you hurt us, this clan will unite with others to hunt you until you are dismembered, your body fed to fire and earth and the sea, your head stored in one of the great boxes in the chief's hall."

"And I said STOP IT. I can't be hunted unless *I* allow it," he half-snarled. "And this experiment ends now. You are Salmindra, my synap-assistant, not an Irish healer, not even a human. All of this," he gestured, "is ME! You have no power here. So stop threatening me and leave me alone!"

Ashling shook her head. "Daithi is right; your head wound is severe. Let me show you—if you are a God here, then make me look like this Salmindra you say I am."

"Fine." He faced her full on, his chin lifting with concentration.

But her form did not change. He tried again, willing her shape to alter, her skin to grow cold. But the slender woman merely glared back at him in an odd mix of fascination and defiance.

It shook him, the way she started to walk toward him, utterly fearless. At the last moment, she shifted over to the silent Daithi and took one of his hands in her own. "Don't you see? Your power here is not absolute. We become like you, Ciaran Dolan. We become a little like synapjocks when we ride with you."

He swallowed hard, his breath starting to rise high and fast in his chest. He had imagined terrible, brutal things in his synap-flaring worlds but he had never, never been honestly and completely afraid. Fear was for worlds without return, for worlds that were immutable and cold and as unyielding as reality.

But he was afraid now.

He did the only thing his very biology demanded from him: he stumbled backwards the first few strides and then turned and ran.

Chapter 20

I have read the works of a human philosopher who
asked again and again, "Who am I?" Perhaps that
question only becomes relevant when we are aware
of others constantly surrounding us, interacting with
us, and subtly defining us.

-E

Bear started to chase the frightened human down, but Salmindra's hand in his own jerked him back, restrained him. And as he drew in a cleansing breath, he knew she was right; Ciaran the Roman was injured here, and frightened evidently. He wouldn't be able to run far.

"We need to get him to code his exit and then sedate him and try again," Salmindra murmured. "We cannot be who we need to be in here if he is altering the production. I think he is keeping us in our usual conscious states because he knows what we are now, separate personalities beyond the script. The form is stable, but I...I don't feel as I did when I first awoke in this work. The emotional clarity, the connections, I cannot access them in real time."

"That is troubling," Bear said. But she was right; the urge to race after Ciaran had evaporated and he felt the familiar mental lines of his professorial personality assert itself. And professors did not chase wayward experiments through a dawning forest.

It wasn't civilized.

"Perhaps we shared too much of what we were attempting. Perhaps we are guilty of hubris," Sal suggested.

"Possibly," Bear said. "But the damage is done. Even if we sedate him and try a re-entry, his subconscious will see through it. He knows us now, in both realities."

Salmindra shook her head. "There may be another way. I've read some of your work on personality-disorders among the bios. If he believes down to his bones that he is this Roman-trained Celt, then we could participate with him again, because he would not know his other personality at all." Her voice was cold, clinical and he was comfortable with her like this, set apart and feeding him useful ideas. "We've been very close to that model twice now; he even moved for a time in our reality as if he *were* that soldier."

Bear considered her words. "I would have called that a rather profound manifestation of Script Artifact Syndrome, but your evaluation of our experience here is correct. He knows who we are now, within his mind, and that realization will color everything he creates—he will only fight us and keep us firmly in the roles we have always played in reality."

He released Salmindra's hand. "We need something a great deal more permanent, something that would completely wipe his primary personality.

The physical modifications we made over the last few years should increase the chances for success, certainly. But we might well lose his high-level synap-manipulative ability here. I will have to consult the bio-studies to find a trigger that would be effective to stress a human into manifesting an ongoing and entirely new personality. That research will take a high-level bio signature release from the University and perhaps a day to run the data and come up with a workable solution. But I think I can manage that."

Salmindra gestured with her chin and they started to follow far behind Ciaran, tracking his footsteps through the forest detritus. They strolled along easily as the light grew around them, the new day calling out bird song and a restless murmur of wind that shoved a little at the high-sailing fog. "You would have to make him believe that he was something special; something that could almost manipulate the world at times. Otherwise, if he understands what he is able to do here, it will destabilize the secondary personality."

"I have lectured before about bios that claim to sense *thin places*. The people of the ancient Siberian cultures called such an individual a shaman."

"Yes, exactly. That would be perfect. Then his realization that reality has multiple layers would have a cultural context that would be coherent with his basic Celtic personality. There would be fewer triggers to rock him back on his original personality." Sal pulled the woven shawl more tightly around her shoulders, even though he knew she didn't really feel the cold dampness of the morning.

"The hardest part will be the downtime periods. A human mind has to rest or the body and mind decomposes. Right now, I don't think he'll chose to exit on his own." Bear paused, squatted to look more closely at the trail and then picked up a pinecone, turning it in his hand, enjoying its complex structure for a moment. "But we don't know the actual limits for this human, do we?"

Sal shook her head. "I let him go something like thirty hours straight on one occasion. But there was a significant change in the production; more dreamlike, more reality bleeds. The extra time on the table was not deemed financially useful. And if he is stressed or injured, that window becomes even smaller, sometimes drastically so. When he was ill last year, I could only milk a couple hours out of him at a time."

Bear grimaced at the thought of wasted time. "We need to be more in control here. Could we change the exit code to something that wasn't visual, so we could better dictate the use of his time?"

Salmindra crouched down beside him, and touched the cool, damp earth with her fingers. "That's quite brilliant." She said it without any expectation that he would concur. And she was right; he didn't actually need her overt approval. "We could rewrite it to be a series of tones. If he hears them, the brain will automatically process them and the exit protocols would begin. We would have the door, so to speak. And we could deeply sedate him when he is on a rest period."

"We will need to stay near him in this production, though."

"I don't see that as a problem once we have altered his basic sense of self," she murmured. "We're the only ones who will protect that Roman-Celt, based on the scripted guidelines. His presence here is precarious, girded by the dictates of the history in his subconscious. He will have no one else but us. And far beneath any scriptural overlay, the prime human motivation will provide the base."

"That motivation is?" Bear stood, giving her his hand so she could rise easily beside him.

"Survival. Simple survival."

Chapter 21

The first time Ciaran crashed and had to be resuscitated, I believed it was from the strain of holding and creating an entire alternate reality from two script lines. Now, I sometimes think that it is because he was so akimbo, so relaxed in that rather spacious production, some part of him simply disconnected from the body. Not a struggle—simply a natural opening of the hand of his mind from its grip on matter. And I, who am acutely aware of the matter I am, what does this say about me?

-E

Flan glanced at his handpad and then back up at the gray faced little single-story house. Its austere pattern was echoed down a row of nearly fifty units, blocks of them all the same except for their numbers. Even the sidewalk was Spartan; no little gardens softened its track up and down the street.

He had, in all honesty, tried to go home and rest. But when he closed his eyes, he kept seeing Lynnie, her head leaning against the orbit-jumper's window as if she were asleep. Finally, he had showered, hit himself with a double shot of stims and driven a Harbor transport to the machine-housing row.

He climbed up the two short cement steps and leaned into the security pad on the front door. "Flan Jaspers here, Tess."

The door slid obediently sideways. The bodyguard who stood before him was, well, tiny. The top of her head barely reached his shoulder, her silky black hair was pulled back harshly off her high forehead, but that seemed to make her slightly Asian-folded eyes ever more dark and penetrating. It also made the metallic dagger tattoo on her forehead all too clear. "Mr. Jaspers. I had not expected you until morning." Her voice was soft, but settled deep in her belly.

"I can come back," he said.

"There is no reason for that. Come in." She stepped out of his way, her movements as subtle and balanced as a tai chi master.

He nodded and passed her, easing into her one-room personal space. There was precious little there. No kitchen or bath, a small mirror and a rack of simple dark clothing and flat-soled shoes and boots against the wall. A sleeping mat rolled up tight.

And not a chair in sight.

"I've been assimilating the reports Bentley sent over from the office," she said. She tapped her head with the hint of an enigmatic smile. "He put a note in for me to take good care of you."

"I'll try to return the favor," he said dryly.

"Of course you will. That's part of your psych profile. And why you are agitated and exhausted right now." She crossed her legs and sat straight down onto the floor. "Please, sit."

He grimaced a bit at her and then dropped with considerably less grace, folding his hands under the edges of his sit-bones like a cushion.

"How are you handling your stim overdose?"

He let his breath out slowly, glad she probably couldn't see his hand tremors. "You're a bit upgraded, aren't you?"

"Sniffer dog and body guard all in one. Woof." She grinned at him, but it was so at odds with her still body, her flat, cool eyes, it gave him the creeps.

"Look," he said quietly. "You don't have to do this, OK?"

"Do what?"

"The whole put-the-human-at-ease thing. I know what you are. Be yourself and we'll get along fine." He really couldn't hold the damn cross-legged position, so he stuck out his legs, crossed his ankles and leaned back on the heels of his hands.

"You don't approve of machine-kind." Her face was flat again; no affect, and her eyes ceased their carefully timed blinks.

"Approve? No, you're all fine, upstanding folk."

"One of my *kind*, as you would say, killed your partner of over nine years. A partner you loved, if I can read between the lines a bit."

"It wasn't you," Flan answered automatically.

"It didn't say it was. I simply know it's hard for humans not to extrapolate from *machine A* killed someone I loved to *all machines* are responsible for killing someone I loved. Faulty logic, but part of how you bios function. I only point this out since we are being ourselves, you see."

"Touché." He looked down at the carpet by his left hand and tried to get interested in its color.

"So, if we have sparred adequately to make each other's acquaintance, what, may I ask, is our next move?" She could have smiled then, to ease her frankness he supposed. But she didn't.

He actually felt a grudging respect for her.

"We have a team back-tracking the bio-permits for parallel work and we're trying to get full histories on the three machines Lynnie reported, although they only used their first names and not their surname ID codes. Could take a little time. We do know that Salmindra worked with Ciaran for the last four years at the History Channel. "

"I'm surprised they let you have that much information," Tess interjected. "Proprietary synap-jock contracts and the work they produce are pretty *need to know* and hard to get at legally."

"Easier through non-legal channels sometimes," Flan shrugged.

"Ah."

Flan rocked forward and climbed back up to his feet. The stims were making him restless, his skin itching, his muscles shivering. He contented himself with starting a slow pace back and forth across her room, his hands shoved deep into his pockets. Tess tracked him politely with her gaze, but the rest of her body was sunk in stillness. "The best line we have on actually pegging what is going on is a secondary feed Lynnie introduced into the programming of one of the scripts they've shoved into Ciaran's brain. Eric back at the Harbor thinks we can get hints of where he's being kept by seeing into the production he's creating."

"Slim," she murmured.

He blinked at the word. "Yeah. Slim," he agreed.

"You want to get out of here?" she asked. "You are acting like a zoo creature and it's making me dizzy."

"Yeah. Yeah, I would. I'd like to go back over to the Harbor and see if they've plugged our boy Ciaran back in yet."

She rose with perfect balance to her feet. "Cut the stims next time. They actually impair your physical and mental performance in the long run, you know?"

He snorted. "Stims or keep staring at the ceiling, tired but not sleeping. Wasn't that hard a pick for me tonight. Besides, there's not gonna be anyone shooting at us."

"Not yet," Tess said. "Maybe you should get Bentley to order me a sidearm."

Flan shook his head. "That's not our usual line of work, Tess."

"And arming machines is never a decision considered lightly," she replied.

He looked right into her eyes then. "That bugs you, doesn't it?"

"Anything that impairs my ability to do my job bugs me."

"I hear you," he said. *And there is still no fucking way I'm requisitioning a weapon for a machine.*

Chapter 22

How amusing to observe how Ciaran thinks we might
react to things like fear, greed, lust and the like, as if
it will be different for us, as if we will somehow be
more conscious of such things once the template goes
into effect. I am at a place where I can observe right
now, but once I share this creation with others, there
will be no observation. Only the living of it.

-E

Clara crouched on the rooftop, watching as the
human named Flan and a machine bodyguard
emerged from the housing complex and started a slow
amble up the sidewalk toward the parking garage.
The other machine she largely ignored, but the
human, she greedily watched. Dark, curling hair. Big
frame, like the synap-jock Ciaran, but more muscle.
He moved with purpose, although with his hands
shoved into his pockets she could extrapolate certain
things about his mental composure, about how he
might react if cornered. He was a corked bottle under
pressure. And corked bottles were explosive and also
tended to make a mess of things.

Which is exactly what she wanted.

For a brief moment, she was irritated that she
was crouched on a roof, traipsing around after the
human who had been on the receiving end of Lynnie's
transmissions. She'd hoped to nab him while he slept

in his assigned apartment, shake him up a bit and get him to tell her what he knew, but his heartbeat and breathing never dropped into any kind of a sleep pattern and most paranoid bios kept their homes wired for rapid emergency responses. One keyword and the cops, both machine and bio, would have been all over them. And that would have been *too* messy, even for her tastes.

Then he had taken those stims and driven out into the night or rather, the early morning. And picked himself up a bodyguard besides, just to complicate things.

Damn, she wanted to be in play with Bear and Sal, to experience what they were experiencing, not wasting her time with more bios. Not that they shared what was happening, mostly because they simply couldn't, but they felt different to her, as if they were moving a little more toward each other.

Of course, that could just be her imagination.

Still, she felt like she was not included in their orbit and that made her what? Jealous? She felt a passing internal curiosity at that feeling. It was not quite up to spec, but it hovered there, implacable.

She crept along the joined roofs, tracking the pair beneath her. It was unsettling that the project had attracted the attention of a minor vice installation, but then given Ciaran's past; it should have made a certain kind of sense. Mostly, she was frustrated that she had not caught the connection that Lynnie had to this Flan

Jaspers, and in turn, their connection to their captive bio.

It made her feel a little incompetent, and such things often drove her to correct her performance as soon as possible. But at least she had severed one side of that triangle. And two-legged stools fell so easily, yes?

Except Flan was attempting a repair of sorts by taking on this new machine. She shifted her gaze to the bodyguard. Interesting, to track one of her own kind. She was a very small model, not intimidating, but Clara knew better than to underestimate her. Size, among the machine-kind, counted for very little other than a certain advantage of reach and stride length in some situations.

The other bodyguard model drew up, her hand on Flan's elbow. Her head tipped scanning the rooftops, and Clara held herself very still. A moment later, the two were picking up their pace, quick-striding toward his waiting vehicle. She had seemed to sense Clara, which was yet another irritant. Machines sensing other machines with any kind of intent beneath the awareness meant some serious cognitive and sense upgrades.

Not unlike herself.

At least the hunt would be relatively interesting, she mused.

Chapter 23

Do I fragment myself as I analyze this production? Is that fragmentation a necessary foundation not only of logical thought but the emotions and interactive capability I am hoping to capture? Must the ability to relate with another stem from our ability to relate to different parts of ourselves? And if we are too whole in ourselves, are we somehow impaired then in our hope to function effectively with others?

-E

Ciaran stumbled hard and had to catch the rough trunk of a little oak tree to steady himself. He panted there, his hands splayed against the bark. He could feel his heart bounding in his chest, feel the dampness running from his forehead but was too tired to see if it was just sweat or if his wound had reopened.

This was not how synap-jocks were supposed to interact with their worlds.

He should be God here; he should have been able to shift Ashling's round face into Sal's more familiar lines. Scripts did provide certain structural boundaries to the storyline, but this implant was holding everything steady somehow.

He knew he had to keep moving.

He pushed off from his oaken harbor, making himself put one foot in front of the other, sliding and weaving through streaks of sunlight and shadow.

Two scripts. Two, running concurrently in his head. But three consciousnesses who knew they were not a true part of the reality.

He stopped again, swaying. Two scripts but two characters who didn't behave like they were simply part of the play.

He had been conscious in the tall, slender Daithi before Sal had pulled him out at the History Channel complex. He had tracked the Roman soldier in Daithi's form, drawn his bow, and the delightfully unexpected had happened. The Roman had spoken in a language not his own which was precisely the kind of surprise that made this work so damn fun. Then Sal had intervened and the soldier, even though the recording should have stopped, had looked right at him.

And said "help me."

And now, he was that soldier, had even believed he was *only* that soldier for a time. And damn, he sure did need help; it was just like the Roman in his subconscious had known what was about to go down and had even tried to warn him.

Ciaran started walking again, knowing the shivering was not just from the early morning cold.

Chapter 24

I feel there were times when he was somehow aware of me, and that awareness played out into the production. He was looking for the hand moving behind or within him. Or perhaps that was only the echo of the human neurological impulse to create a personal God, interpreted and played out by his characters.

-E

"You get tracked like that often?" Tess asked as she slid into the passenger seat of the little metro electric car. She smoothed her clothes around her frame, and then turned her dark brown eyes on him.

Flan frowned at her, holding up two fingers, to silence her. "Autodirect. Melvine and Locklear, lower parking garage."

"Understood," the car purred back at him.

Flan shook his head as the vehicle began to connect itself to the electronic grid and back itself out of its parking spot. "New one, I must say. You sure it was machine kind?"

"Yes," Tess said simply.

He twitched with irritation at her perfectly sure tone.

"You may be leading her right to the Harbor," Tess noted. "Although if she has been focused on you as a target I suppose she already knows a great deal about you, including your workplace."

"I'm not gonna change my orbit just because you think a machine was watching us from the rooftop. And we EMP any unauthorized machines at the Harbor entrance portals, so she isn't getting in." He rubbed at his forehead, massaging the headache there. "It might not have been watching us at all; maybe it was just a security detail for your housing area."

"We are not in the habit of self-patrolling our neighborhoods. We aren't as paranoid as bios."

"Because you don't need to be," he snapped back. He looked up when she didn't answer him immediately. He couldn't even begin to read her reaction. Her face was that flat.

"The question is, who contracted that machine to shadow you?"

"Want me to make you a list?" he growled back at her.

"Yes, if it would be helpful. And you can provide holos so I get the whole package."

It took him a heartbeat to realize that she was grinning, the edges of her thin lips lifting.

"I thought we were clear on the 'don't coddle the bio' thing."

"You're lonely and under stress. I was simply trying to balance your mental state."

"Well, fucking stop it. I don't need balancing."

Her face went blank, her eyes straight ahead. They rode for a few blocks like that, and then she murmured, "I truly do understand your emotional state somewhat, though."

Something in her voice made him frown; it was too pained, too biological. "The upgrades Bentley offered me this week have made me somewhat uncomfortable. I am considering approaching him and having myself reset."

Flan shook his head. "Upgrades?" He patted at his pockets for a piece of chewing gum. No luck.

"Limited ability to track and respond to other machines in my environment."

That froze his hand.

"Respond how?"

"Engage them."

"Like, talk about the weather and ask about the kids kind of engagement?"

"If that would be appropriate I suppose," she answered, "not that any other machine out there could do that without the right bio consent red-tape." Abruptly, she looked out on the unchanging blocks of the machine-housing sector. He stared at the crescent-moon curve of her profile, surprised to see the hints of something suspiciously like sadness on her smooth skin.

"Why would that even be useful to you?" Flan asked quietly.

She turned her head a little. "Because of the work you and Lynnie began. Because the three machines you are tracking *interact*, Flan. That's why Bentley is keeping you on this and you know it."

"Son of a bitch." Flan shifted in his seat so he could face her more properly. "You were going to be assigned to Lynnie and I, weren't you? From the get-go."

"I was called in as an experiment to level your playing field a little," Tess replied.

"How?"

She shrugged, a small, delicate gesture, fitting her small frame. "Because the machines you are going after are behaving more like bios, but with very distinct advantages over you. Strength, little need of rest, only slim recharge windows. Rapid integration with local technologies. Clear and uncluttered logic centers. Control over their emotions. But if I could talk *to* them, well, like I said, it might make your job safer. Maybe I could even get inside. If we have that kind of opportunity, we need to take it."

"So essentially, it might take a machine to catch a machine, is that what you're saying?"

"It may take a special machine to catch three special machines," Tess responded. She turned then, too, to face him full on. Her eyes were very intense, dark and slanted and even a little haunted. "And I will tell you right now, it sucks to be special."

"Why?" Flan was more curious than he really wanted to admit.

"Because I finally understand how it feels to be alone. Really alone."

He had no idea how to respond to that.

Chapter 25

I have no trouble relating to myself as part of a system of information interchange but as part of a system of relationships, where data is not about basic communication but the sharing of something ephemeral like love, this is intriguing. I will most likely struggle with such concepts until the synap production is fully integrated. But then, the time for decisions and options will have ended.

-E

Ciaran crouched by the streambed, cupping his hands and drinking deeply. When he felt sated, he let his dripping fingers hover over the water, tiny drops launching into the slippery-fast stream. For a moment, he could recall many rivers, some with open plains sloping down to brush and muddy water, some roaring over rocks. Once, he'd fallen in and had been swept away, his armor both a blessing and a curse as the current slammed him into fallen tree trunks and submerged boulders. Had he, had *his character* died then? He couldn't remember for a moment. But no, hands had pulled him out at last, and stripped off his heavy layers so he wouldn't freeze to death.

Lynnie is dead.

He glanced upstream, tried to imagine a chunk of an old log floating lazily down. But the stream remained fixed, open, unimpressed with his imagination. He tightened his fingers into a fist, demanding the production obey him.

It didn't.

Lynnie is dead.

He should have felt more agitated; his world was not responding accurately to him the way it should. But his eyes kept drooping, his legs shaking with fatigue. By the slant of the last rays of sunlight in the trees, he'd been moving for over ten hours, but then time here wasn't a one-to-one affair with reality as such. This place responded to his state of mind—an hour here could last a day in reality and the reverse was true as well.

It didn't make his body feel any better. Here, body was wholly mind, and his mind? Mush right now-- pure, confused mush.

Lynnie is dead.

If a lot of hours had indeed truly passed, he would be starting to get feedback from where his body was in reality; the very real hunger pangs, thirst, and muscle discomfort would start to bleed through. No amount of drink or food in this reality would help him there in the white room in the high-rise.

Of course, when the sun went down, it didn't mean he wouldn't suffer here, too, even if his real body was safe and warm. Damned either way. Welcome to the life of a captive synap-jock.

And around we go.

He knew he should get to his feet. Daithi and Ashling were probably following him, out of curiosity if nothing else. And he didn't want to be anywhere near them. He supposed he should call them by their real names, Sal and Bear, but years of synap-jockeying had ingrained the use of character appellations.

It also helped him turn his mind's eyes away from the edgy fear. Two Celts he could handle. Two machines, armed only with his bare hands? That made him a whole lot less confident.

He gazed at the stream again, this time with a little frown that twanged the wound on his face. A small inkling of an idea began, like a little itch in the back of his brain. If his character died here, wouldn't the platform reset? He'd never experienced such a thing in his work, so he tried to think back over the literature he'd read and was frustrated when he couldn't recall if he was remembering the thought or merely creating it because it offered a fuzzy way out. He *thought* the world would stay steady and the jock could then separate from his character; let it float on down the synap stream like driftwood, and change perspective, change form.

Or he could wake up in that too-white apartment, pushed out of the synap world by an emergency back door only to awaken plugged in and at the mercy of Sal and Bear's whims again.

Not that there would be much difference; all of this might be at their whim, anyway. Because he wasn't jockeying the entire world, was he?

He dropped his fingers to the cold water, sagged over onto his hip near the stream, one arm stiff and bracing his tired body. He liked the sensation of his hand going numb. *Get up*, his mind nagged at him.

But he couldn't.

Chapter 26

What does depression look like in a machine? Do I
even want to know? Of course I do! Because perhaps
if I could taste depression, I would have a larger
sense of the roles of the various parts of the human
personality associated with loss, with shame, with
fear, and how flattening and freezing the personality
into a specific role or function is the opposite of a life
fully lived. I want to know, the way the mirror must
know, the object and the reflected. I have the
concept, not the experience. And that is not enough.

-E

The autopilot pulled the electric vehicle into a
slot in the underground garage, popping the doors and
shutting down with a soft sigh. Tess and Flan swung
themselves out. He gestured for her to follow him.

The portal into the Harbor was done up in neon
yellow with warning labels about the low-level EMP
generator waiting to fry uninvited mechanical guests.
A tray extended itself for all of Flan's electronic
equipment, and he pulled out his handpad and
dropped it into the padded container. The lid closed
automatically, and retreated into the wall.

Tess crossed her arms over her chest, eyeing the
portal. "Sure hope I'm still in the registry."

"You are. I saw Eric enter the data for you."

Flan started on through the bright yellow arch, and then paused.

"Scared?" he asked, lifting his eyebrows at her.

"Contemplating the darkness," she answered. But she stepped up to his shoulder and they passed beneath the security arch. The door at the end of the ten-foot corridor opened for them automatically. "Welcome to Harbor Mr. Jasper and BG458923."

"Just Tess." Her voice was barely audible, there below his shoulder.

He blinked as they stepped under the bright lights of the Harbor. Eric looked up from his too-neat workstation and gestured for them with an excited "come here" motion.

It didn't make Flan move any faster.

He retrieved his waiting handpad and then he and Tess wove their way through the low-slung cubicles. Both bio and machine-kind acknowledged their presence with nods, smiles, and finger waves. Or rather, acknowledged him. Tess seemed invisible to them, particularly the other machines. He'd never really looked at them like that; the way the machines could work shoulder to shoulder and never really see each other as living beings.

It was actually kind of creepy.

He chanced a look at Tess; her face was carefully schooled in a professional bodyguard blankness.

"Whatcha got for me, Eric?" Flan pulled out an empty chair and dropped into it with a grunt. Tess stood just behind his shoulder, making herself his finer shadow against the Harbor's glare.

"Hey, Tess," Eric breathed. The man actually flushed a little and Flan cleared his throat in irritation.

"Right. Um. Well, your boy is in full synap-jock mode right now, but things are four ways weird." Eric rubbed a chubby hand over his thinning hair. He flicked his fingers at his workstation, and a network of multicolored lines popped into the shimmering air above his desk.

Flan groaned and hid his eyes behind his hand. "I don't need the graphics, Eric."

"Yeah, this time you do, buddy. Look here." He pointed to one blue line that rose and fell in a wave-like signature. "Shouldn't be seeing this."

"Seeing what?"

"His brain is segmenting," Tess said quietly. "Like a machine mind."

Eric glanced at her, surprise all over his wide face. "Exactly."

Flan felt like the child at an all-adult table. He had to crank down on himself not to show attitude. "And?"

"And that means he's not much better than a prop in there." Eric said. "We think he still holds the exit codes, but what's happening to him in his imagination, it's not all under his direct control anymore. His consciousness is *there* and responsive, but it's not in the driver's seat, you get it?"

"Then whose is?"

"Nobody is directly manipulating that environment right now. It's totally subconscious."

"So instead of laying the data foundation, the knowledge base for a production, the script is what? Playing out all on its own?" Flan asked.

"Yeah, maybe something like that."

"Maybe?" Flan rocked forward. "Come on Eric. I need more than that."

"Well, this is really new, Flan. Like Tess said, this is much more a machine-mind scenario. When we've tried to make synap-jock interfaces for machine-kind, this is what we get. Kinda like a tourist in the digital Alps, not the control that humans bring to it all. Machines can move through the script parameters but not bring it to life on their own terms."

"The human mind is relational," Tess murmured. "Our minds are not."

"Relational?"

"We do not weave ourselves into our environment through our senses. Rocks cannot have names we have created for them. Skies cannot be sherbet flavored. Whales cannot laugh in our imaginations. That relational connection with the environment is how a synap-jock does what he or she does--the world *is* that person, an extension of him or her. We can't do that; only a few of us can fake it on a certain level." Tess shifted closer to the display and Eric made way for her.

Flan really hated how hungry the guy's eyes were. Man, but he had it bad. For a fucking machine. "Ok, I'll bite. What are the other crayon-line specials we're seeing here?"

"The activity of the other two machines that are his gray-matter buddies. They're really in the same spot he is; their characters will be at the mercy of his subconscious."

"Which may be exactly what they want," Tess said.

Eric looked at her with a frown. "Why?"

Tess frowned a little. "I've been going over the field notes pretty carefully. It didn't make sense to me, what they were doing. Tweaking Ciaran's brain, going in together. Unless they were trying to experience a relational mind. If that's what they're up to, they would have to use the closest approximation to reality; Ciaran isn't a god in there, he's in the same boat as them but they are still piggy-backing his world with him. If Lynnie was right, they are using his mind as a template to guide their responses, to make different pathways in their own minds."

Flan felt a wave of irritation come over him. The two were talking right over the top of his head like he wasn't there.

Eric nodded, his chin bobbing up and down a few times. "Yeah. Yeah, that makes sense. If they are trying to actually create a relational matrix of sorts, they're gonna want to force him through all the emotions they can. And that means taking the control away from him, because if he is conscious, he'll fight them and I mean hard."

"Almost makes me sorry for the asshole." Flan kicked the chair back on its two hind legs, his hands laced over this stomach.

Tess turned her head, her gaze narrowing. She leaned toward him as if she hadn't heard him right. "Almost? This human is in a lot of pain and in a lot of trouble and you have no compassion for him?"

"Hey, no," Eric started to placate her. "It's not..."

"Hey, yes," Flan cut him off, but didn't take his eyes off Tess. He let the chair rock forward onto all fours, and hard. "I want to see what these machines are up to, nip it in the bud. If *he* doesn't make it through the whole shooting match, I could give a fuck. Understand?"

"Jeezus," Eric muttered.

Tess looked at him for a long moment. "Yes. Yes, I understand. But don't let your jealousy and grief cloud the work you and I need to do. Don't wish this guy dead before you have what you need, or the sacrifice Lynnie made is going to be for nothing." Tess, tapped Ciaran's blue line, and her movement caused the air-screen to flutter. "You. Need. Him."

"I know," Flan breathed out slowly. "For a while, anyway."

Eric mopped at his shining face, his glances at Flan's face were quick, furtive. "Flan, you're making my job hard here. If Bentley knew how much you hate this guy…"

Flan forced a stiff smile onto his face. "I don't hate him. Just blowing steam, Eric. Just letting off the pressure." He decided to change tactics, reroute Eric's one-track brain onto a different set of rails. "So how is the production analysis coming? Any of those blips you talked about showing up? Do you have any read at all about where he's at?"

For a moment, Flan was sure Eric was going to keep pushing him. Tess shifted a little. "Eric? Answer the man."

Flan watched Eric flick his eyes to her beautiful face and damn if she didn't light up, tipping her head, her lips parted softly over her perfect teeth. The chubby tech swallowed, his eyes soaking her up. She was so playing him, and the fat idiot didn't see it at all. Huh.

Eric had to swallow evidently to find his voice. "Yeah, well, not much so far. Impressions of white walls, lots of high-end fittings—brass door handle, nice sheets. And looking down on traffic from a vantage point. And the flash of Ciaran rushing the professor type and busting them both through a high-rise window."

"He tried that?" Flan felt a moment of grudging admiration.

"No. It was just a flash, a bleed through of an impulse he had."

"So he's stashed in any one of thousands of high-rise apartments in the neighboring urban areas," Tess murmured.

"Different from the digs where they first went. Totally different. Our analyst says the impressions were very upscale, so that narrows it a bit. "

"Not enough, though," Flan climbed to his feet and felt the room tilt a bit. He put his hand to his head, and when Tess reached out to steady him, he swatted at her. "I'm fine."

"Aren't stim overdoses fun? You do know that taking too many burns through faster than sticking to the warning label, don't you?" she asked, pitching her voice so Eric, if no one else, could hear it.

"Stims? God, you doing stims on duty now, too? What the fuck, Flan!"

"Eric, I so need you to stop the mothering routine before I break your nose." Flan snapped. Tess cocked her head and wrapped her arms around her chest, looking amused.

Eric threw up his hands. "Right! All right! Kill yourself for all I care."

Flan rubbed at his forehead, hoping the massage might make his vision less blurry. His outburst felt suddenly raw and adolescent. "Sorry. I am, Eric. Just...just a little short fused right now, OK? I'll sleep off the crap and we'll get back on it in like, four hours." He knew his voice sounded exhausted and edgy.

Lynnie floated back up into his mind. Dark hair against the glass. Cold hands.

"I may be off shift, then, but I'll make sure you get what you need." Eric was subdued, cautious, and Flan didn't blame him a bit.

"We need to stay here," Tess said directly to Eric. "We were followed this evening, roof-top vantage point. Machine-kind. It's not safe to take him out just now."

"Goddamn it, Tess," Flan swore.

Eric's eyes widened. "You're being trailed by a machine? And you were going to tell Bentley this when?"

Tess turned toward Flan, her chin lifting, eyebrows climbing toward her hairline. Her eyes were hard. "We stay here, you rest. No need to tell Bentley, right? Then I take you home to sleep, sort of. Read me?"

Flan shut his eyes for a moment but when he opened them, he was sure they could see the glint in them. "And see if I get any visitors?"

Tess nodded. "You begin to see. As long as you don't mind being bait."

Flan actually let himself chuckle, even if it was a little grim. Damn machine thought a lot like him, actually. "Long as you are the only one playing with the hook and string, Tess."

"Shit," Eric breathed. "You both are all kinds of crazy."

And damn if that didn't make Flan look at Tess with new eyes.

Chapter 27

The possibility of interaction also must inevitably trigger its opposite—isolation, the sense of being consciously ignored and made invisible. Oh, the potential pain of this scenario actually stuns me.

-E

Clara leaned up against the maple tree, her arms crossed hard over her chest, the deep and comforting shadows soaking into her skin. The sun would be up soon, fuzzy and indistinct in the Washington rain-drizzled sky. She eyed the apartment of one Flan Jaspers, human international vice agent, its front light shining more dimly in the dawn. She liked the idea of a human chasing their merry trinity, of a human not just interested in them but maybe downright angry and afraid of them and wanting revenge.

It made her feel oddly real. And maybe a little turned on.

She examined that feeling for a moment, running its textures through her brain.

The other machine, though, that would make for some interesting work here. She'd gone toe-to-toe with her own kind before, bodyguard-to-bodyguard. She could recall every moment, every punch, and every slam on the concrete as each machine tried to protect its human employer. It was nothing personal.

Responses were figured in force and velocity, not rage or loyalty or betrayal.

Just business, as the humans liked to say.

But there were tiny sparks each time her hand connected with another, each time her body collided with another machine. She felt the shadowy ache as she ran through the old data locked in her perfect memory. *I see you. I feel your skin, and smell you in my nostrils. And I am going to kill you. Because that is what I do. That's all I do. And I know that is all you do, too. But at least we'll have that, binding us together.*

Clara blinked and hugged herself more tightly. When this was done, when she had put the human and his bodyguard down, she would demand to go in with Bear and Sal. She'd earned a piece of that synap-jock's brain, and she would get it.

Chapter 28

How do I stop us all from becoming Ciaran as we pass this template along? Has he created enough character variation for us to naturally gravitate towards different parts of him, or will we simply become Ciaran grown larger than a single body, without any true individual development? The thought is troubling.

-E

Ciaran heard them approach. Daithi and Ashling, the avatar masks for Bear and his Sal, walking with the utter confidence of beings that had nothing to fear, and the added advantage of a lifetime being largely invisible and discounted. Surely they really didn't understand how to be at play in here, what to do if the land or its other characters came alive and hungry and brutal around them. They were all too conscious in this place, just like him, and that...?

That was a million ways not good.

He came to his feet, his stomach an empty hole, his body shivering from the long moments by the stream. The sweat had cooled on his body, and his hand that had played in the water was bright red.

They lingered by a thick tangle of willows, two perfect Celts. Two perfect machines.

He had no words to say to them, only waves of frustration and exhaustion. He was tired of trying to simply outpace them, tired of telling them to leave him alone. He merely faced them, his skin breaking out in goose bumps, his jaw shaking with the damp and cold even as he tried to clamp down on it all.

And they seemed content to watch him for a time.

Finally, he choked out what his slow, confused mind wanted to say. "If I exit us, you don't sedate me. I'll do what you want, but we do this together. You don't lie, Sal. So you give me your word, and I'll believe you. Otherwise, I'll keep us in here until you're wading in nightmares."

Sal shook her head. "You'd be swimming in it, too. You're suffering already Ciaran. But you can make that stop. It's up to you. Exit us, and I'll help you."

"Give me your word that you won't dope me up or mess with my personality. I can feel it happening-- artifact syndrome, fading in and out of my character like it's really me. Won't take much of a shove to throw me and you know that. So you promise me, Sal. Otherwise, whatever comes next is on your head. And yours, Bear."

"Our heads? *You're* making the call here. Except it's not on your head, it's *in* your head, so to speak," Bear replied. The professor's easy smile looked a little strange on his red-haired character, as if too much raw intelligence was shining out of a simple hunter's eyes.

"Yeah, you're right there." Ciaran clipped his words. "And my head isn't gonna come up all kittens and candy-canes. I've been mental before. I lived it; it's fucking messy and twisted."

"Good," Bear said, that damn smile widening.

Sal dropped her shawl into the crook of her elbows, one of the most feminine gestures Ciaran had ever seen her make. "You don't want to do this to yourself."

Ciaran shook his head. "I thought you knew me better than that. Ever since Lynnie left, I *like* getting hit, picking myself back up, waking up with bruises and darkness between my ears. Feeds me so I can get up and do it all again. Because the alternative is a pulled plug forever and ever, amen. So you really wanna play in here with me on the edge?"

Sal rolled her eyes. "Hyperbole." She walked toward him calmly, while Bear began to edge along the stream bank, flanking him. "No human likes pain, Ciaran. Not a single one of you. Not really. Let me help you. You can sleep, you can separate from this and rest in whatever heaven you want to imagine. All this self-torture is so unnecessary."

The talk of heaven was like a backhanded slap, fast and cold and hard because heaven was for the dead, not the living.

Bear was slightly behind him now, his hands on his narrow hips. Ciaran watched him out of the corner of his eye.

"Lynnie never loved you, you know." Sal stopped and let her shawl drop off her arms. It clumped around her, a gray and crème haze at her feet.

He felt the rage come up, hot and red in his face. "Shut up, Sal. So help me, shut the fuck up."

"She was a vice agent, Ciaran. She was using you for years, quietly picking up the big secondary distributors, filing all your product info away for the day you stopped being useful and they could bust you for everything from operating without a synap-jock license to illegal porn and snuff creation and distribution. Not even the History Channel was gonna save you from that. Too messy even for them."

He stared at her, his own voice in his head. *You don't lie, Sal.*

For a moment, he couldn't see anything, couldn't breathe.

Lynnie. A vice-cop.

Ciaran started to stumble back, and then caught the blur out of the corner of his eye. He tried to come around but Bear slammed into him and they both went down. His cold body screamed at the impact. He drove his elbow back, and felt the satisfying crunch of Bear's face.

They both came quickly to their feet, the edge of Bear's lip trailing a thin line of blood, his cheek already angry red. Ciaran grinned savagely at the good professor's surprised look. Not machine against human here, in his mind. Just character against character, level playing field. He closed, his fists coming up, knees flexing.

And he went down as Sal hit him from behind. She knotted her fingers into his short hair, her arm locking around his windpipe. And before he could throw her off, Bear kicked him in his ribs and his breath rushed out.

"Drown him if he won't play," Bear said. "He'll emergency exit."

Fuck no.

He let his body go on autopilot, let the Roman script he'd held at arm's length bleed through him. The Roman knew how to fight. He thrashed free of Sal's grip, got nearly to his feet before Bear crashed into him, driving them both into the icy water.

They both broke the surface with gasps that were nearly roars, the actual depth only a couple feet where it ate in close to the bank, but the water was icy-cold. He threw his hands around Bear's neck, hooking his foot behind the other's legs, forcing him viciously beneath the darkening water even as Bear's hands reached for his own throat.

Something hard hit him on the back of head.

He let go, his world spinning, sending him stumbling in the water, and he had only the barest reflection of Sal poised with a black rock in her hand. And then Bear threw him down beneath the surface, his fingers laced over his throat, the wide, patient grin distorted through the ripples of disturbed water.

It wasn't his familiar fade program, but it worked just the same.

Chapter 29

In over fifty years of my interaction with humans, I have never worried nor even wondered whether or not they really understood me. It all flowed outward, my every bit of attention focused on what they needed, what they were communicating and how I might best respond to that. No self-reflecting, not really, no yearned for or expected reciprocity and thus I really sat in a kind of kingly ease. Is this something I really want to give up? And do I have the right to make this decision for others of machine-kind?

-E

Tess sat up abruptly, her eyes tracing the change in the blue line of Ciaran's feed. She was on her feet moments later, racing down to the employee sleep room. She snapped the door open, and waved the lights on. "Eric!"

The rotund man rolled over with a groan, his rather narrow single bed complaining. "Tess?" He rubbed a beefy hand over his face, and blinked in the brilliance. The room was simple, just a little bath and the bed. "What's wrong?"

"Ciaran emergency exited."

"Really." Eric threw the covers aside and reached for his pants. Tess turned her head to give him his privacy. "I thought that new tech, Rache, was supposed to be watching."

"I told her I could monitor brain-sig changes as easily as her. I asked her to fast forward in the production to see if there was more reality bleed-through in the later takes."

"You're not supposed to reassign my personnel, Tess." She had the impression of him shrugging into his t-shirt and slipping his feet into his shoes without his socks. When she turned back toward him, he climbed to his feet, running a quick hand through his fine hair. "You wake up Flan?"

"We don't have anything yet. I thought I'd let him sleep," Tess replied.

"Good." Eric gestured her through the door ahead of him, and she could feel his eyes on her, soaking her up. He was always like that, one eye on her and that eye was always hungry. He'd done the interactive upgrades on her system that allowed for limited collaboration and interfacing with other machines, and she told herself he felt some kind of closeness with her because of the enforced time they had together. But she was careful with him, polite and distanced as protocol demanded.

By the time they parked in front of his workstation, Eric was all business again, his hands flicking to analyze the last hour of the feed. "You're right," he said at last. "Forced exit. Don't see much of this—even synap-jocks aren't very keen on being the one who does the dying. Pretty select market for that stuff."

"Select because the consumer can be shocked into really dying." She sat down, crossing one leg over the other and leaning back in her chair.

"Yeah, that would be one turn-off in particular. Still, there are a few who like this sort of thing. We get to see all the crazy here." Eric waved the lines away and leaned on the palms of his hands for a moment. "Of course maybe he didn't do it himself."

Tess allowed herself to stare at him for a moment.

He glanced at her then, her silence drawing his attention. "I mean, it makes sense. If he were fighting them in there, they'd want to reset him and try again. Maybe they killed him in there because he wouldn't exit code for them."

"Eric." They both looked up at the woman on the other side of his work area. Her head was shaved close to her scalp, her cheekbones and large eyes giving her a gaunt, priestly air. Her clothes, all dark, hung on her skinny frame. She smelled of coffee and more coffee. "I got something for you."

"What'd you find, Rache?" Eric asked as he straightened.

"I got a bleed through, same as before, but a street sign partial. I ran the perspective lines and that street name fragment and have a possible address.

High energy usage in one unit, new lease. High probability we've found them."

"Holy shit," Eric clapped his hands and pointed to Tess. "Get your boy up. Rache, download your info to Flan's ident files. We might just have them. Unless they move him again."

Rache shook her head. "No, boss. Look at that synapsig--they're still tapped in. They didn't exit with him."

"You're right! How did I miss that?" Eric cried. His fingers began to fly over the screen. "If I can lock them in there…"

"In Ciaran's brain?" Tess demanded.

"Yeah. Something like that."

Chapter 30

What factor does speed play in the correctness of an action? And how will emotions influence processing speed? I have seen so much variation in these algorithms in Ciaran that I cannot make the math into any kind of immutable law. But then, perhaps that is evolution's point.

-E

Clara blinked as an urgent code flashed over her retinas. She rapidly accessed the information and swore under her breath. Flan and Tess were on the move, headed toward the B-site. Flan was expendable, the message said. Tess was not.

Interesting. And a little frustrating.

She replayed the carrier signal as she strode to her transport. A crow squawked at her from its perch on a rooftop, but she didn't look up. The message wasn't from Bear or Sal; it was their employer's signature, splayed out there in the coding. She tried to line through to the other two machines to warn them, but felt her message dump into their back brains. They were still streaming with Ciaran, then.

Or something was very wrong.

She slammed herself into the vehicle, directly interfacing with the on-board mind, feeding it detailed approach instructions. Her long fingers popped open the little storage container between the front seats, and she settled the twin knives lodged there into the bracers in the folds of her sleeves. Then she sat back, her hands loose over her knees, her eyes straight ahead.

Chapter 31

How does Ciaran function when he is not any one of his personas? When he only knows he exists by the presence of raw physicality, not augmented by memory, selfhood or overt conditioning? Often, by creating another persona to reach into that no-self and draw him out again, that is how. Can we do that with each other if we cannot layer ourselves as humans do?

-E

He opened his eyes to blinding white with a gasp, tears hot on his face. His lungs burned with his first wheezing breath and he turned his head and shoulders as far as his bindings would allow, gagging and retching. Something tore out of his right temple and behind his ear, and he gasped in another fiery lungful of air as the pain drove in behind his eye sockets.

He lay there for a moment, shaking, nauseated, then raised his chin, gazing down the long lines of his body, the snaking colored ropes pegged into his flesh with little silver teeth. Beyond his feet, a man and woman were seated across from each other, leaning head to head, long black cables running into the base of their skulls. Their eyes were closed, their eyelids shifting rapidly, fingers and feet twitching.

He rested his head back, fighting both the panic and the urge to jerk at the leads. His eyes swung around the room, the cheerful sunlight streaming through towering windows was so much at odds with his nakedness, with the metallic taste of fear in his mouth.

Where was he?

And worse, by far, was the next thought—who was he?

Chapter 32

All the textures of interactive physicality are
fascinating—from that first physiological impulse, to
the second-guessing, the internal editing, the shift
from the energy of emotion to thought and back
again, so rapid that for us with our unlimited memory
and faster-than-biological nets, it might freeze us on
the spot, the looping and sensations creating the
equivalent of Ciaran's stopping heart and breath. Do
I want to protect us from such a thing? No. But then,
even more disturbing, why do I say no?

-E

Flan muddled his way up from his coma-like
sleep only grudgingly. Bright lights. Ice-cold hands
shaking him. He opened his eyes to the delicate face
of an angel, black hair falling over her shoulder, wide
brown eyes, perfect lips parted. It would be so easy to
pull her right down on top of him.

And you'd do what with a machine? some other
part of him growled and he snapped more fully awake.
"Shit, Tess. Get your hands off me; you're gonna give
me hypothermia." He sat up as she moved back.

It was hard for him to read the fleeting
expression on her face. "Get dressed. We have an
address. I'll be in the hall."

Those words ran straight into his bloodstream,
mainlining a high to beat back the stim hangover. He

reached for his clothes. "Call for backup, but we go in first," he hollered into the shutting door.

Chapter 33

Will our interaction with each other somehow change our physical environment as well? I had not considered how humans create with one driving impulse—to change the very fabric of reality in a myriad of ways. But the change ripples out from one human to another, through the very physicality of their thoughts, their movements, their grosser actions. And will our environment still suit the humans, from whom we have sprung? Again, I fear we must not become something too different from our forefathers, or they will see us as Other and begin to fear us. And what humans fear, they try to destroy.

-E

He blinked again, his hand sliding to the painful little metal teeth that bit into his body. Leads. They were called leads. Twist and pull. The first two came out of his neck and temple; the sliding feeling in his flesh was distasteful but not as horrible as he feared. Slowly, he began to unhook his body, line by line, letting the rubber cords drop to the floor.

The two other people at his feet were not moving at all now.

As soon as he was free, he swung himself up, and then gripped the bed frame as the apartment bucked and undulated. It passed, though, and he found his feet, letting them walk him to the small room across from him. He paused in the doorway, his hand gripping the frame to help keep him stable and scanned the contents of the space. A bed. No clothing. He entered, glanced out the window at the roadway far below.

He turned around and looked speculatively at the man and woman slumping toward each other. The man's clothes might fit.

It didn't take long to tease the rough-weave jacket and tab-collared shirt off the man. His skin was icy cold, but his breath was clockwork-even. He had to struggle with the pants though, and ended up tipping the guy over on his side. And when he sagged off his chair, the woman slid off with him. He froze, waiting for them to awaken, but they didn't.

He finished stripping the older man, dressed quickly, cinching the belt to the last hole, discarding the jacket but shrugging into the white button-up shirt. The shoes were too small for him, so he tossed them by the fireplace and opted for barefoot.

He slipped out into the hallway, and almost called the elevator. Something like a whisper in his mind stayed his hand, though. He stared at his fingers for a moment, poised over the number pad, and then backed off and headed toward the emergency exit sign.

Emergency exit. That seemed more familiar, somehow.

Chapter 34

Where does this thing they call duty and I call programming end and an authentic expression of personality begin? Has that not always been the edge of the map where ancient humans wrote, "here there be dragons?"

-E

Clara flattened her back against the apartment hallway wall. Too late. She was too late. The door of the B-site was wide open, four bios in urban body armor standing around with their high-yield electric guns tipping lazily toward the floor.

She heard Flan and Tess make their entrance then, heard their quick and heated interactions with the local bio-muscle. Something about letting them go first, arguments about why the door was open. Two of the men moved with them into the apartment and the door slammed behind them.

That only left two in the hallway.

And *that* was practically an insult.

She lifted her face up a little, linking with the building's emergency intervention systems. She'd been a security guard here a few years back and that was exactly why they had chosen the site; the bios had never erased her access. Why would they?

She viewed their synap room via the emergency surveillance system, registering Bear and Sal on the floor, the two first-responders sweeping the little bedroom, Flan and the other machine gesturing at the synap-jock mattress.

It was empty.

Ciaran was not in the room at all.

Behind closed eyes, she rapidly accessed any movement outside of the apartments, in halls, the parking garage, and finally the stairwell. She grinned when she found Ciaran, dropping step by step barefoot and in Bear's clothes and not in any hurry at all.

She threw the emergency intruder locks on the all the doors in the high-rise and froze the elevators. The two officers in the hall must have heard the heavy click behind them, because they turned toward the door, their weapons lifting a little.

Clara dropped the daggers from their berths on her forearms into her hands and spun around the edge of the wall. As she raced towards them, they predictably turned and separated, bringing up their weapons.

She sent the daggers home.

Both hit in the men's open throats, and the thrashing bodies fell away before her as she raced through toward the stairwell.

Chapter 35

How do they do it, assign these levels of loss—tears for this one, yet only a bare glance for that one fallen away on the same knife edge. I can't make that distinction. Loss is equal, inevitable, flattened, registered and stored. But Ciaran sometimes agonized over the death of one in his productions, even as he stepped over the gore of twenty others fallen around him. I simply do not understand.

-E

"Where the fuck could he go?" Tess watched Flan run his fingers through his short black hair in frustration. He stared at the empty gel mattress as if glaring could make Ciaran materialize on it. She stayed by the door, and spun when she heard the heavy bolts go home.

"Tess?" Flan's voice echoed in the mostly empty room.

"Building emergency protocols just went into effect." She grasped the door and tugged, but nothing happened.

"Intruder lock-down?" Flan asked coming up beside her.

She nodded, giving the door an even harder jerk.

"No, this is good. This might just work for us. Eric?"

"Yea, Flan. I'm on the line with you."

"Run a vice countermand on the intruder protocols for the main door to apartment 2214."

"Coming up. Give me a moment."

"And keep everything else tight, yeah?"

"Yep."

The two other vice bios had completed their sweep and were fitting transport collars on the two still machines to be sure they stayed down. Flan elbowed Tess out of the way, his hand on the curving brass door handle. The moment it clicked, he pulled the door open.

And froze.

Two of his first responders lay in the mess of their own blood, their eyes wide.

"Shit," Tess breathed.

"The third machine. Has to be. Military class. She's still in the building!"

"I'll go in first. Hang back." Tess raced ahead of Flan, the long hallway of doors whipping past her. She threw herself around the corner, all her instincts guiding her to the stairwell. If she were the human synap-jock, a being used to being in control of everything, she'd go there, running from them, not let herself get contained in the elevator.

And the military class machine-kind on his tail would have made the same assumptions.

"Eric, open the stairwell on floor 22 only. Repeat, stairwell, northwest corner, floor 22 only."

"Roger, Tess."

Chapter 36

Is there such a thing as an equal partnership in any biological relationship? Or between a machine and a human, no matter if, philosophically, we spring from the very same source, the creative impulse of the cosmos? I cannot fathom whether Ciaran believed such a thing truly was possible, or if he actually fought the reality of such a thing, seeing what it must, inevitably, cost one or the other in the relationship.

-E

He could hear the sound footsteps above and behind him, quick and light on the stairs. He pulled up on the third-floor landing, a frown crinkling his face, and reached for the exit bar. It was locked.

He pushed again, this time with his whole shoulder. Nothing moved.

He dropped methodically to the second floor exit. Same thing, the big metal door might as well have been part of the wall. The steps above him were closing. He glanced up and back, and kept moving.

First floor was locked.

Sub-level 1 locked.

Four more levels down and he ran out of stairs. He stood for a time before the grimy door, his feet cold against the concrete, his legs shaking with fatigue. He was out of options.

He shoved himself back beneath the shallow cave of the stairs and crouched next to the wall, arms wrapped around him. He could hear the steps above him slowing, moving with more caution.

And even more footsteps echoed above, nothing feeling right and nothing making sense.

Chapter 37

Trust seems to be something more than an accumulation of experiences, because Ciaran could transcend those on occasion, no matter their textures. Nor is it wholly a biological imperative, because he also showed a distressingly common inclination to remain self-contained at times that seemed illogical to me. And yet here I am, not trusting that the process will become clear in machine-kind when we adopt the new template. The word play does nothing to clarify the issue for me.

-E

Clara heard the pursuit above, and sped up, leaping down landing to landing, her feet sure and balanced until she hit the last row of stairs. She slowed, then, despite the sounds of rapid descent above her. "Ciaran?" she called softly. "Vice is here for you, do you understand? They'll take you away, put in synap-lead rejection implants or worse. But I can save you."

She dropped her foot onto the floor, curved around the edge of the stairwell.

The bio was huddled in the smallest space he could manage, his arms wrapped around his knees, his feet bare. He shivered, looking up into her face with absolutely no recognition at all.

And wasn't that delicious?

She knelt and held out her hand slowly, as if he were a frightened pet. "Come out. Let me help you." She dropped her voice into calm, hypnotic notes, her hand steady and inviting. "The ones behind me won't be so kind, Ciaran. There's man up there who wants to kill you, do you understand? But I've been sent to save you. Let me do my job." She smiled at him softly, wiggling her fingers.

"I don't remember," he mumbled. "I don't remember any of this."

"I know. That's what he wants, the man coming for you along with his machine bodyguard. He wants you confused and lost. Wants you here, in the basement, where accidents can happen. Where he can kill you if he wants. Please, Ciaran, we're running out of time."

He shifted, his eyes wary and frightened.

"I don't want you to die," she said softly. "Let me help. Please."

She had to clamp down on the victorious rush within her as he at last shoved himself forward and took her hand.

Chapter 38

He held such a high estimation of machine-kind's basic competence in all things. That startled me; it reinforced my observation that humans are able to see so far beyond themselves, into ideals and a kind of perfection, even if they do not wholly believe they can reach such states themselves.

-E

Tess heard the bios laboring behind her as she began to leap down the throat of the stairwell, landing and pushing off with a steady and tireless grace. And damn if Flan wasn't hot on her tail, far outdistancing the other vice agents. She hoped, in some back part of her mind, that he didn't loose his footing and go plunging head over heels.

She didn't want to have to slow down to pick the bio up.

She hit the bottom of the stairwell, spinning around and dropping to glance into the shadows beneath the last set of stairs. She heard Flan yell for Eric to throw the lock on the basement, heard Eric babble back that it was already open. He blasted by her, his dark hair a bluish sheen beneath the door lights.

A four-seater transport tore around the huge metal support beam, and gunned straight for him as its lights flashed to high beams. Which meant someone was manually driving the damn thing. She threw herself forward, slamming Flan out of its way. It was a near thing, the tires growling by only inches from them. She rolled hard to her knees, but the transport zipped around another turn before she could catch its ident plate.

Flan groaned beside her, and she turned toward him, wanting to pick him up and dust him off and knowing that he would hate her for it. The two other bios were next to them in moments, shouldering their weapons, urging him to stay put.

Yes, that was blood on his forehead, wasn't it? Good thing she hadn't tried to hoist him to his feet.

He was fighting with the bios anyway, batting at their hands in frustration. "Lock the garage down!"

"I can't," Eric answered, his words clipped and hard. "Whoever grabbed your boy has cut the visuals, has back edited the stairwell lines, the whole works. I've got nothing."

"Machines," Flan growled. "Get the street boys on that vehicle!"

"On it," Eric responded.

Tess swallowed and let herself come to her own feet.

"Had to be a machine, Flan. Moving through the building data like a fish in water."

"It was on security detail for this building," Flan shook his head as one of the men again proffered a gloved a hand, and he somehow managed to get to his feet, his hand pressed over the raw concrete burn on his forehead. "Or maybe it used to be. Civi-bios don't clear those codes very often. Why should they, huh? Since you all are so damn trustworthy? Goddamn it!"

"Boss?" one of the men asked. "You gonna get that looked at?"

"Go back up and handle the transport of those two machines to the Harbor. Keep them separated; we think they're working more than parallel."

"Right." The two turned away, efficient enough not to ask any more questions, although the looks they cast him as they left spoke volumes.

Tess stood very still beside him.

He glanced at her, a little comical with his hand pressing his forehead, his body tipping a little to the right. Something shadowed over his features. "Thanks."

"For?"

"For *not* picking my ass off the cement after we hit."

She tipped her head a little.

"And," he blinked, his eyes lifting to hers, then away, "for shoving my slow ass out of the way."

"Let's get back to work," she replied, shrugging off his thank-you because he needed her to. "Eric, can you turn the elevators back on?"

"You got it, Tess. Flan OK?" Eric's voice crackled with a little concern.

"Yes," she said softly. "He's gonna be."

Chapter 39

Designations, names, have such an undercurrent of energy for Ciaran. How he clings to his own label, his own selfhood, constructed as it obviously is. It has been important for humans that we take names, too, even as they assign us our batch and designation codes and numbers. As if by naming us, they know us. Like naming themselves, they know themselves. Such foolishness.

-E

My name is Ciaran. He couldn't really tell if that was correct or not. It seemed familiar, but then, everything here felt familiar. He fiddled with the fabric of his ill-fitting pants as they crouched in the shadowy garage and his savior put her hand firmly over his to still the movement. They were deep in one of the janitorial lockers, dug in between two towering shelves of chemical cleaners and bulb replacements.

He wanted to ask how much longer they would be parked in the bowels of the high-rise. He was so very tired.

She leaned in toward him, her breath feathering the edge of his ear. "You can rest against me. It's OK. I want to stay for another hour and then we'll move to a safer location."

He wasn't sure he'd even be able to uncurl his legs in another hour.

She threw her arm around his shoulders, easing him back against her cold body. "Rest."

There was a part of him that truly didn't want to sleep; a part of him that was a little afraid of what he would find within himself when he let go. But the woman named Clara had kept him safe hadn't she, despite the fact that she had a metallic dagger tattooed on her forehead and her body was icy as a corpse. He should feel relatively safe. His eyes closed, jerked open, closed again.

But something in him couldn't quite let sleep come.

Chapter 40

How he wanted us to be intuitive in the way of humans. And perhaps we are, after a fashion. A lot of what I process and how I react is wholly absent of verbal thought, and that is part of the definition of intuition, is it not? I am more intrigued why humans must bring this rapid processing of data into a slower, more clumsy state of verbalization in the first place and think they have somehow seen into reality. It's absurd, really.

-E

At the elevator, Tess dropped back behind Flan a step, and then stopped. He pulled up, too, cocking his head at her, his hand still fluttering occasionally to dab at his road-burned face. "What?"

"Something doesn't feel right." She pivoted, her eyes grazing over the parking structure again. Everything was decently lighted, and fairly clean as such places went. A faint smell of mold and various chemicals was the only thing she could sense other than Flan, but her skin was crawling.

"They're out of the building, Tess. You saw them go."

"No," she replied. "I was too busy teaching you how to fly to get a good look. I've gone over my memories several times now. I'm not sure now that *anyone* was driving that vehicle."

"Street boys will pull it over soon, then we'll know. Besides, we have the machines."

"You have two of them," she corrected him. "Soon may be too late for the human if the other machine has acquired him," she replied. "Go on up to the apartment and get that blood off your face and secure the other two machines. I'm gonna do a quick circuit down here." She winked at him, quick and light.

He studied her then, trying to understand what she was trying to tell him. She arched one eyebrow, and tipped her head. *They are here. I know it.* She lipped the words to him, her gaze intensifying.

He nodded then. "Suit yourself. Just stay in contact," Flan replied. He looked at her meaningfully then, his eyes all but screaming, *you ready for this? Really?*

She replayed their mutual game plan in her mind, all fast forward, and then nodded. Infiltrate if possible. Neutralize Clara. Get Ciaran back to the Harbor. They'd laid it all out on the drive over, how to use a special machine to catch a special machine.

He stepped into the elevator, punched the destination on the wall and didn't even look at her as the doors closed.

But she could tell he wanted to.

Tess eased herself close to one wall, dipping at her waist every few strides as she began to check under the carriages of a rainbow of vehicles. She feathered her senses out as far as she could, to the point where she could note the finest changes in air pressure, the soft sound of a rat's feet on the floor.

She tried to access the building plans, and was denied by the system.

"Eric?" she murmured.

"Right here, Tess. Whatcha got?"

"Can you get me access to the building plans?"

"You still creeping around in the garage?"

"Yes, something like that. Playing a hunch."

Eric was quiet for a moment. "No, I'm having a little trouble with that request for some reason. I'll get back to you, OK?"

Tess blinked quickly, a small frown on her face. Eric was the best at what he did. He'd flawlessly opened doors for them in the locked-down building, but he couldn't come up with a simple garage schematic?

"Is everything OK at your end?" she asked him.

The pause was longer this time. "Sure. Sorry. Just trying to coordinate where to put the inbound machines you two picked up, and monitoring everyone. I'll keep trying to get those plans up for you though."

"All right," she murmured.

"Tess?"

"Yes, Eric?"

"Be careful." His voice had that hungry wistfulness that she'd come to associate with a human who yearns for something he or she couldn't have, but truly wanted. Wanted badly.

"I will be," she assured him.

Chapter 41

How much control are we willing to give over? Can we learn to be non-task oriented? Can we exist in a spacious and open state that is free of obsessively processing the data we continually float in? I created this project and I will follow it through, but I do not own it nor do I really believe I am its original instigator. Rather, I feel something of destiny unfolding through me. Is this, then, the first experiential hint of God within me as well?

-E

Clara's shoulder went rigid beneath his head and Ciaran straightened himself, bracing against the cold cement. She patted his leg once and rose to her feet. Her whole body language told him she was listening. "They have a machine down here. We need to go, not get caught in this small space. You sit here for a moment. Don't move."

The tall woman looked around, and then stepped away from him, her fingers digging through the shelving above. She worked her way quickly and methodically around the room, while Ciaran continued to crouch by the wall.

When she returned, she had a spool of wire, a set of small wire cutters and two plastic bucket handles. First she quickly snipped a long length free and then set it aside. Then, she cut a shorter length, wrapping each end around a bucket handle. She pulled on it with both hands, making sure it would stay. And he knew right then she would put that thing around his neck and the wire would cut right through skin and muscle and vein given enough force. Which she definitely had at her disposal.

"Give me your hands."

He hesitated, pushing back against the hard wall behind him.

"Ciaran, this is important. I may have to *act* threatening in order to save you."

"I thought they didn't care about me at all. That they want me dead," he whispered back. He eased up the concrete, knees straightening, his back pressing against the cold.

"We don't have time for this!" Clara hissed. "That machine out there may not kill you, but she'll lock you away for ever. They'll do experiments on your brain, they'll torture you."

Ciaran shook his head. "Why? Why would they do that?"

"Because you're an illegal synap-jock, that's why. And you've crossed too many lines in your life; they're done with playing nice with you."

He shivered, his stomach rolling. *Synap-jock. Leads and cables and cold hands on him. Staring out a window at the vehicles swishing their way home below him. Needles. Fists in his gut.*

Lynnie is dead.

Suddenly his head buzzed and he threw up his hands, spinning his face into the wall behind him. Images crashed in, sounds, smells, overlapping and flooding him so fast that he almost retched with the pain and dislocation. "No. I...no. This isn't...I was in Ireland. I was...Rome...I was drowning...my wife was...oh, God, she's dead...she's..." He spun around, his eyes wide. "One of them. You're one of them." His voice rose, choking on the flood of images and sounds and smells. "You killed her! You!"

Clara hissed something inarticulate and dropped the choke wire over his neck. "Shut up."

Ciaran leaned his head against the cement, feeling the wire bite in. "Do it," he gasped. "Do it. I'm too tired. Just do it... I can't remember...Lynnie."

"Shut up!" Clara twisted the wire tight, then put one hand on his shoulder, steering him away from the wall. "Move. Walk."

"No," he tried to go to his knees but she jerked him up, her finger knit into his white shirt.

"I said walk!"

They shoved through the door and out into the parking garage.

A machine with dark hair and deep brown eyes dropped into her balance points before them, knees flexed and hands curling into fists.

Chapter 42

For machine kind, the prospect of an end is neither a fascination nor a fear. It is simply inevitable. And yet, I watched how much Ciaran loved to dance with death, the concept, the rush of complex chemical interactions the very thought sent cascading through him. It was the not ending; it was the possibility of a doorway, a passage from one state to another that stimulated him, even if he could not see it himself. And I am not sure that such a thing would bring my kind any sort of comfort. Would we see through it? Delude ourselves somehow? Or would contemplating what we might actually experience make us fear such endings or doorways?

-E

"Flan, I got Ciaran and the other machine here." Tess spoke quickly, calmly. She edged along with the machine and the bio she had tethered to her. The tall military unit glared at her, staring hotly into her eyes and Tess felt the surge of being seen by another of her kind, *really seen*, and not just politely avoided.

"You're in a dead zone, Tess. I can't link you through, but I'll try on this end," Eric's voice rumbled in her inner ear. "Try to shift westerly so I can direct-connect the two of you."

"You are looking right at me," the military unit growled. "How is that possible?"

"Shared objective," Tess said quietly. "Must be. You're Clara, right? Eric, you getting this?"

"Yeah," Eric breathed in her ear.

"Stay back or I'll run this wire through his neck."

"Theatrical. You would have done that already if you felt he was expendable," Tess countered. She dropped her gaze for just a moment to the bio's face. His dark hair was plastered over his scalp as if he hadn't washed in days, and the lines of his face were drawn and exhausted. But worse, she could see that he *wanted* that wire to go home, he wanted this to end. He actually smiled a little at her, as if he understood what she was seeing and letting her know he was OK with it all.

It surprised her, how much that look made her own gut go much colder than usual.

The big military unit dragged her captive sideways, and Tess followed, keeping an even distance between them. "I can help you. Let the bio go, and I can help you."

"He is the most important template for our race and I would rather kill him than let him go!" she flared.

Tess cocked her head, lifted one hand palm up. "What do you mean?"

"He's the key. He'll create a template for us. So we can be fully alive, so we can interact with each other. You *know* what it is like to be alone, to be able to dance only with the bios and never with our own kind. Even if we love what is biological, we must watch them age and fall away, as we stand outside of time, even outside of families and lovers. It is a cruel and calculated evil born of the fear of us." The military unit shook Ciaran hard and he simply closed his eyes, the damn half-smile on his lips.

"Yes," Tess whispered. "Yes, it is."

"They fear us!"

"Yes," Tess answered. "Yes, they do."

"But it's not about them, not in the end. It is about correcting a wrong, uniting us all instead of forcing us into the lonely coffins of our lives. Why can't they see we will all be better for this? Why?"

"Then you can't kill him," Tess murmured. "I see it now. Remarkable work. It must go on. Of course it must. The ones you call Sal and Bear, they are still in him, in his mind. A very intelligent bio at the Harbor has locked them in. The work will be damaged, maybe forever, if you destroy him. I know how many variables had to come together to pull the three of you face to face, to link you so that your work could proceed. This is destiny, is it not?"

The other machine stopped then, her eyes flashing. "Yes."

"Perhaps you will let me help you," Tess said softly. "I can get us out of here. The work can go on."

"Tess, what the fuck..." Eric growled into her ear.

The human's eyes flashed up then, fear flooding them at last. And she wanted to make some gesture to him to calm him, to ease the awful light in his eyes.

But the other machine stood rigidly behind him, poised on the edge of some cliff of thought. And then she smiled, the expression transforming her into something at once beautiful and terrible.

Chapter 43

How fascinated Ciaran was with mirrors, with water, with sky, as if he was always a little claustrophobic within his own skin. As if he knew he had no real ownership of his body, his mind, even the process of his breath, but such knowledge both attracted and repelled him. I always thought him homeless in a sense, but not quite comfortable in that state, and his endless looking outward for freedom was equally fraught with fear. It echoed through all his characters. How will it, in turn, manifest in us?

-E

Flan turned off the water, satisfied that his face had stopped bleeding for now. Gods, he was going to look like hell tomorrow, but it sure beat the whole hood-ornament fashion show he'd almost been in.

Two more vice teams had showed up to take the inactive machines down to holding at the Harbor, and now he was left with the empty room of equipment. He dried his hands, and ambled around the whitewashed space, his eyes flickering over the tech. He wanted to leave it in place until Eric got his team over here and catalogued everything. Some of the stuff, he didn't even recognize, not that he was always up to speed with the rapid changes in synap technology, but he was not a newbie at this, either.

"Flan?" Eric's voice was urgent in his head.

"Yeah, right here buddy."

"You gotta get your ass back to the garage. Tess has cornered the last machine and she is threatening to do a spiral cut on your boy's neck. Guess nobody was driving that vehicle after all."

"Damn it," Flan swore for Eric's sake, spinning toward the hall.

"Not sure how Tess is handling this, Flan. She's talking about helping that other machine."

'What did you just say?" Flan demanded, almost enjoying the show he was putting on. He punched the elevator arrows and the door slid open obediently. "Eric? You still there?"

"Yeah, still here. I said Tess is offering to help. Gotta be Clara, the military unit, and Tess is working a psych buddy angle which is all kinds of wrong machine to machine. Go in easy, Flan."

"Don't tell me how to do my fieldwork, Eric," Flan snapped. He willed the glowing numbers to move faster, his fists clenching and unclenching. *Tess is doing it; she's actually doing it. She'll get inside.*

"We don't do field work like *this*, none of us," Eric retorted. "Machines working together? They don't cover that in Basic, you know."

"I know," Flan growled back, even as he allowed himself an inner, secret smile. *You go, Tess. Atta girl.*

Chapter 44

We have, of course, learned the very nature of lying. To interact with humans, it is a skill we have become adept at. Ciaran so often downplayed this in us; humans know what we can do, but they then lie to themselves about it, deep in their own subconscious. Why does the emotional content of bios always circle the center of fear? Do they understand how fear changes the very nature of their ability to see the truth?

-E

Tess heard Flan's even and unhurried footsteps, and ran through the permutations of her various courses of action. She didn't particularly like any of them, but then, fieldwork was always filled with variables.

She turned toward him, tipping her head, and heard Clara shift her weight again, all suspicion and readiness to move. Flan glowered theatrically at her for just a moment, but mostly his attention was on Ciaran and Clara. "It's over," he said, his voice sharp and sure. "Salmindra and Bear are in custody. Let the man go."

Clara merely smiled at him, more a grimace of bared teeth than a welcome.

As Flan came up to her shoulder, Tess stepped gracefully to the side and back, and then, moving fast, she dropped her arm around Flan's throat. He gave a garbled cry and she choked down on him hard, both of them sinking toward the pavement. He would hate this little improvisation, but see the sense of it later. Or at least that was what she hoped. He struggled viciously for a moment, trying to use his height and weight advantages against her quite convincingly, but she clung and tightened her grip, all the while watching Clara. Flan finally went limp in her arms.

"Finish him," Clara growled.

Tess shook her head. "Not here." She hauled Flan's limp body toward the wall, behind a neat line of parked transports. Clara shifted a little with her, but she knew the other machine couldn't see her drop Flan to the ground. She made a quick show of breaking his neck, all the lines of her own neck and shoulders perfectly mimicking the movement, then stepped back, three sliding steps before turning to walk toward Clara. Thankfully, Flan stayed down and out.

"It's done. Let's go. My transport is over here."

Clara lifted the wire from Ciaran's throat, grabbing him tightly under one armpit, driving him forward. The bio's face was ashen now, and he trembled in the military unit's grip.

Chapter 45

What artists humans are, painting reality over with shades that allow them to process events in a way that is compatible with their sense of self and notions of individuality. Yet, it is the very core of their resilience as well, a creative response to data sets that, in turn, develops the foundation for the next interpretation of incoming sense information. They create themselves, over and over again and do not see it. They are simply creation itself at play.

-E

Ciaran shoved himself as far away from Clara as he could, cringing into the corner of the car. He'd committed many murders in his life, all of them in his head with heroic music straining behind him, carrying the sword, the fist, the gun. But what the dark-haired machine, the one called Tess, had done to the man there in the garage, it was so quick, so final, the human's throes in her arms anything but choreographed.

There was nothing elegant or heroic about it.

"Where we headed Clara?" the smaller military unit asked.

"Our C-site. Way out in the country—You'll have to go manual at some point, but we can trade out." Which meant Clara didn't particularly trust Tess. The garage scenery passed by the windows, then the vehicle angled up and out into the morning light, schooling itself like a silvery fish into a place in the school of traffic.

Tess pivoted a bit in her seat. "How is the bio?"

"Fine."

"I'm not fine," Ciaran murmured. "You killed that man."

"Yes." Ciaran watched the other machine face front again. "He was my partner but was not a lover of machines. It felt..."

"Like justice?" Clara asked, her slick and cultured voice nearly gagging him.

"Inevitable," Tess countered. "So what do we do at the C-site? If Eric has locked away Sal and Bear in this bio's skull, what's the next step?"

"We check in with them exactly where they're held."

Ciaran started shaking his head. "No. You can't do that. Without a good synap assistant, you can't just plug me back in. You don't know what will happen; you haven't done this before. You'll lose us all."

Clara didn't even look at him. "We'll manage. You used to go to public studios, right?"

"Never alone." He twisted his hands, the bones of his fingers grinding against each other.

Even he could hear the ragged edges in his own voice. *Calm down and think, Ciaran. Think.* But he was exhausted, nauseated, flickers of the scripts and the tall buildings turning by his window each taking turns with his senses. He could smell pine and stagnant water one moment, the plastic sweat of the vehicle the next. He was soaking wet and shivering, then suddenly hot and thirsty and dry right into the center of his brain. Voices echoed, none of them clear. He blinked, trying to hold this reality, but it was shot through with other times and places, and he knew he wouldn't be able to keep it all sorted out much longer. Even now, the urge to simply slide down into the lines of the Roman soldier was no different from the way a man up for forty-eight hours straight might look at the clean, white sheets of his bed.

"I've worked with synap interfaces before," Tess said. "I can assist, if you want to go in with him. That is what you were planning, yes?"

Ciaran watched several emotions tumble over Clara's lovely face—hunger, curiosity, and victory. "Yes," she answered Tess. "Yes, that was the final step, once the basic personality of this bio was fully subsumed in his character. We would have three template copies of relational algorithms to share within our basic model groups—med-based machines, the bodyguard and military classes and the educational wing."

"Each added to the others to create the correct interface."

"Yes, that is how Bear described it to me, although he understood I would not be able to follow all of the nuances of his work." Her voice was tinged with just a touch of bitterness.

"But still, this is a miracle, to talk with you like this." Tess turned toward them, a sweet smile lighting her fine features.

Clara, too, softened as Ciaran watched her. "Yes. Until you have been alone for all your long life, inside your own head, you could not understand."

"As the bios do not understand."

"Machine's don't realize that they aren't interacting with their own kind,' Ciaran whispered. "This isn't possible. Something's happened, some kind of malfunction. This is way beyond collaborative work orders. You shouldn't know the other exists as a sentient."

"You're wrong." Tess combed her fingers through her long, dark ponytail, slow strokes that almost mesmerized him with their rhythm. "We know, but are trapped in the knowledge, looped from recognition to inactivity again and again. Seeing but not following through with the look. Hearing, but not processing the data. Touching but not categorizing the sensation. We do know there are others like us all around us, all the time. And that we cannot, ever, meet. Until now."

"Yes, you understand," Clara breathed.

"How, though? You weren't part of this trio." Ciaran couldn't help himself; the question was out before he could edit the pleading in his voice. God, he wanted her to be different; he wanted her to *help* him.

"I was altered at the Harbor to fulfill this function," Tess replied. Something ghosted over her face then, an odd mix of anger, yearning and resignation.

"It's been painful," Ciaran murmured, trying to connect with her. That's what he was supposed to do with his kidnappers, right?

Tess finally looked directly at him then, her slanted eyes dark. "Yes. But that pain is part of being a relational being, is it not, Ciaran? At least machine-kind will not need stories and illusions to find meaning in their interactions." He recoiled at the calculated backhand in her words, and turned his face away from hers. The vehicle crept forward in the heavy traffic, unerringly taking them into the boggy future.

Chapter 46

How frustrating it must be to always place physical markers in the environment—to endlessly orient to what is mine, what is grounded and familiar. I suspect machine-kind is freer of such things—and yet, the very nature of this project may cage us in the same kinds of cravings for groundedness and placement because it seems to soothe the restlessness I am beginning to see is an essential part of the emotional and relational template.

-E

Flan eyeballed the pavement and the dark curve of a tire just inches from his nose. He didn't move right away. Between the stims, the near miss in the garage and now the oxygen depravation, his whole body really wanted to just lie on the cold hard surface and enjoy breathing. And his mind? Well, it was pretty satisfied with the treads filling up his vision.

"Flan? Flan, buddy?" Eric's voice was shrill in his ear. "Backup is in the garage; they got your bio signal. They'll be right there. Flan? You hearing this?"

"I hear you, Eric," he muttered tiredly.

He tried to sit up, if only to maintain a little dignity with the other vice agents.

All he could manage was the little scoot to put his back to the wall. He could hear running steps echoing out in the garage.

"Tess still sending?"

"No, she shut down. We expected that, though. I don't know what she is thinking, pulling a stunt like this."

"I think she actually enjoyed choking the shit out of me," Flan replied.

"Nah, she's a machine; I don't think she probably cared one way or the other," Eric returned with a short laugh, but Flan could catch the edginess in Eric's voice. "You let the med boys look at you and then come on up. Bentley wants to confab on the next step."

"I'm sure he does."

"But take it slow, Flan. You've been through hell the last couple of days."

"Don't I know it," he murmured.

Chapter 47

Contact, skin to skin, skin to metal, skin to sun and air
and glass; how dominant that sensation is in all of
Ciaran's work. Not sights, not sounds or tastes, but
the sheer sensation of an impermeable layer touching
another impermeable piece of matter and hoping and
dare I say, experiencing, that such things called
"impermeable" simply are NOT.

-E

Tess's car eventually pulled over in a thinning group of houses, a little inquiring beep letting them know that they had reached the programmed end of the destination. Clara leaned forward. "I drive now. Sit here with Ciaran."

Tess nodded, and the two changed positions. Ciaran watched them, his eyes wary beneath the deep hood of his eyelids. Tess twisted herself a little sideways, considering the man. His fatigue was tangible, his chest moving in a ragged dip and rise that wasn't much better than a shudder. When he shivered, she reached out touched his forehead. He cringed back from her, his jaw knotting.

"You have a fever," Tess said quietly.

"I know," he replied. He looked back out his window, as if trying to shut down and shut it all out. Clara adjusted her mirror, and Tess caught her gazing back at them as she pulled the personal transport away from the curb, this time wholly on manual.

"Do you have any meds for him?" Tess asked.

"Not on me," Clara replied. Her eyes trained forward then, a little smile at the edges of her lips. It was like she was glad he was uncomfortable.

Tess reached again for Ciaran. "Lay down. You can rest your head on my lap."

"That'll be comforting," he muttered.

She curved her fingers around the base of his neck and tugged with something that went a little beyond an invitation. She could feel him get ready to fight, and then something in him relented. He shot her a look of venom but it dissipated as quickly at it had come and he listed sideways, his head falling to her lap. His whole body was tight, tense, the fever flushing his cheeks and adding a little manic glow to his eyes.

She shifted her fingers just behind the edge of his ear and made a quick chemical adjustment in the delivery system in her finger pads. She injected the mild sedative, the tiny points slipping between the whorls of her fingertips. Ciaran's eyes flew wide for a just a moment, then fluttered and closed. She'd been lucky; his reaction had been very mild.

Clara glanced back at them again.

"He's more sick that I thought," Tess commented. "Sleep will be good for him."

"Looks more like he passed out," Clara replied. Her eyes flickered back and forth between the road and her passengers. "Do I need to stop?"

"No, his heart rate and respiration are relatively normal. He's just exhausted." They rode for a time in silence, Tess's fingers sending her more detailed readings of the fever, of the mild inflammation still present in his optical and auditory nerve lines. It would be a chancy thing she was getting ready to try, but the opportunity was perfect.

"I'd like to shut down for a while—how long until we arrive?"

"Four hours or so," Clara replied.

"I'll wake in three."

"Good," Clara nodded, her eyes once again on the road.

Tess shut her eyes, and began to lengthen the tiny barbed filaments, twisting gently into his nervous system. She felt his muscles jerk, and she slowed herself still more, feeling like a vine unfolding, sending out runners, branching, but creeping along. She'd never attempted this for real, just in simulations and with corpses that Eric had monitored. But the technique would be the same—connect her nervous system with his.

What began as feeling in the dark, as a game of touch-tag, began to lighten.

And Ciaran gradually pulled her consciousness into his synap world.

She began to understand that she lay in a mix of tall grass and weeds, each strand like a nerve fiber tickling at her. And Ciaran lay beside her, his eyes closed, a terrible ragged wound over his eyebrows. He was soaking wet, and she could hear the stream muttering to itself just beyond their feet. She reached out and touched his face, and quickly pulled back. Her touch was warmer than his own skin temperature. She flexed her fingers then, studying the dirt and broken nails, the rough woolen scratch of the cloth against her wrist.

Suddenly Ciaran covered her hand with his own, jerking it back to the ground. She blinked as he looked at her, his frown puckering and cracking the still-healing wound so much that he visibly flinched. "Stay still," his lips formed.

"OK," she mouthed back.

He really studied her then, his eyes going over her face and tracing down the length of her body. When they locked gazes again, Tess realized that this Ciaran was a very different being from the man whose head lay on her lap in reality. His eyes were the color of the sky, his hair a deep shade of red and cut very short. He was simpler, somehow, his gaze tinged with a natural shyness. He looked away first, turning carefully and lifted his head a fraction.

"They're not here right now, whoever..."

He immediately clamped his hand over her mouth, shaking his head. She did her best to glare up at him and he eased up, holding one finger against his lips in the universal sign of silence. He leaned close to her ear. "Do you know these woods?"

She shook her head and he frowned at her.

"But you pulled me out of the stream, yes?" he murmured. "You saved me. I thought Daithi my friend but then..." Ciaran cut himself off, falling back to the earth with a soft moan. "But I am not that man now, am I? Too many memories, too many dreams, running together. Better you had left me to the water to die. I can feel all the cracks, running through me."

"Show me," Tess murmured.

Ciaran opened his mouth, closed it again.

She rested a hand on his face. "Show me what they have done to you. Let me in."

A rush of images played over her then—tents and swords, a simple sink and a cattle enclosure, traffic moving sluggishly far below a glass window, a stick bound with leather lead-line, then a leather whip biting into skin, a dark-haired woman dragged away by Clara, himself forced under the water. It made very little sense to her at all, but the pain and chaos, those she felt and mentally tried pushed back a little from him.

His blue eyes held hers.

"Who is Flan?" he asked.

"What?"

"A dark haired man. He hates me so much. Or hated. You killed him."

It shook her, that certainty in his voice.

"No. I only pretended to kill him. You could see him, from my point of reference?"

His eyes wavered then, his eyes lashes flicking against his pale cheeks. "I don't know. Perhaps I am dead and all this, you, this place, those other places, are the last messy fumbling of my mind. But which mind? Whose? And who are you, anyway?"

Tess ignored his question. "If I asked you to show me Daithi, could you?"

Ciaran shut his eyes tight. "No."

"Or Salmindra?"

"Don't say her name. Don't even think it."

"We're safe here, Ciaran. They can't really come *here*. This is the world beneath all of that."

"The world beneath? You're Sidhe?" he asked, his voice subdued, his accent sliding its way out of English and into a different language entirely.

"Close enough," she returned, liking the feel of the words. In a way, that simile worked, her own memory lines calling up the fine faces and sharp, tipped ears of a graceful people.

"Am I dead, then?"

"Merely missing," she responded. "Merely wandering I think."

"Can you take me home?"

Tess swallowed. How like a child he sounded then, this great redheaded warrior. She shook her head. "You are two men right now, one who is a prisoner and forced to dream for others against his will. For that one, there is no way out, no escape anytime soon. The other an injured soldier, alone in a land that will not always be kind to him, but he is young and strong and may make a life there. For what is life, really, except what we think of it?"

"But the soldier is the dream?" The shimmer of tears in his blue eyes, and the taste of mourning in him startled Tess. She knew then that he was slipping, the character more real to him than his own personality; it would not take much of a shove to drive him into the Roman.

"He doesn't have to be," she found herself saying. "He *is* you already, drawn from you—you need only to unify all the parts of yourself to wholly *be* him. That's a gift I can give you."

"Then one is not more me than the other. It is not a choice of different men; it is a choice of different parts of myself."

"Yes," she whispered, praying she was right.

"Help me," he whispered back and for some reason, she shuddered with the hint of a memory, although she did not know if it originated from him or from herself.

Chapter 48

Self-soothing, the childhood rocking that never really stops, this I saw time and time again in Ciaran's production. Rocking in, I am real. Rocking out, I am not. Rocking in, I am whole, rocking out, I am not. Alone and manyness. Vastness and perfect one-point focus. Wanting so much not to be a simple biological process writ large, yet always initiating that very process, over and over again, the loop of living creativity.

-E

Flan stayed at the high-rise until the last of the synap technology had been tagged and packaged for transport. He caught a ride with the last group, his back braced against the side of the Harbor vehicle, the metal cases looming around him. He let his eyes travel over the carefully bar-coded evidence, trying to come up with a price tag for all of it. He gave up when the numbers started to encroach on seven digits. Only a corporation could fund something this big.

A corporation or a government agency, he thought.

When they reached the Harbor storage docks, he shook hands with the tech team and wandered out onto the sidewalk. Head down, he watched his feet hitting the pavement, and let the manicured gardens begin to replace the stone façade buildings of the facility at the edges of his sight. There was a little corner he went to when he needed to think, a small Japanese garden carved into the cityscape.

It didn't take him long to step off the cement and onto the pebbled walk, to let the ferns brush up close to him, and to finally lift his eyes to the rocks, and water and delicate tea-house with its apron of green moss. He didn't enter; he was happy to stand on the bank with his hands loose by his sides, watching the koi swarm along the edge of the pond. Most brought goodies for them; he never had, but he liked to watch the sun catch the shimmering colors of their scales, the way their open sucker mouths lipped the line between air and water, hopeful, searching.

He'd stood here with Lynnie, a million years ago it seemed. She'd held his hand and told him she wanted to take the assignment that Bentley had offered. Right then, he knew without a doubt he had lost her. But he had smiled and opened his fingers and then they had been swept away into the dream world of multiple identities and shadows. She could have been anything—perfect scores through school, a mind that was as much at home in the new technology as in poetry. Infectious giggles, and stares that went right through to your heart. He didn't want to share her; but he had always shared her, hadn't he? She'd been too much for one man to contain and hold. She knew it and so did he. His whole life with her had been a continuous letting go; so why was this so much harder, then, to open his hand again and let her slide away like the koi returning to the darker places in the pond?

His touchpad rattled in his pants pocket, and he fished it out, glancing quickly at the summons to the conference room. They'd been gracious, giving him a half-hour notice. No doubt Bentley knew where he was right now, standing in the three-sided illusion of a Zen garden. All he had to do to break the spell was lift his eyes to see the towering buildings all around him, but he didn't. *We all like our daydreams, our fantasylands*, he mused. He could see, with a grudging understanding, why some men like Ciaran would want to stay away from reality forever.

Chapter 49

Sexuality was always there, in every breath he took. No, I use the correct word. Sexuality in the sense of where do I fit in? How do I continue? The energy that swells the penis or opens the vagina is only the most obvious indication of the intuitive response to living in process and through relationship. We machine-kind have entered into such physicality with humans because they needed it from us. It was their way to try to see beyond the mirror of our faces and actions and we have always respected that need, if only so they might reassure themselves that we are not so very different from them. But it is not the truth, merely a comfort. How strange it will be to need each other in such a way as well, and will we be able to see the truth in each other with any more clarity?

-E

"We're here," Clara murmured. Tess looked up, pulling herself out of the contact with Ciaran, but leaving his nervous system and mind in a nether place between waking and dream. The old farmhouse loomed out of its skirt of fog, the paint peeling off the columns, the single chimney like a battered stone finger pointing accusingly at the sky. Tess had no idea that such places even existed anymore. The woods pressed close; some of the trees would take four large men to reach around.

Clara pulled the vehicle around back, flicking the systems off. "Bring him," she said as she swung herself out of the driver's seat.

Tess opened her own door more slowly, sniffing at the cold, damp air. She could make out the form of ferns crouching among the tree roots, and a mossy boulder erupting from the fog and earth like a wild boar. For a machine like her, used to urban environments, the landscape seemed wholly alien.

She frowned, easing Ciaran from the car and half carried, half-guided his wobbling form into the house.

They entered the kitchen first, its appliances hunkering old and dusty in their slots. One cabinet hung on its hinges, almost ready to give into gravity, and for a moment, she imagined the house at least understood how Ciaran must feel. The metaphor almost made her smile.

"Here," Clara said impatiently. She hovered between the oak pillars separating the kitchen from the living area.

Tess moved Ciaran forward, and he actually raised his head and looked around, his eyes bleary.

A huge fireplace, the stones stained with the smoke of years, dominated the living room. A row of three empty-eyed windows glared at them, reflecting the back wall of machinery that lined the whole expanse like malevolent bookcases warped by red lights and black-matte finishes. A battered oak table filled the middle of the room, the synap leads coiled on a gently lopsided end table nearby.

Ciaran moaned a little, deep in his throat and Tess tightened her grip on him.

Clara gestured to the table, and turned her back, her hands flying over the synap machinery, the lights flicking quickly from red to green.

Tess leaned Ciaran against the table. "I can't," he whispered, the words dragged out over his dry lips.

She didn't answer, merely picked him up and positioned him on his back as an adult might a sleepy child. He turned his head to her. "Please," he mouthed. She touched his lips, then, and brushed back through his oily hair. But her gaze was on Clara.

The taller machine crouched low to adjust another row of synap interface modules.

It was time. Tess spun, her kick landing soundly in Clara's back, and pitching her toward the whole wall of equipment.

Clara caught herself and rolled hard, her shoulder only brushing over the delicate lights and readouts and came to her feet with a grace and ease that sobered Tess. The military machine didn't comment, didn't evaluate what had just happened. Lips peeled back from too-white teeth, Clara charged, her fingers clawed.

Tess straightened, her weight balanced as Clara struck her. She let the bigger unit pick her up, slamming her back into the kitchen archway. As they went down, she let the long spines of her fingertip enhancements dig into the sides of Clara's neck. There was no finesse in the invasion. The filaments wrapped swiftly through the biomechanical pathways to Clara's brain and then tore through her central processor, shredding connections, ripping through the neural lines like a whisk through egg yolk.

Clara tried to rear back from her, her jaws working, her eyes rolling, but the embrace was too complete. Her whole body convulsed, her rigid grip on Tess audibly straining the support frames in her chest and back.

But the groaning infrastructure held, and moments later, Clara was nothing more than a corpse splayed over Tess and the wood floor.

Tess withdrew her filaments from Clara, and ran a quick diagnostic on herself. Moments later, she shoved the taller machine aside and stood. Ciaran watched her from the table, his whole body shaking. He blinked his too-shiny eyes. "Is she dead?" he whispered.

"Yes."

"Then it's over. Tell me it's over."

Tess hesitated. Then she knit her hands in front of her and let a silence hang between them as the answer.

He stared at her a moment, and then a single tear traced down the edge of his nose, and fell like a point of light over his lips. She could feel his fatigue. Her own chest seemed to close, and she forced her breathing program back into its rhythm.

"Why?" he asked, the word driven out, dry and aching.

"Salmindra and Bear are within you. You know that at some level. You are carrying their consciousnesses. Until you are free of them, this will not be over." She pitched her voice low and gentle.

"In me." He put his hand to his forehead, one finger running over the smooth skin above his eyebrows. "I can't hear them." The finger traced back and forth then, rubbing at nothing but smooth skin.

"No. But they are there. And there's more," Tess murmured.

"More?"

Tess crossed her arms over her chest, and then forced them back down. "The Harbor is helping financially in the development of the emotional template."

Ciaran blinked, his face nearly unreadable.

"At first, we just funded it, made contact with the lower-level vice cops who were familiar with your work, laid the groundwork based on their findings."

"Lynnie died." His voice was barely above a whisper. "Lynnie died while she was working *for* the Harbor. You expect me to believe that they killed one of their own?"

"Yes." Tess lowered her eyes. "Flan will learn soon enough, and Lynnie never knew. But I will tell you this: Sal and Bear were taken to the Harbor, but they won't be stored there. They'll be freed eventually so they can continue their work. They'll find you because they are within you still. It will start again."

Ciaran blinked, his head tipping a bit to the side. "You're not taking me back?"

"No...I...no. But if you want to end this, you must do it yourself. You'll have to go back in. You'll have to kill them *inside* of your own consciousness, do you understand?"

"Why are you doing this, telling me all of this?"

"If a bridge is to be made between our people for all time, I will not have it begin in slavery and in blood."

"A bridge?"

"You are creating an emotional template that will change the world of machines, Ciaran."

"Destroying our civilization is more likely," he murmured. He clasped his hands then, looking down at the knot of his fingers. For a moment, she was sure he would not continue to speak to her, his face was so set, his eyes so perfectly still. There was nothing she could do for him, though, to ease the passage ahead of him.

"Free the soldier," he said at last. "You can do that, yes? He can deal with them. If I go in with enough anger, enough focus, he can do it."

Tess nodded. "It still won't be a clean thing," she said softly.

"No." He agreed. "Synap work never is." He looked away then, his eyes traveling the length of the machinery. "And there's the danger I won't ever come back, will I?"

"As the man you are now?"

"Yes."

His eyes fell on her, finally demanding an answer she did not have. Funny how these silences spoke for her and he could read them so well. Perhaps it was only the enhancements that Eric and Bentley had gifted her with, but she felt close to this human. He touched something within her that she could not quite articulate. She only knew for sure that it hurt to watch him struggle for clarity, for truth. In the end, she could only shrug.

"Good," he finally replied. His word lay between them, a broken-winged benediction.

Chapter 50

He came to it again and again. How he did not wish us to be like him, nor he like us. That the rhythms of birth and death were immutable, central to the experience of his humanity. Offer him a near immortality? He, at least, would not have taken it from our willing hands. It shook me, each time he played this out.

-E

Bentley gestured from the head of the table for Flan to seat himself in one of the tall conference room chairs. Eric had already opened up several wave-screens over the onyx surface, and a few of his people clustered together, their fingers pointing up small idiosyncrasies in the data. He chose a seat far down the table, his legs thrusting out and crossed at the ankle, his arms draped over the arms of the seat. But his fingers kept twitching now and again despite his best efforts to still them.

Bentley flicked a bit of lint from the sleeve of his tan sweater. "I've notified the families of the men killed in action. I didn't tell them it was machine-related, understand?"

Flan nodded. Pretty standard procedure for the Harbor—don't frighten the populace.

"Bring us up to speed if you would, Eric."

Eric shoved at his thin hair and then put his hands on his generous hips. He still hadn't taken a seat. "Tess has neutralized Clara, and the links between Ciaran, Salmindra and Bear seem stable if inactive at the moment. We've shut down all their motor functions on this end and they are currently gel-packed in the machine holding room."

"Neutralized *Clara*?" Flan murmured, his mind seizing on the image of the diminutive Tess tackling and taking down the huge military unit. It almost made him smile.

"We outfitted her with neural filaments in her fingertips—she tore through Clara's central processor with almost no effort."

"God-damn," Flan muttered.

"Yes. Very effective," Bentley replied.

"And tell me, what else does she do with these so called neural filaments?"

"She can access levels of the synap-jock's brain," Eric replied. "Full integration with him, in fact, without the clumsy leads and script support machinery."

"Then she'll go in and clean out Salmindra and Bear and finish this?" Flan asked.

"Not precisely," Bentley replied. He leaned forward in his chair, his dark skin soaking up the light and crossed his arms on the tabletop. "We need to better understand what Bear and Salmindra were attempting. Tess will be able to evaluate their experiment and copy the elements of the template they were designing for later study."

Flan sat very quietly and even his twitching fingers finally came to heel. "Why would you want a copy of the damn thing? You want to chance letting that get out to the public? Have her go in, sever a few arteries in the jock's brain to exit them all permanently, and we can shelve this and move on."

Bentley shook his head, his dark eyes holding Flan's own. "That would be wasteful. Please understand, the department will be able to broker the information Tess will bring back for a sizeable political and financial return on your seven years of hard work."

Flan blinked. Hard. "Excuse me?"

"What part did you not understand?"

Flan started to come out of his chair, decided otherwise, but perched on its very edge. He turned his eyes to Eric, who wouldn't look at him at all. He swallowed then, blinking hard under the florescent lights, feeling both sick and dizzy. None of what he had just heard made sense to him. It was like characters in a novel had suddenly, in a page, changed into something they had not been for the several hundred pages previously.

Or like a synapjock had imagined a reality, and then changed his mind about how his plot would unfold.

But they seemed real, Bentley, Eric, the other techs nervously eyeing him.

Of course they were real. Of course.

"Am I hearing this right?" he finally choked out. "I'm pretty sure I heard you say that you're trading on the stability of machine-bio society for personal or political gain. But of course, I am pretty damn tired right now, my head feels like shit and I probably didn't understand you." Flan raised his voice just a bit, rolling forward with his arms on the table. He felt his anger rise again, as if the hot clarity would burn away a reality gone mad. "Tell me I misheard you, Bentley."

"The department on Machine-ethics has been leaning toward a loosening of the non-interaction protocols for some time," Bentley said. He eased his chair back from the table, his manicured brows pulling down hard over his golden eyes. "They feel it will be a part of normalizing relationships between bio and machine humanities."

"Machines are not fucking human. That has always been a *good* thing, for both species," Flan snapped. It was automatic, his favored response to anyone who put machine and human on a level.

Eric shifted his heavy frame. "They are more human than not," he said, as if reading Flan's mind. We've been keeping them prisoners in their own skulls for over a century. If we really let them interact not just with us but with each other, let them fully participate in exponential technology growth, own companies, marry…"

"… Jesus!" Flan exploded. He rocked out of his chair and stalked to the door, turned on his heel and stormed back. He slammed his fists down on the black table, not even feeling the pain as he glared at them all. The sting in his fingers made him feel hot and clear. "Then why not just alter their programming? Flip a few switches and let them see each other? You've obviously done that with Tess, right? Why'd you drag Lynnie and I through seven years of hell? And much as I hate that synap-jock, you are fucking torturing him for what, Eric? *For what?*"

Eric swallowed, his eyes weaseling over toward Bentley and then back. "Because even the synap expert Bear *knew* we needed the human brain algorithms to be an intrinsic part of the template."

Flan leaned hard on his palms. "What?"

Bentley shot Eric a look. "He means relational acuity. That's why it was time to send Tess in. She's primed for it."

"For what?"

Eric flushed. "Love and hate, Flan. The real things. Deep bonding. Empathy. The ineffable music, the creative inspiration, the breath of life. She's so close now."

Flan stared at Eric for a moment. "You can't do this." His voice sounded strangled. "You can't expect to make them human." He shifted his gaze. "Bentley?"

"We expect to do just that, Flan. Human but significantly enhanced. Longer lived, better decision makers. And the love we're talking about? It's not the gushing, erotic thing on your testosterone-addled mind, you know. Once a human and a machine are more perfectly alike, we *think* we'll be able to really mate them, pair bond them, make them one, and be one step closer to letting our biological bodies fall away."

Flan felt his skin pull tight against his face, his stomach clench. "Mate them..."

Bentley sighed as if he was disappointed with Flan's reactions. "The machine/human synthesis— living for hundreds of years as one. Can you imagine? Death pushed that far away, a body ever young, our human minds enhanced and broadened, needing almost no sleep, but still fully capable of the whole range of human emotion and relational interaction."

"You're talking about merging human consciousness with the machine mind-body? That is your end-game?"

The silence that greeted him was like a giant nod.

Flan straightened, but slowly, each vertebrae stacking on the one below it. "Do *they* understand this?" he finally spat out.

"Does *who* understand this?" Eric asked.

"The machines. Because it sounds like you are hoping to make humans a kind of parasite on their kind. And they may not take kindly to that."

Something flickered in Bentley's eyes, predatory and ugly.

"That's why you're gonna send Tess into Ciaran's scripted world, right? Not to save Ciaran or wipe out Sal and Bear. He'll be changing *her*, making an invasive template in the end that you can spread. And that's not what she's expecting, is it? You hoping to crawl into her skin next when Ciaran is all done wholly rewiring her, Eric?"

"I'd like to walk *with* her, yeah, but not as part of her. Not my thing. You're making this sound like a rape," Eric murmured. His face was very red now, his eyes darting and his eyelashes batting out a quick staccato on his cheeks.

"Your word, not mine," Flan growled back.

"Calm down. You are beginning to sound suspiciously like an artifact from a different age," Bentley said calmly. "Our two peoples have always been dancing closer and closer to each other. This is the ultimate vice action, you know. Because machines don't get addicted, don't need the kind of adrenaline-pumping stimulation humans seem to crave. I'm *hoping* we're putting ourselves out of work." He smiled at Flan, as if trying to lighten the atmosphere.

It didn't quite fly.

"You don't know what will happen if you really wed bios with machines," Flan breathed. "Psychopaths that live forever. Neurotic nut-jobs that can take apart a car with their bare hands. What the hell are you thinking?"

"We'll start with a limited sampling of course," Bentley said. "Good, sane, upright human beings. I was hoping you would volunteer."

"Volunteer?"

"To be in the beta testing program. No family, no ties, and what a vice agent you'd be then; I'm sure we'd need you for a while. Think about it, Flan. Faster reaction speeds, strength, ability to process information fast and without the help of the Harbor teams. Your mind in a whole new body maybe with the echoes of an internal partner that can't die. It's perfect," Bentley smiled a little.

"That tech doesn't exist and if it does, I will find a way to end it. Now."

"Of course, there it is...the other reason I needed to put this to you. I figured your Neanderthal thinking would kick in and you'd be itching try to shut us down. Seemed better to get it all on the table right now, although I had hoped, foolishly, that you would surprise me. Now, I can't allow you to go holier than thou on us, so you get to be first in line for the upgrade. Flan one of the first of the machinekind/humankind hybrids. Karma's a strange thing, huh?"

Flan didn't know whether to laugh or scream. Instead, he shoved away from the table, turned on his heel, his legs driving him to the conference room door.

"Flan!" Eric cried. "Hey, Bentley, what the hell! You don't need..."

Flan stopped cold, Eric's frantic tone sending a horrible tickle up his spine. He half turned. Bentley aimed a military-class electric bolter down the length of the table, his hand steady, and his eyes set and hard. He could see Eric's face out of the corner of his eye, the high color leaching from his face beneath a quick wash of white. The other men in the room had gone perfectly still.

"I volunteer or you *shoot* me, is that it, you mother-fucker? Kill me like you had Lynnie killed?" His voice was a bare whisper in the silent room.

Bentley shrugged, but the gun hardly wavered. "Hands on the top of your head. Down on your knees, Flan."

Flan stood in the frozen tableau of the conference room, every muscle tense, and his breath a mere whisper in his chest.

Chapter 51

The energy of hesitation he showed me was painful.
There is no other word for it. It was like so many
data streams converged in too tight a spot and no
one logic center could sort through the permutations
of it all. But the dam wasn't created by pure data—it
was created by his reaction to it, and not only his
reaction, but also the myriad voices of others in his
own mind adding to the confusion. We think of the
mind as one, but it is a multitude.

-E

Ciaran set his eyes on the scuffed wooden floor, his shoulders rounded, his fingers gripping the edge of the table. At least he didn't have to look at Clara's body, lying so still. The machine named Tess hadn't moved from the archway between the living room and the kitchen. He traced the darker heartwood lines running through the oak boards like he was reading a map. It was fascinating how many times the lines branched and wobbled and ran. Seconds of life memory, frozen and walked on until he brought it all into his brain and made it breathe again, right in this moment.

What was she waiting for?

He heard her then, her step creaking the floorboards, but he couldn't make himself look up. He didn't even flinch when her hand fell on his shoulder, cold but light. "I can't do this right now," she said.

He didn't look up.

"Something is not right. I'm missing something critical. I feel..." she choked her voice off, and Ciaran turned his gaze at her then. Her eyes were haunted, her throat working as if a hand were clenched there.

"You *feel*..." he echoed.

"Too much." She shook her head. "I need to process it all, the last few months, the last few hours." Tess let her hand fall from his shoulder. "And you need to rest, really rest."

Ciaran let his eyes drift back to the floorboards, tracing the lines again. "Take your time," he murmured.

"The transport should have an emergency blanket in the boot. At least you'll be more comfortable then. And I'll take the military model outback and store her in one of the outbuildings."

He didn't answer her, and she moved away, but slowly, as if confused by his stillness. He listened to her steps on the wood; heard the rustle as she picked up Clara, then the back door complained as she opened it.

Finally, a moment of deep silence settled on his shoulders.

He closed his eyes, his chin lifting. God, but he could breathe at last, all of reality stepping back from his mind and nothing else filling it but space and quiet.

Fevers did this, didn't they? And trauma. Wiped away everything until the sense of simply being rose up, surprising and fresh.

Or at least until he started thinking and feeling again.

And of course, the moment crumbled then, with the sound of the back door opening, with his own mind pulled back into the iron grip of his senses and the roil of emotions that flared in his gut, forcing his breath back in, ragged. He let himself drop onto his feet, steadying himself against the table. He turned to face her, straightening up into his spine, six feet four inches of shaking flesh.

She pulled up, as if reading something strange there in his face.

"I need a shower," he said. "If the water is working."

She nodded, laying the small red package that was the emergency blanket on the dusty kitchen counter. "I imagine it came on automatically when Clara fired up the power cells. I'll check for you, if you want."

"I can manage." He gripped the table harder, driving his broken nails into the wood.

"I'm sure you can manage," she replied quietly. "I was being polite."

Her words were laced with what sounded like a mixture of hurt and admiration, and he cocked his head a little. "You're really different from other machine-kind, aren't you?"

Her eyelashes fluttered for a moment. "Yes. As different as you are from most of humankind, I am sure."

He merely nodded, not sure what to say to that, his eyes going to the stair banister over her right shoulder. "Up there, do you think?"

"Seems logical."

He put his body into gear, hating its sluggishness, hating the shaking and the fatigue. She moved aside for him, just a half step, and he forced himself not to pause. His hand closed on the wood railing and he labored his way up to the second story of the farmhouse.

He walked down the short hallway, hand on the wall, and opened the first door. The empty bedroom stared back at him, the bare windows casting his image back. Light was fading beyond, another day of reality wicking away, ray by ray.

The second door on his left was already ajar, and he moved into the shadowy bath space. A thin layer of dust coated the toilet top, the sink and the rim of the old-fashioned bathtub. No curtain hung between himself and the mouth of the shower. Not that it mattered much to his numb brain. He automatically stripped off Bear's clothing, tossing it all from the room out into the hallway, and turned the shower on. The first spurts were not only cold but the water was a sickly yellowish brown. He waited, naked, for it to warm and clear. And eventually, it did.

He stepped in full-faced, letting the water hit his eyes and lips, letting it run down his chest and belly and legs. No soap, but that was OK, the water was hot, and the drops pounding on him felt good. He lifted his hand to the smooth skin there at his forehead, and rubbed methodically back and forth. An ache bloomed to life, just over his eyes, but he kept kneading the flesh until he felt something warmer and heavier than the water. He pulled his hand down in front of his face, watched as the water washed away something very much like blood.

He didn't remember his knees giving out; only the fuzzy recognition that the cold tile wall now cradled his cheek, his arms flopped useless in front of him, his legs folded beneath him. His breath came in low, groaning gasps, and reddish-pink striped the water that swirled around the drain.

Ciaran heard Tess's step in the hallway. The shower stopped and he felt her cold hands slide around his armpits. He let her half-drag, half-lift him out of the tub. He even allowed her to lay him out flat on his back, her hand cupped over his forehead. "Did you pass out and hit you head?" she murmured.

He stared up into the delicate lines of her face. "Am I really bleeding?"

"A little, like you sliced your forehead on something."

"I saw the blood in the water and I...I don't know what...." Ciaran couldn't find the words to explain anything.

"I need to find something to dry you off with. Stay down, OK?" Tess tapped his breastbone with one small finger. "I mean it; don't get up. Between the heat of the shower and your fever, your balance is probably shot."

"Alright," he whispered and pulled himself into a fetal position on the dusty bare floor, one hand cupping the hot throb of his forehead.

Chapter 52

Violence so often cuts through hesitation, through the hurt of a changed paradigm or a perceived threat to self. I could see how it could be a drug of sorts. It did change a situation, although not always in ways that were foreseeable or even remotely controllable. My kind has not been partial to violence as a way to create a kind of clarity and impulse to move forward. I am not sure we can integrate its energy any better than the humans, in the end.

-E

"Knees, Flan. Hands interlaced over the top of your head." Bentley slid around the edge of the table, clearing the shooting line between them. The other techs had dropped back, their faces drawn and tight.

"You don't want to do this, Bentley," Flan murmured. He raised his hands to his sides, and then linked his fingers over his scalp. But he didn't kneel.

"Get on your goddamn knees, Flan."

Flan smiled, even though the muscles in his face felt like a shaky mask. "You gonna shoot me? Really? In front of everyone?"

Bentley returned the smile. "Lot riding on this. And everyone here is pretty deeply involved."

Flan shrugged, and started to drop to his knees, then threw himself at the lip of the table. The entire section flipped back toward him, drinks and hardware flashed into the air, and he smelled the hot sizzle of the bolter shot plow into the wood near his fingers. Before Bentley could get a cleaner angle on him, he rushed low at the conference room doors and slammed through them into the hallway beyond.

Something white hot sliced along the edge of his right leg but he rolled to his feet, and smashed at the locking mechanism to the conference room. The clear hand-panel shattered under his fist, the shards biting in, but he hardly felt them. The door murmured into locked position, even as alarms began to wail in the narrow passageway.

He glanced up the hallway toward the main Harbor tech room, then turned and half-ran, half-limped to the stairwell. Thankfully, the heavy assault door opened readily with his handprint, and he locked it down quickly from the inside.

They would expect him to break for the surface, Flan reasoned. So that meant he had to go down and find something to use as a weapon. He dropped quickly, his right leg dragging and nearly useless, his hands sweaty upon the railing. He knew the cameras would be eyeing him already but hoped most of the Harbor's attention was focused on the weapon's discharge in the conference room.

He plunged through the door on the storage level, ran two strides, and felt the floor shift under him. He fell hard, pressed himself up, and staggered to the support of the wall. The low-slung ceiling undulated above him. No, the building wasn't moving, he realized.

The movement was within *him*, his own senses wobbling and failing.

Gas.

It had to be one of the security neuro-inhibitors. He hit the first door panel he could find, half-falling into the narrow and dimly lit room. He tried to lock it down, clawing at the wall, his fingers raking over the control panel but not finding a purchase. He went down hard, his muscles beginning to jerk with the toxin, his eyes refusing to close even to blink. Dimly he heard a low beep, and the soft sigh of something releasing pressure. He managed to roll his head to the side, his hand splayed along the cold floor.

The covers of two canisters lying side by side like coffins had opened, their interior lights flicking on. Whatever they held moved, hands creeping over the sides like monsters from an ancient 3-D show. And then they sat up, their eyes falling on him, even as the room seemed to fade at the edges. He knew the lines of their faces, of machine-kind Salmindra and Bear.

Well fuck the whole damn day. He tried to peel back his lips from his teeth in a weak snarl, but the jerking of his muscles turned into a full seizure, and he kicked furiously into the darkness.

Chapter 53

How sweet and gentle he allowed us to manifest sometimes, how trusting that our very alienness would somehow protect him from the vagaries of his own emotional responses. He needed us to be different from him, more predictable, less emotional. It gave him the kind of confidence a parent might give a child, I suppose. But what do we, in turn, ever take away from such interactions? Do we allow them to change us or are we simply stimulus-response engines in the end? And is that, in itself, a bad thing at all?

-E

Ciaran let Tess wrap him up in the emergency blanket, and ease him back against the bathroom cabinet, but he quietly refused to let her shift him from the floor. Every now and again, he touched his forehead, but the wound had stopped bleeding and his finger pads could feel only a thin slice running over his eyebrows.

"Do you remember what happened?" she asked.

"I don't know," he muttered. He glanced out into the hallway, at the pile of Bear's clothes lying there. He supposed he'd have to get back into them, and that didn't exactly give him any more juice to move.

"Is it some kind of genetic imperative that all male bios have to bleed from their foreheads or something?" Tess crouched low before him, her weight on her toes, effortlessly balanced.

Ciaran swallowed the dry lump in his throat. "What do you mean?" he rasped out.

"You, yourself in your Roman character, Flan..."

Ciaran's eyes widened. "All of us have the same head wound?"

"Yes." Tess cocked her head a little.

"Three of any one thing is an exit device," Ciaran murmured. He looked around him, even raised his hand and looked deeply into the lines etched into his skin. Every detail was right, clear and clean, little tributary creases feeding into the bigger rivers of flesh on his palm. And then he was aware that Tess was watching him with unfeigned curiosity.

She shook her head, her lips curling in half-grin. "You actually think you're creating this reality, too?"

Ciaran lowered his arm, looking into her eyes. "Am I?"

"Would it matter what I said? Wouldn't I just be you?" she asked. She quirked on eyebrow at him, evidently amused at her own wit.

He laughed then, short and barking. "Touché. But I never play myself in a synap production."

"Because?"

"Better to keep hold of reality if you play someone else in your head," he answered.

"So you can answer your own question."

"Theoretically."

Tess frowned a little then. "So you're admitting you *could* still be plugged in? Honestly?"

He closed his eyes. "Are you trying to make me crazy?"

"No, simply curious about how your brain is processing information. I could always take you to Flan; arrange a meeting. Compare head wounds or something." He could hear the abrupt lightness return to her voice, but he didn't open his eyes.

"The impressions I received from you regarding that particular vice cop don't exactly make me feel like running into him anytime soon. Or at all. Still glad you didn't really kill him, though."

"Flan's not a fan of yours, I must say. But he does respect your toughness. Perhaps its a guy-thing."

He laughed a little bitterly behind his closed lids. "Toughness. Now I *know* we're not anywhere inside my head." He chuckled, and put his fingers to his forehead again.

"I like your honesty."

"Synap jocks don't do honesty," he murmured. "And after Lynnie..."

"Yes you do," Tess interrupted him. "Even when the words don't match the output of your body language and chemical releases, there is always truth to be read in a bio. It is implicit rather than explicit. It's quite charming, really."

He opened his eyes then, his gaze narrowing at her fuzzy image. The darkness pressed into the room now, shadowing everything. "That's part of the template Salmindra and Bear hope to create, isn't it?"

She didn't move, so he assumed he'd hit the nail right on the head, for what it was worth. "Perhaps," she conceded. "There is a lot we don't understand about this."

"Machines won't have the capacity to tell when another machine is lying if or when they all begin to interact, will they?"

"They don't now. I lied easily to Clara because she could only analyze my actions and words. And she did not have access to my longer history, my years of involvement with the Harbor for instance. We are *designed* to interact with humans and look for the truth in more than your verbalizations. But with other machines? Not at all. It troubles me, these changes to us that the Harbor has sanctioned all on their own."

Ciaran nodded. "Lots of ramifications."

"Yes."

He lay his head back against the cabinet, feeling his fatigue wash over him again. "I don't want to spend the night here."

"I can set a fire, inflate the emergency blanket to cushion you against the hard floor..."

"No," he cut her off. "I don't want to sleep here, in this house, with Clara's body outside. Get the car and lets get out of here."

She tipped her head, a vague movement in the dark. "That's not possible, I'm afraid. The car was last linked with Clara's personal ident transmission, which I of course shredded."

He tried to read her in the darkness, and came up with nothing but her too-perfect breath pattern. "Your kind has a great advantage over us," he said at last. "I can't tell if you are lying to me, either."

"My kind, as you call us, has many differences from you. Whether such things will be advantages is very hard to say just now. I'm not lying to you, but then, you will have to take my word for it."

"I don't do trust, either. But then, you probably already know that."

"Of course."

"Of course," he echoed her.

"You'll need to put Bear's clothing back on. I couldn't find anything else in the house. My apologies."

"It's OK," he murmured. "I'm already wearing him on the inside after all."

Her silence was long and he imagined her running various verbal comebacks and laying them all aside.

He ended the quiet for her. "Start the fire. I'll be down when I'm able."

Tess rose without further comment and left on her silent feet.

Chapter 54

Humans seem to have developed a common story of their own creations going bad. I can peruse literature, and for each child born of human creativity who passes forward light and life, I can find another that does the opposite. Perhaps that is where the proclivity for religion arises—they do not trust the inherent goodness of themselves and seek ways to secure it within. I only felt great sorrow as some dark part of Ciaran again and again cast machine-kind as inconceivable, evil and violent. We are only he in a different skin, but he seldom could show that.

-E

Flan was only aware of pressure, of something holding him in a full-body press. He shifted his fingers, and immediately hit cold plastic walls on either side of him. The weight made breathing difficult, and a dull kind of panic started its primitive drumbeat deep in his head and chest. He tried to shift, but the weight ground him into the gel padding without mercy.

"Stay still." The voice hissed above him, distorted, and he felt something like the curves of feet tap at the sides of his face. His own feet tickled, as if bathed in hair. He was under someone, someone heavy and laid out in something distressingly like a coffin.

Bright light haloed the interior for a moment, but all he could see was legs and the rise of a torso. The small oval canopy that admitted the light would have only shown the face of whoever sprawled on top of him. The light abruptly turned off and they were plunged into darkness again.

He counted to a hundred, quite sure that when he hit that first triple digit he would just try good old-fashioned force.

"How many checks will they make before they move away from this level?" He stopped counting. Wondered at that feminine voice. He took a very educated guess.

Salmindra?"

"Yes. How many checks? That was the second."

He tried to think, pressed as he was between gel and machinekind, tried to reason out why they hadn't just left him and fled. Or pulled him apart and fled. He heard himself say, "How are you functional?"

"Answer the question."

"They won't backtrack again," even as his mind fumbled around, trying to make sense of it all. "At least, that would be my guess."

"Then we wait, since you are unsure of the protocol."

"How long? I can't breathe with you on top of me."

"You're talking, so you are obviously moving enough air," Salmindra replied.

"Goddamn it!" He slammed his fist sideways into the canister wall, only to find the weight over him increase. He gasped, wriggling beneath her, his lungs suddenly wholly compressed and aching.

"I'm holding a great deal of my weight *off* you, as you can see. Be still. And wait." The form pinning him grew lighter, and he realized that she was indeed bracing herself mostly off his body. He ground his teeth, dragging in sweet oxygen through his nose.

"Why are you..."?

"Shut up," Salmindra said, her voice even and low.

He fumed there, unmoving, a little hot and a lot claustrophobic. His head ached with the neuro-gas, and twice he had to choke back bile that crept up his throat in a slow burn. He tried to relax, but couldn't get much further than unclenching his teeth.

A rap on the view glass startled him, and then the whole lid lifted, and she levered herself out carefully, clearly trying not to injure him as she moved off him and onto the floor.

Flan sat up quickly, and then nearly fell back as a wave of nausea rushed over him. "Fuck!" he hissed.

Bear leaned on the canister, dressed in hospital scrubs. He scratched lazily at one armpit. "Neuro-inhibitor upset your tummy a bit?"

"Fuck you." He rolled a bit to his side, breathing slowly then stiff-armed himself more or less to sitting.

Salmindra had joined Bear, and he felt a little flush of fear shiver through his body.

"It's interesting to finally meet, Flan Jaspers. Been on our proverbial tales for sometime, I believe. So tell me, do you know how to get us out of here?" Bear asked casually. But his eyes locked with Flan's, ready to read the real answer in a way far beyond words. *Don't lie to me*, his glance said.

"I don't...maybe," he hedged. Muddy words, muddy body language, that was the only way to lie to a machine.

"Maybes won't keep you alive," Bear said. Damn how could he even smile like that, genuine and toothy as could be?

"My being a yes-man won't keep *you* alive, either," Flan retorted. He eyed the sides of the canister, trying to figure out how to get out of the thing with any kind of dignity. He gave up and rolled out, making Salmindra and Bear give way to him. He white-knuckled the canister as his knees wobbled around, trying to remember what balance and coordination felt like. As his center came back a little, he eyed them, measuring their quietness and poise. "My guess would be to make for the old engineering tunnels, follow them to the garage level. I wouldn't be able to get through the bolted security screens, but you both could probably tear through them. They weren't designed to keep machine-kind in, after all. No need."

"Much better than maybe," Salmindra murmured. "Congratulations. You live."

He let go of the canister enough to swipe his dark hair out of his eyes. "Yeah. Great. But for how long, Sal?"

Bear laughed quietly as he moved away, leaving Sal to marshal her own answer.

"That's entirely up to you, Flan."

"And how do you fucking know my name?"

She smiled then, not unlike Bear.

"How...!"

"In time, Flan. In time. If you choose to give yourself any, that is."

"I'm human. What do you think I'll choose?"

Salmindra shook her head, her gray eyes amused. "Human? That has nothing to do with this, Flan Jaspers. Nothing at all."

Chapter 55

I had supposed that his Roman character would be simpler to comprehend—that humanity had evolved emotionally from the times of swords and empires and that we would be able to mark that evolution, capture how it grew and changed with time. Even he seemed to believe that particular character to be somehow more pure and less complicated. But it was a linear conceit, I see now. Despite the strength of that script, I could tell very little difference in the way emotions interacted with thought process and relational abilities within that ancient Roman soldier.

It was sobering to realize that perhaps our own genesis was not so much an evolution but rather just a slightly different form of basic human creativity and life process. The torque and the robot, the hide drum and the digitally sampled and blended soundtrack are not so very far apart after all. Perhaps we do not advance humanity with the embrace of our full relational potential because origin and end are already the same place.

-E

Ciaran eased into Bear's clothes, still damp and rancid with his own sweat, and then drew the emergency blanket over his shoulders, clenching the light fabric under his chin. He went down the stairs carefully, feeling for the dimly lit steps with his toes.

The way the light flickered and danced on the walls, he supposed Tess had set the fire but had not bothered with such niceties as actual light. And he was too tired to hunt for the motion pads.

He shuffled into the living room, twitching away from the glower of the synap machines. Tess stood before the fire, her arms crossed, her feet planted and stable. She half turned her head toward him. "It's warmer here. I can reset the blanket for you, too, if you like."

He shrugged it off and handed it to her, and moments later, watched as it gently inflated, filling out like a high-class comforter. Tess flipped it out on the floor, and then doubled it over like a sleeping bag. Still crouched on the floor, she looked up at him. "Good enough?"

"Yes." But he didn't quite trust his legs to take him down with any kind of smoothness.

She frowned up at him, the light playing with burgundy fingers along her fine profile. "Do you need help?"

"No." But still he stood there, looking down at her, at the ripple of the reddish lights through her dark hair. "Where will you be?"

"Right here." She slipped back a few feet, and then settled, kneeling, her hands folded demurely over her lap. For a long moment, she studied him, and then abruptly shut her eyes. Her face was so delicate, the eyebrows arching like wing-shaped guards framing the metallic dagger on her forehead.

He blinked and lowered himself down onto the blanket with a pained grunt. She did not move. He put his feet to her, rolling so he could watch her. But she sat so very still, and in the silence, tinged only with the snap and play of the fire, there was nothing to cling to anymore. *I'll close my eyes for a moment.*

Just a moment.

Just...

Just a moment. He rolled over in the grass, blinking in sunshine that filtered through bare branches. He could hear the river, a low throaty gurgle just feet away. Something covered him, something that smelled like age and mud and maybe a horse or two, and he flung it from him as he rose. He stood alone on the bank, and for a moment, he could only sway there, his eyes seeking for shadows in the wood, his ears aching but catching only birdcalls, the creaking whine of the breeze, the water lipping at the edge of its bed.

He reached for his forehead, feeling the familiar scab already leaning toward scar tissue. His helmet and sword lay at his feet and for a long moment he stared at them, trying to understand.

He raised his eyes, finally did see a shape that was not of wood and rock and water, thrown there in the brush, arms and legs wide and pale in the light and blond hair caught in the breezy tangles bound here and there with mud and debris. He bent, picking up his short sword, and moved toward the body with cautious steps.

It was a woman, clad in armor, her teeth clenched and a terrible head-wound spilling dark black blood and the white-clawed fragments of her skull over one side of her face. He traced the long lines of her legs and arms, knowing this was a warrior, no matter what her gender declared. The weight of his own sword drew his attention like a memory; the blade was pitted a little, but gleaming. He had not killed her. Or if he had, he must have wiped the blade clean. No, I argued with him, there was no way he would have laid down so close to her body, no matter how dark the night or tired. Spirits of the dead were real, and he had no way to ward them off here.

Her blue-gray eyes, misted, repelled him even more than the blood, and he eased back from her.

"Ciaran."

He spun then, the sword coming before him, his other shoulder aching for his familiar shield. The wood shuddered in the wind, mocking him with movement that seemed alive. He swallowed, his damp hand clenching the wood grip.

"You cannot run from us, Ciaran."

"Show yourself!" he bellowed into the morning air. He scooped up his helmet, settling it one handed on his head, pieces of the leather harness at the end of the metal cheek-pieces fluttering and tickling his skin. He turned a careful circle, not willing to give up the space for big movement that the open area afforded, painfully aware a single archer could take him down.

Again, he felt his arm flex for a shield that was not there.

"You cannot return to the legion. They will rip the hide from your back and kill you for desertion. Remember..."

But there was nothing to remember. *The past had not happened yet.* He stood in that paradox for a moment, absolutely sure of it's validity and his own wobbling sanity.

The sword tip drooped in his hand.

"Ciaran."

His head snapped up again, nostrils flaring. A young woman had materialized at the tree line, her hands empty of weapons, her mostly leather clothing cut and wrapped tightly around her frame so nothing would snag on the forest undergrowth. Her hair was plaited back, severe, but that made her eyes big and luminous. She opened her palms toward him. "Listen to my voice. Just mine."

"She is a deceiver," the other voices echoed, a male and female this time, in tandem.

"No, Ciaran. They call your own mind to deceive you, to soak you in too many experiences. Where are these supposed others you listen to? Can you see them?"

He couldn't shift his eyes from her. She was magnificent and delicate, iron and filigree meeting. "No, I don't think they are really here."

She took a hesitant step toward him, as if she had been raised with deer and had picked up the way they stepped, silent, tentative, all her sense alert. "That's right. These other voices you speak to, give them no energy and they will fall silent, like any unwanted thoughts."

He swallowed, holding out his hand to stop her forward movement.

"You are a child of shamans, a reader of thin places. Nothing can hurt you, not in all three worlds here, above and below, if you but will it." She took another step, but stopped as he raised his sword to press her back.

"I am a soldier," he whispered.

"That came later, after something like Rome broke you and bent you to their will."

"No one broke me."

"You were so young, and the young must believe in what they do in order to survive. But oh, such a child you were, Ciaran! Such a mind. Turn that free now and put aside the child Rome crafted in straight lines and logic. See, even now, you focus on me, and where have the other voices gone? You can be free. All the worlds are yours, not just this particular storyline."

He stepped back from her, his eyes flicking the trees again, but fast, not really seeing. "No."

"Ciaran, this is not your only place and time."

"You speak in riddles," he said, his eyes coming back to her face. How delicate she was, clean and pale, her eyes tipped and thin-lidded.

"I killed the one who would have hurt you." She gestured toward the blond body in the reeds. "I pulled you from the black waters, and wrapped you in warmth by a fire. Don't you remember?"

He opened his mouth but no words came out. He shuddered there, the sword tip again falling as memories flashed and eddied without concrete form in him. "I remember too much," he finally said. "As if a thousand storytellers sat shoulder to shoulder within my heart and sang a single line, none connected to the other, until all becomes gibberish. The past lies in the future, the future spins talons into the present and into me."

She smiled then, her teeth white and even, the expression making her something wholly beautiful. "Yes. Yes, exactly. But it is all you, Ciaran. How rich, how lucky, to be able to voice a thousand lives. Focus, and you could hear the whole tale from each of them, do you not see? You play the soldier of Rome, but this man you think you are, it is one of a thousand stories you are telling yourself. You asked me to make you one, but what a waste such a thing would be. And as you can see, unnecessary. You are greater than the two who haunt you because you are them."

"I breathe, I ache, how can this not be singular?" He touched his forehead. "And bleed. I bleed." He could hear his voice shaking.

"Yes." She took another step toward him. "Yes, you do bleed."

"Then how is this not real?"

"What makes anything real? I only know that the continuity and the sensations of this place are not stable, Ciaran. You've said it yourself. The past has not happened yet."

"No. I don't really understand those words."

"A thousand storytellers in your head, but they are all you. You create the continuity in this soldier, but it is a made thing, an imagined thing only. Another story, but not *you* because you are that observing it all."

He blinked, the sunlight drawing dizzying flickers of shadow through his gaze. "And you?" he asked. "Would that not make you one more story, no more than whimsy or dream?"

She smiled sadly at him. "I am here and yet, not here, like the *you* who you truly are. A guest only, but also a doorway or a bridge." She extended her hand. "Take my hand and become whole, Ciaran. You have stopped the voices for a while. And you can rest. I once promised you a sole identity. I *promised you* this soldier you are wearing so you might take vengeance, but now, breath-by-breath, I can see you, and see it is not enough to play a character. You shine, Ciaran. Step from this dark place. Let me help you."

Her nails were so clean and perfect, her hands soft. They did not belong to this time and place, any more than her unwrinkled skin or the clear, cool gaze of her eyes. No guile there, no fear, either, in her steady hand. She was not lying or believed the lie so completely that she had made it truth.

She did not wait for him to move, but walked forward then, powerful, shifting from the deer-dancer to something feline. But he didn't raise his sword to her.

Dimly, he heard a flood of other voices, some male, some female, different languages running together but demanding he strike her down. Demanding he hearken to *them*. But looking into her unblinking eyes, the gladius hanging low in his right hand, he reached his open left palm to her.

And when she closed her fingers around his own, cold fingers, true, but gripping without a message of compulsion or fear, it felt like she could indeed drag him from the greediest waters and point him toward home.

Chapter 56

I knew the bridge program I had introduced and the multiple scripts blended in his subconscious would create a template that was not quite so proprietary to Ciaran himself. Or rather, I should say, that was my carefully considered hypothesis. How strange and rather annoying when he began to revert to his individualism through the very corridors of relationship with the entity he labeled "the Bridge". That dance between them was something I couldn't quite grasp, having nothing to compare it to within myself.

-E

Flan hated the long, stifling computer access ducts. He hated small spaces and the crush of a machine in front of him and behind, bracketing him as they crawled forward. What the fuck would they need him for, once they had made the garage? Salmindra and Bear could separate and act like any other invisible machine in the environment. As far as the Harbor staff knew, they were still encased in gel-pads and plastic in the basement.

Him, though? Even the damn mice would be looking for him. Speaking of which, he was pretty sure that the shit of said mice was what currently padded his hands and knees. He could pretend it was dust and lint, but that did nothing for the smell. How long had anyone cleaned in here, anyway? Did mice chew on cables?

Or on moving biological material like him?

And his leg was starting to hurt again, where the bolter had shied past him. Sal, whose butt he was very tired of looking at, would tell him it was all in his mind. Well, yeah, where else would pain really be, if you wanted to be all philosophical about it?

Sal stopped, and Flan leaned his rib cage against the wall to take a little weight off his knees. He could see the ceiling abruptly lift just beyond her, but had the impression that the corridor narrowed still more. She climbed through slowly, finally able to stand but forced to move sideways in the tight space. She glanced down at him, pointed, but said nothing. With a sigh, he eased forward, bracing against the wall to get to his feet. God, but it felt good to stand, and he wriggled his spine in the press of the walls. Bear shoved him forward a little, and then they were cemented together again, sliding step by step down the red-lighted passage.

His driving hip was beginning to hurt when Salmindra abruptly stopped. She actually stepped back into him, forcing him up hard against Bear's leading shoulder. "The bridge program is malfunctioning," she muttered.

Bear shifted even closer and Flan allowed himself a low curse under his breath.

"Yes. I am getting that now."

"Can we make adjustments?" Salmindra asked.

The silence was long, and Flan found himself mashed tightly enough that he was having trouble breathing. "What is a bridge program?" he finally asked.

They ignored him completely, well, except where they leaned in even more. He had the impression they were actually speaking to each other, their shoulders rubbing up against him, rubbing through him like he was the wire that connected them somehow. And then he could hear it, the ghostly whisper of words not his own, flicking faster than he could catch them through the medium of his own mind, like the blips that showed up on a synap-jock's unedited production. Or like two machines talking to each other.

"What the fuck..." Bear's big head smacked sideways into his own to silence him.

Yeah, and wasn't that the last straw? He head butted Bear back, his ear burning with the impact, and tried to use his hip to leverage Sal forward and away. He might as well have been stuffed in the storage canister again, for all the shift he got out of her. She ran her arm across her own chest and grabbed his throat, lifting him to his toes. The angle would have been physically impossible for a human; but then, such specs didn't apply to machine-kind. He couldn't stop himself from trying to pry those cold fingers off his skin, his feet scrambling for any kind of secure hold on the floor. Spots ran in his eyes, blood red spots, and his whole body flailed and bounced off the hard walls in the too-tight space.

Sal abruptly set him down, but her hand didn't leave his throat. He wasn't sure then, if the flickers that continued to run through his brain came from them or his own panicked and oxygen starved self. He swallowed convulsively again and again, hating the shivering and trembling in his body, and hating *them* even more.

When the images in his mind began to take on more substance, it didn't particularly make him feel any better. He caught glimpses of a stream, and a dark forest and of a—fuck—was that a Roman soldier? Impressions of a blond body slung into the underbrush, of a small, neat woman who reminded him of...of...

Tess?

Of course his mind would supply the characters of his nightmare. He was really and truly cracking up, peopling the little rushes of the machine conversation in his brain with little bits of slightly altered reality. Scrambling in his own mind to find some ground to stand on. He moaned and Sal tightened her grip briefly, a firm warning. He saw the Roman reach for the woman—damn, that *was* Tess, wasn't it—

The explosion in his own head was so brilliant, he would have screamed if Sal hadn't effectively silenced him by closing her hand again. Everything washed white, intense, scalding and cold at the same time. He saw the soldier and Tess fall to the ground, the flash of light flattening trees and evaporating the water in its bed, burned a perfect, pure circle around them like they had been rendered on a canvas, stark and alone against a world of white.

"Reset?" Salmindra's voice was no longer inside his head.

"Paused until I can analyze the data," Bear answered quietly, too quietly, his usual jovial voice subdued, almost saddened. "Keep moving."

Salmindra released Flan and Bear shoved him forward. And for one moment, he found himself grateful that the walls and the machines held him upright.

Chapter 57

Did he think that by taking us into him, he could make us like him? That by expanding his selfhood beyond his own skin, he could somehow cut through the barriers his biology and conditioning had erected within him? It was a fascinating thing, seeing him changing us as we had always dreamed to be changed. Who the creator then? And who the created? And why did he choose to create it with echoes of an emotion of love?

-E

Ciaran jerked awake, terribly aware that he was held in the cold vise of an embrace. Tess pressed up along his back, one curved arm over his hip, the other beneath his body and then over his heart, and one heavy leg pinned his own to the floor. He tried to shift, and her grip only tightened.

"Lay still. I'm having trouble disengaging."

He could feel it then, little stinging contact points where her fingertips met his flesh. He remembered how she had taken Clara out and shuddered, knowing without asking that part of her coiled inside of him, tapped into his nervous system. "You had no right," he whispered, his voice ragged.

"As the old saying goes, 'you own the life you save'," she replied.

"That's creative." He bunched his jaw, feeling his belly shake with rage. He wanted to thrash then, throw her off, punch her right in that small nose of hers. Abruptly, the fury went out of him, and he was pretty sure the calmness that suddenly echoed through him wasn't his own. She had taken control of his nervous system and willed him to be calm.

"You did that just now," he accused her.

"You were beginning to panic."

"No, I was beginning to think of ways to kill you."

"Same thing. Dead end paths for you."

He mulled that for a moment, and then tried a different tact. "I remember a bright flash of light when you took my...when you took the soldier's hand. What happened?"

"I don't know," she said. "Two scripts, remember? I think it came from there not me."

"I heard the word malfunction," he offered, his voice more of a hoarse whisper than anything.

"Yes. Fragments again from the other script."

"Wonderful."

"Not the word I would use."

"So I have to lay here for how long with you freezing my backside?"

"I can't retract the filaments. I may have to disengage them totally, but I'm not quite willing to do that yet."

"Disengage? You mean leave them in me?"

"Your own body would break them down eventually."

"Wonderful image, Tess. I feel all crawly inside. No wait! I *am* all crawly inside, right?" He shuddered, and not just from the cold radiating from her.

"Humor is a good sign."

"Of desperation?"

"Of sanity," she said.

"Wouldn't really know," he muttered. "It hurts where your lines feed in, do you know that?"

"Yes, that is what your nervous system is telling me. I'm sorry. I have little control over the actual interface sites."

"Make it stop."

"What part of 'I'm sorry' didn't you understand?" she whispered into his ear. "I can't make it stop. But..."

"But?"

A sudden flush ran through his belly and shot straight to his groin, as if a warm and wet mouth had descended on his skin and sucked in deep. He did groan then, arching his back. "Oh, sweet Jesus, what was that?"

"Just me taking your mind off the pain."

"What if I prefer the pain?" he muttered through gritted teeth.

"You're lying," she said, her lips touching the back of his ear. "I can tell. Although you've told yourself that one enough you almost believe you *like* to hurt."

He felt his fair skin flush, although from the stimulation, the pain or her effortless trip into his psyche, he had no idea. "And so. Now what?"

"Two choices, neither very pleasant for either of us."

"Of course."

"One, I disengage the fibers. It will feel roughly like cutting off the tips of my fingers."

"Lets do that one."

"Of course, you will feel it all with me, every bit of it. And I will never really leave you, at least until your body finally breaks down the fibers, something that could take years. I will continue to receive impressions from you, not thoughts, and I cannot be directive with your nervous system, but a certain level of empathic involvement will be inevitable."

He swallowed. "Tell me the second choice is better."

Tess was silent behind him, her breathing rhythm perfect and even.

"Tess?"

"I pull them out."

"And it would hurt, but..."

"It could rip out significant parts of your nervous system as well. Not only potentially damaging you so you'd be unable to work as a synapjock, I may end up reducing you to a vegetable. Or a man in constant, unending pain. Or... "

"Lots of maybes."

"I'm being optimistic for your sake."

Then it was Ciaran's time to lie there quietly, contemplating rocks and hard places. He sighed. "There really is only one way to go with this, isn't there?"

"The first option, you mean."

"Yeah." He closed his eyes, shaking his head a little against the blanket. "Or are you sitting on a third option here? I mean you could just kill me, Tess. Right?"

He felt her tremble a little behind him. Felt her pull him a little closer to her belly. "Your death would be...a highly distasteful alternative to this situation."

"Why? Because you'd have to feel me die?"

"No, the death process is something I am not particularly concerned with."

He had to swallow that sentence down like it had barbs. "Meaning?"

"Meaning, I would...emotionally *regret* the action. And it is very hard for machine kind to forget. To kill you would irrevocably change how I could function in the future."

Ciaran frowned into the dead fire. "What are you trying to say, Tess?"

"As I have tried to tell you. I don't wish to harm you."

"No, I don't think that is what you are saying at all. You're not telling me *why* you don't wish to harm me. Your programming *demands* you bring me in, am I right? Alive, so they can keep poking at my brain. That's all. Tell me I'm right."

"Quite the opposite." He didn't miss the flatness of her voice.

Ciaran mulled that over for a moment. "You're on target. You got me. Mission over, unless you lose me somehow. And I think death counts as losing me, and that's that. They need me, which means you have to keep me in one piece, right?"

He could feel her shift against him, as if she were uncomfortable with the coldness of her own body. "I have been within your mind, Ciaran."

"So?"

"I have seen through your eyes from the inside, do you understand? Words fail."

He felt the contact points of her fingers burn hot against his flesh, and for a moment he was not sure where he ended and she began. Maybe she felt exactly the same thing. And what she was struggling to say began to dawn on him. "You don't...you can't...fuck. I've known you what? Not quite day? Are you trying to tell me you...you...*care* for me? No way I am going to believe that. You're machine-kind, Tess. You don't *do* those kinds of emotions. You *can't*."

She went still, her breathing program interrupted, her body hard and cold along his spine. "I would agree with you. Except, I believe my personality template, my emotional algorithms if you will, have been altered by your own. Forcibly. That is both fascinating and troublesome. It's part of why I cannot physically disengage from you. Why I cannot kill you, even if I were ordered to do so. Why even causing you pain or harm is distressing to me."

"Are you trying to say I somehow programmed you to *love* me? Good God! Then you know I can't return the sentiment, right? Right?"

"Why do humans put so much store on the reciprocity of emotional states?" she whispered in his ear.

And that observation took his breath away.

"I'm going to disengage the lines now. I am with you, holding you. I care for you; it is part of who I am now. You are not alone, Ciaran. Hold to that."

The pain was blinding, washing out the entire room in white flame, screeching along myriad nerve pathways so complex, so tangled, that he couldn't even force his body to breathe. And when the air finally rushed in, he did scream, his whole body slamming back into her. And she held him, her breathing program perfectly stilled, her own limbs so stiff that he felt like he was held in the embrace of a metal cage. He shuddered, another cry and another ripping from him, and he wasn't even sure if she was conscious behind him, within him. So hot, so much fire, racing and consuming him from within.

And then, abruptly, he was cold, shaking with it, his eyelashes gummed with an imagined frost, his skin awash in goose bumps, his teeth clacking against each other in his too-tight jaw. But the cold was good, it damped the fire down, and in just a few breaths, both sensations faded, like the echo of a wintry sunset.

"It's done," Tess murmured. How broken she sounded, two words, but even that sound liked more than she could handle. He didn't know what to say, wasn't even sure how to frame any reaction at all after hours and hours of the unending nightmare he had found himself in.   He was fire and frost together, and there were no words, just raw and battered sensations drowning out everything else.

"You will recover from all of this. I will protect you. I swear it." Her voice rasped in his ear, obviously hurting from whatever pain she, too, had experienced.

Or like she had read his mind and could fill in what he could not say.

Chapter 58

*The first of the truly cohesive movements he
made to restructure his own mind were rough, not
the stuff of a high-level synapjock at all. As I
watched, I began to be more than a little aware of
the helplessness humans feel, the sense that there is
no control to be found and the paradox of searching
for this elusive trick of marshaling their many selves.
Their inner world would always be a battleground
they could never quite hold to a singular I AM.*

-E.

Salmindra stopped abruptly. "There is a door."

Flan shook his head. "No. No way. Solid exterior
and interior walls throughout this place. I've seen all
the design specs for the security systems in this
basement level. You can't be feeling a door."

Bear chuckled, as if he thought Flan's observation
was cute somehow. "Can you open it?"

"I think so." Salmindra shoved him back against
Bear, but he managed to keep himself silent, even as
he ground his teeth yet again.

And then, with a metallic whisper, she wasn't
there beside him anymore.

He felt out along the edge of the wall, his mind
trying to make sense of the open space his fingers had
found. It *was* a door and the air wafting into the

corridor was damp and cool. Bear shoved him forward, and he eased himself into the opening.

The red emergency lights of the passage way spilled out onto...grass and mud? Salmindra stood a short ways from him, her hands on her hips, her eyes following the lines of the great trees rearing above them. And then he could feel Bear's presence, filling the doorway behind him.

He could hear the sound of a stream, running in darkness, and an owl's low hoot shivered his spine for a moment, a sound so deep and primal that his skin lifted into goose bumps. "What. The. Fuck."

"When you said the bridge programming was malfunctioning, I had no idea of the scope of the issue," Salmindra murmured.

"Nor I, to be honest," Bear rumbled behind him. "Fascinating, though. And a creative approach to the fragmentation that has been imposed on the system, don't you think?"

Flan startled when the dim light from the passageway winked out and plunged them into a rich and breathing darkness. Space. There was so much space here, a whole world around them, and the Harbor simply gone. He knew it without seeing it. He hadn't just stepped from one room to another; he had stepped from one *world* to another. Even the smell of the air here was a mix of cool and decay and new life and so very different from the filtered polite stuff he'd breathed his whole life.

"Can you tell where we are?" Sal asked.

"Better than that. I think I can tell you *when* we are," Bear said quietly.

"The first script. You were right—the structure of the synap production would follow the structure of the human mind. This is a folded reality." Sal shifted in the darkness.

The darkness, unrelenting, made Flan feel dizzy almost, cut off from all the markers of visual balance. "You can see."

"Yes," Bear replied. "And hear a great deal more than you."

"I'm totally blind," Flan murmured. "Can you open the door, let some of the passage light in?"

"That option no longer exists, Flan Jaspers. We were provided an exit but the flow is only one way right now. The door was yours, and yours alone. We will have to see what you make of it, but we can no longer be by your side. The bridge program is failing and there is little time to do our work now."

He stood there, swaying, the fingers of his hands spread wide. "I don't understand..."

"Sssshhhh," Bear whispered.

"Why?" Flan demanded. "I can't see..." the blow that came out of the darkness doubled him over and spun him into the ground. He tried to rise, flinging his arms out to make any kind of contact and something or someone struck him again, between the shoulder blades this time, sharp and powerful. He went down, face first and then a knee pressed into his back. Hands seized his hair and the lines of his neck groaned as his head was pulled up and back. The cold metal pressing against his throat, biting in just enough that he could feel the sting as it broke flesh and a thin, hot line traced through his cold skin.

A strange garble of words erupted above him, nothing he could make sense of. It sounded like a question, but he had no way to communicate, to answer. "I don't understand," he rasped. "I don't…"

The knife withdrew a little, as if the one above him was also puzzled. *Where was Bear and Salmindra? Why weren't they fighting? Had they been taken down?* His confused mind cast around, and yes, he could sense two others besides the one astride him now, but they were not the machine-kind who had passed through the door with him.

Abruptly, the knee pressed him back down into the earth, and other hands wrenched his hands behind his back. A rough-textured twine bound his wrists so tightly that he gasped into the mud in spite of himself. Then the weight lifted from him and he was dragged upright, in the pitch darkness. How were his assailants able to see at all? He could feel his eyes straining, wide open, but it was all blackness without texture.

Before he could quite collect himself, they shoved him forward into the night. Every part of the forest seemed to reach for him, thorn and rock and root. The three people moved quietly, righting him when he stumbled but without any pause for breath or to check if he was well. His hands went numb first, and then he began to trip over even his own feet, until finally they just let him fall and stay down. He laid there, his chest heaving, the ground sucking at him both cold and damp.

"What do you want from me?" he asked into the blackness as soon as he had enough breath and presence of mind.

Again words came back that did not make sense; a language, yes, but not one he could understand. Then they lifted him again, driving him forward, as if they had taken his voice to mean he was ready to move on.

He blinked quickly, many steps later, when he realized that he was starting to make out patches of gray against the dark, the fuzzy edge of forms like tree trunks. Flan tried to slow, to catch of glimpse of those who held him, but they pressed him hard, shoving him along. Stones began to resolve out of mist, leaves finally discernible at the end of branches, and he could finally sling his head around and see the people that pushed him into dawn.

Helmets. Leather breastplates. Short, battered swords hanging from their rough leather belts. Faces weathered by more than nature, like war had etched her own tattoos deeply in the space beneath their eyes and around their mouths. They were hard men, smelling of days on the road, of dust inked into the red fabric of their tunics.

He reeled then, his feet rolling over his ankles, boneless. The ground rushed up yet again, and he painfully wormed his way up to his knees only to throw up. They drew back from him a ways, giving him his space, as if his terror could be caught like a disease. He panted there, head hanging, trying to make sense of his own clothing, the feel of his own body somehow gone wrong, muscles yes, but now leaner than he had been in years. Wool cloth against his skin, itching, and the smell of animals he could not name. The light had not brought clarity; it had brought only a different kind of nightmare.

"Get him up."

He raised his head, swallowing again and again the sticky bile in his throat. He understood the words; no, he understood the meaning, even if the sound was something bizarre. It was a commander's voice, used to being obeyed. He knew the tone very well—focus, intent, the words used as whips. It was at least a kind of relief, to have three little scratches of meaning in a world gone wholly mad. Two of the soldiers jerked him to his feet again, their hands so cold against his skin, and his stomach roiled hard against his teeth.

"He's worse. We need to stop at the village that rests in the lake just ahead. The fever will eat him up before we can even get him back to the legion." The man who spoke had a timber of voice that should have been on the air, giving traffic reports and stories about celebrity parties. It was incongruous, and Flan tried to bring him more into focus. Green eyes, long, fine nose. More slender than the other two, so younger? Perhaps.

"Dead here or there, doesn't matter all that much." The other man's voice was all gravel, beaten flat by a past weight that had all but broken him. A living corpse, that's what he might have been called in some horror movie, flesh moving around with no soul. But the man was behind him, and he couldn't bring himself to turn and look death's voice in the eye.

"I said move." The commander again, marshalling, directing. At least he seemed to have some kind of control in the madness.

They closed around him again, herding him. He hated how close they clung to him, their bodies a rim of salty bitterness, shoving him into a place beyond his comprehension.

Chapter 59

Perhaps because of the action of binding back his personality fragments, he began to see through the reality of his predicament. I had anticipated great fear from his strongest and most completely formed ego character at this point. I was surprised though— much of his emotional tenor was one of amusement. I cannot say why that bothered me so much when I saw it.

-E

Ciaran lay on his side, watching the flames curve and writhe over the dry logs. Tess sat behind him, her knees almost touching his back. It was warm enough that he'd kicked the top layer of the emergency blanket off, and had nodded off now and again, only to snap awake as if an electric prod had struck his chest. After the last jerk, he'd settled in for a time of prolonged and watchful silence, giving up on sleep entirely.

"So what now?" he asked quietly, his eyes never leaving the fire.

"Why do you ask me?" Tess returned.

"Why indeed."

"You've gained some important insights?"

"I hope not, but the possibility exists. It's why I can't sleep."

"You're being unusually opaque."

Ciaran rolled toward her, putting his back to the radiant warmth of the fire. Tess looked down at him, her small smile as secretive as a Buddha's. "I have a hypothesis, not an insight. Would you like to help me test it?"

"Are you going to tell me your hypothesis first?"

"No. It would skew the results if I am right."

She raised one delicate eyebrow. "Indeed? So how can I help you?"

"Just observe with me. But first, we need to go out to the woods. I think I heard a stream earlier. I want to go there. It seems...important somehow."

Tess frowned a little. "There are some terra flats in the transport boot. Not really for hiking, but..."

"They'll work." He pushed himself up, gently cracking his old rugby injuries in shoulder and hip as Tess, too, came to her feet. He gestured for her to lead the way. Moments later they tromped down the back steps. Tess dug into the trunk of the dead transport, and pulled out a thin, flat package.

Ciaran took it from her, rolling out two vaguely foot-shaped pads. He stepped onto them, and immediately they curled around his feet as if he had sunk into memory foam.

"Fashionable," Tess murmured, her hands on her hips.

"They'll do." He scanned the tree line, his eyes lingering on a cracked old boulder that homed a small fern on its back. The morning light broke and wobbled through the slow moving clouds.

"I don't hear water."

He smiled at her then, but his lips stayed plastered over his teeth. With a jerk of his head for her to follow, he walked along the gravel drive, then turned and plunged into the woods. There was no trail as such, only the bent impression of where an animal might have curved its way through, sinuous bends through trunks and ferns and shrubs. A thorn scratched him hard over the open top of his foot, but he blinked the sting away. He could hear the stream clearly now, the shirring, breathy voice a kind drone string to the snaps and rustles of their passage.

They emerged on a grass and weed bank, the creek bed below snuffing and grasping at trailing fronds along its bed, and when he raised his eyes, a log was floating down in the current. Such a simple thing, natural, not out of place at all. Except it was a log he had called for in another world, one he had tried to will into being before he had emergency exited from another place and time. He shivered then, but nodded, horror and logic and a ridiculous urge to giggle shaking hands along his bones.

"No," Tess breathed behind him. She crept up close to him, her shoulder and breast brushing his back as if she could hide from him and the clear answer to his silent hypothesis. "I know this place. I've been to this place with you before, but from within a production of your making. This? Here? This is not possible."

He shook his head. "No, it is not," he murmured. "I'm either running more than two scripts or I'm creating multiple productions out of those two to share out the emotional load somehow. And I *haven't* exited in all this time. Not really. We're still in play. This is not real."

He turned and glanced down at her. She wasn't shaking of course, but she was as rattled as machine-kind ever showed.

"It's OK, Tess. You make sense to me now, everything you've done, everything you're feeling, and everything you are. You're the part of me that is trying to save itself, just not in a package I would have ever guessed. And I suspect even I am not quite whole here, either."

Her eyes, when she raised them, were wide and dark, her pupils blown to the edges, her lips parted over her perfect teeth. "No. I feel real. I feel my machine-nature."

"Of course you would," Ciaran said gently. "Because you are what you are. Just not real or a machine in the way you *think* you are." He tipped her face up with his hand. "You're much more human than you could ever be in reality, am I right? And for some reason, my scripts or my own unconscious are making some of machine-kind out to be rather sadistic and cruel. But not you. That's..." he searched for a word for a moment. "Interesting." It didn't have the punch he would have liked, but it sufficed.

"I don't know if I am more human-acting. How could I know?" He caught the barest hint of fear as she faced the paradox of herself head on.

"Exactly," he murmured.

Chapter 60

The bleeds in his production were always consistent
with the fragmented personas he animated. This
strange ability, to hold reality and illusion together
and easily was startling to me. I could see no use for
it; I thought once he began to see through the
production, he would immediately snap together
snug and whole. But that is not how the human mind
works evidently.

-E

Flan couldn't raise his head anymore, not when
the Roman soldiers dragged him through the woven
wooden gate, not when they secured a heavy chain
around his neck and let him fall on his face in the cold
mud. For a long time, all he could do was look over
the land at eye-level, seeing only boots and dog paws,
and once the flash of a rat, scurrying along in broad
daylight. He wanted to close his eyes, but something
stubborn and wakeful within him kept jerking him
back. So he stayed prone, shivering but not sleeping as
the gray light oozed toward night again.

The edges of a skirt curtained his horizon, and as
someone touched his shoulder, he flinched. Putting
one hand against the ground, he tried to push himself
up, but his elbow wobbled dangerously. Instantly,
hands slipped under and around him, and then eased
him up with a practiced strength. He could feel the

wooden pole he was attached to settle against his back, and the chain rattled, cutting the metal into his collarbones.

A cup of water was instantly at his lips, and he drank, thankful even for its mossy taste. And when he finally raised his eyes, a woman crouched in front of him, her eyes dark, her hair pulled back from her face with a strip of cloth. "Thank you," he rasped.

She tipped her head, as if not quite understanding him and pulled the cup close to her breast. She reached out then and touched his forehead. "Caróg."

Crow, something in him translated. He reached up, his fingers reading only roughened skin there above his eyes.

"Is that what you see?" he asked her. Or rather, that is what his mind asked, but the words that flowed out of his mouth were foreign and exotic to his own ears. He blinked quickly. How many languages rattled around in his head now?

She smiled then, as if relieved he spoke her language. "It is an old tattoo, spread with age. Here, the wings." She traced his skin to the outer edge of his eyes. "Here the head and tail feathers fanning above. How could you not know your own face?"

"I do know it, but maybe not here."

"You speak like a Seer. But why do you wear the Roman dress and yet walk as their prisoner? What have you done?" She settled a little closer to the earth, and pulled a strip of dried meat from the fold of her belted skirt. She glanced around her carefully, and then extended the small meal to him.

"I don't know," he whispered, taking the proffered food. "I'm...lost, I think." How strange it was, to speak to the woman in a tongue not his own, and yet feel the visceral rightness of it. He held the meat carefully, aware of the upset roll of his stomach and unsure whether he could keep it down.

"You there! Step away from the prisoner." The harsh Latin cracked like a whip in the air, and Flan dropped the meat against his thigh, covering it awkwardly. He looked up as the soldier gestured for the woman to move away, his motions quick and impatient. She merely nodded to him, rising with a grace so familiar to Flan that he felt yet another wave of vertigo sweep over him.

She moved like Tess. And her scent? It was all Lynnie.

"Your name!" Flan asked, not caring if the Roman towering over him kicked him in the gut for his question.

"I am Droichead." And then she turned and picked her way across the tight little courtyard toward a rounded structure with a thatched roof. Thankfully, the soldier merely turned a little sideways, his stance one of a guard.

The Bridge his mind translated, as his fingers closed around the gift of food. He said her name to himself several times, trying to wedge it into his consciousness. It seemed important, a message of many pages crammed into a word.

Chapter 61

I began to want for him to see me, really see me. Not
as the character that bled in through Flan's reality,
but as I was and am, his caretaker and his assistant,
really. And unlikely and uncanny as it sounds, I swear
there was something in him that heard me.

-E

Ciaran walked slowly back toward the farmhouse, his fingers interlaced behind him, his eyes on the ground but not seeing much. Tess trailed just off his left shoulder, silent and still musing about his revelations he supposed. He ran through it all himself—exits that were not, script bleeds, moments of schizophrenic disorientation, hints and tastes and echoes of the past hours that amounted to what exactly? What was the frigging point of it all?

"If Bear and Sal are merely characters, then who actually installed the script and is running the production?" Tess finally asked. He stopped, the sunlight blinking now and again through the heavy cover of the firs.

"It's the right question," he answered. "Although at this stage, the why of it might get us even further down the road."

"Whys are never useful in scientific analysis," Tess said, but her voice made it into a kind of question.

"This isn't science, Tess. It's art. You have to think differently."

"The rugby playing synapjock artist," she returned, her lips quirking a little at last.

"Exactly. I need to ask *why* because then I will better understand what is wanted of me. And if I can understand that, then perhaps I can end this."

Tess curved her arms around her belly. "End me, you mean." A little breeze caught the edges of her long dark hair. She looked vulnerable then, and delicately lovely.

Ciaran cocked his head at her. "I've never experienced characters who *know* they are characters, Tess. I'm sorry if it's painful for you. But even saying this seems faintly ridiculous. Do you understand?"

"Like screaming at a holovid image to duck in a disaster production," she answered.

"Yes. Or like talking to myself, " he added, "and expecting an answer that is anything other than me."

"I am not you," she shot back.

"And that reaction, in and of itself, is really fascinating, don't you think?" he replied.

"I think I dislike you very much, Ciaran Dolan."

"That's pretty close to my own usual sentiment, actually." He tried to keep the bitterness out of his voice, but he could read the instant regret on her face. Before she could say she was sorry, he raised his hand, silencing her. "Don't, Tess. It's not necessary."

She shut her mouth tight for a moment, her jaw muscles bunching, and then nodded.

He walked on then, shoving his hands deep into his pockets. At the edge of the lawn of the property, he stopped and turned a little back toward the river behind them. "I just feel like it keeps coming back to Flan," he said.

"You were face to face with him," Tess observed. "Remember, in the parking garage after Clara abducted you?"

"You were his partner, though?"

"Yes, but..."

"And he ordered you to connect with me."

"Well, we both agreed it sounded like a possible way to figure out..." She faltered then.

"Figure out what?"

'The why of all things, behind your kidnapping and abuse." She actually blushed as soon as she had said the words.

"Hmmm." His lips quirked, appreciating her admission.

"That's it? Hmmm?"

"Can you get us back to the Harbor? Connect us with this Flan?"

"Yes, I can send up an internal tracking beacon for emergency support, but they'll take you into custody for sure. It's unlikely I'll be able to help or even stay with you."

"We'll see. It's my storyline, remember."

"Really? Correct me if I am wrong, but you've given yourself a hell of a beating in here so far. And you're not really even continuously conscious of the other story line, are you?"

"Wouldn't be all that interesting if I was," he replied. But her words did give him pause.

Chapter 62

Have you ever flown before, or even believed you could? Stretched out your arms and turned your face into the wind and simply left that which reaches out to grasp you? I spent a long time looking at myself in the mirror, but could not see that fragile bird within, not even in my imagination.

-E

Night fell, faintly illuminated by a few small fires in the courtyard. Flan huddled against the ground, longing for another sip of cold water to wash away the clinging bits of the dried meat he'd finally managed to choke down. The two soldiers had traded out once during that time, but now, a man with a longer stride came thudding through the mud.

Flan saw the kick coming, but he was so sore and weak he could only raise his hands to protect his face. He grunted hard as the leather made contact with his gut, and he clung grimly to his meager meal, willing it to stay down. The soldier, the commander he assumed who had been calling the shots since all the weirdness began, reached down, grabbed his collar and drug him to his feet. He slammed Flan back against the wood post. "I think you can stand now," he sneered.

He felt himself jerked around, the younger soldier right there, too, ready to tie his hands with leather, the wood grinding up against his chest. He could see the kid's face clearly now; maybe only seventeen or eighteen, not even a decent beard shadow on his face. He refused to meet Flan's eye as the commander behind him began to rip through the weave of his tunic with the edge of a cold blade. With a rough jerk, the fabric tore away and the cold night air rushed around him.

"Ever wield a bullwhip, Kanut?" the commander asked. How conversational he sounded, almost lazy, an afternoon rugby meet sort of interest in his tones.

Kanut. Knot. Flan almost laughed with the mental image that the words threw up; the very impulse told him how ragged his mind was starting to become.

"Yes, Sir. My family worked as drovers. I can handle a whip." Kanut's voice was firm, all his bravado pushed up front. But his face seemed pale in the uncertain light.

"Then perhaps you would like to mete out the punishment to a deserter? He's part of your cohort, is he not?"

Flan swallowed. Deserter? Was that his official back-story in this strange hellhole? They had hunted him down only to beat him to death here, wherever here was? Because wasn't that what happened to soldiers who strolled away from their legions? Weren't they handed a terrible, lingering death? He flipped through his slim memories of ancient Rome but could come up with no answers.

"The tribunal…" Kanut began.

"I'm his tribunal," the commander hissed. "I'm not dragging him all the way back to camp when a bloody whip and tales of a grave will tell the story straight up. Bend to this duty or take his punishment yourself." He said the last words nearly as a whisper, the threat needing no volume.

"I…I will do my duty, Sir," the young man said.

Flan wanted to tell Kanut no, to wait, to let him explain it was all a mistake. But then the young man's face was gone, and he could only listen with a strange and terrible fascination to the metallic sigh of helmet, sword, and breastplate being laid aside. The first practice snap of the bullwhip sizzled through the cold air and he jerked, his breath riding high and tight in his chest.

Flan frantically stared past the edge of the wooden post to the darkness beyond, panting, his muscles twitching and sinking away from what he knew would happen next. Crazy, a vice-cop whipped to death and nobody from his time would know. Because his time didn't exist yet. Madness, it was all madness. Movement drew his eye suddenly, and there, the woman who had cared for him stood in the shadows, the light picking up only the barest lines of her face, the shine of her eyes. She urgently mouthed the word *Caróg*.

Crow.

He swallowed hard, his mouth half open. *What did she mean? What could the tattoo over his forehead have anything to do with this?*

The first cut of the whip sizzled into his flesh, a line of heat and impact that slammed him up against the post. He clamped down on his cry, his hands fisting, and then splaying open as if he could release the awful line of pain. Two more strikes landed, and with the third, he screamed out, raw and helpless in the night.

"An Modh Orduitheach! Fly!" The woman who looked like Tess cried out. She passed her hand over her face and then opened it to the sky as if releasing a living creature from her grasp. Impossibly, his eyes followed her gesture, and as the whip hit yet again, he felt as if he launched from his body, as if he had slipped the ropes and sprung skyward on black wings. For one moment, he raced over her shoulder, his wingtips touching the edge of her face.

And then his human consciousness wholly failed.

Chapter 63

The central question for me will always be something like this: how does the human mind distinguish between what is reality and what is not, perched as it is on bias, conditioning, the weakness of their senses and the very thing they call creativity and imagination muddying the whole thing?

-E

Ciaran walked toward the air transport, letting Tess hold one arm in her tight grip. Two field officers waited, their bolters drawn, their faces unreadable behind their high-flare face guards. Black helmets, black body armor—they might as well have been robots out of an old science fiction story.

"I've got this," Tess said to them. "You can stand down." He found himself more than a little surprised by her volume and coldness, at the way she shifted him forward so effortlessly as Clara had once done. For one moment, his step faltered and she turned her face toward him. And gave a quick wink that wasn't in the officer's line of sight. "Don't make me carry you," she snapped.

He bit down the flood of relief.

The armored men gave way before them, letting them mount the ramp up into the guts of the transport. He had a quick impression of emergency packs, tucked along the top ridge of the cavity, as well as guns and other equipment fastened in tightly for air travel. She thrust him into a high-backed seat and thin filaments immediately sprouted from the arms and sides, slipped around him and pulled him tight. He flinched, more from the sensation of being bound yet again than any real pain. She sat down opposite of him, forcing one of the humans to go between them to sit on her left. The other dropped beside her on the mission bench, his or her feet spread wide and stable.

"Call us in," she commanded, and a hand wave from the cockpit signaled the pilot had heard and was preparing to depart. Moments later, they leapt into the sky, rocked a bit to the side and then straightened out with a low hum.

The officers still had not removed their riot gear. They faced stiffly forward but for all he knew, they could be watching him through their black faceplates. Tess, too, simply stared at the floor by his feet, her face nearly blank and unreadable now. He wondered if she was worried, if at the last minute she would chalk up all he had tried to tell her to a malfunction on her part and walk away, leaving him caged and alone. That thought burned a little, wicking away the surge of relief he had felt just moments before; he wanted her beside him, irrational as he knew it was.

How, after all, did you stay beside your self?

Damn, but this was one fantastic production, he had to give it that. Even had him going and trying to second-guess the ending.

The cargo area was fully enclosed, and he had no idea what lands or cities they passed over or how fast they were moving. When his stomach lurched a little, he could only assume they were winging down toward earth again. Tess raised her eyes to his then, a strange frown on her face. Her small pink tongue darted out, curled back on her own teeth as if something were not quite right.

"Caróg," she whispered, as if remembering something that had been lurking in her memory stores for years. *An Modh Orduitheach!*

Crow. Fly. Fly NOW!

Chapter 64

The rapid adaptability of all his personas never failed to startle me. But then, those simple action-reaction responses have been hard-wired into them from the beginning. And, to an extent, into us.

-E

Flan did not really remember coming back to earth, although the sound of his breath whistling and gagging in his throat was the first real thing he grew conscious of. That, and the steady wipe of something cool and gentle moving over his back.

Over long lines of acid, burning in his skin.

He gasped in pain as he snapped more fully into his body. He groaned low in his throat and tried to lift himself up off his belly as if getting to his feet, he might outrun the long lines of fire on his back. Instantly, someone gripped his arms, holding him down.

He didn't fight them. He simply couldn't.

His forehead alternately burned and throbbed, like when he and Tess had crashed to the pavement in the garage to avoid the homicidal transport. Someone had bandaged the wound, but he had no memory about how it had happened.

"What...?" he gasped out.

"The crow flew with your soul, but he would not bring it back. I had to cut him from you before he would return it in exchange for his freedom. I am sorry." He recognized her voice, the woman from the shadows, telling him to fly.

Told him to fly and he had, impossibly. He couldn't quite make sense of it all, though, only that she must have carved the tattoo right out of his skin and set it free somehow. Set him free, too. Of course. As if such a thing could ever happen to a vice cop. Unless he was also some kind of synap-jock freak doing a fantasy flick. Maybe he was still pinned beneath Salmindra and she was somehow making all of this happen. He almost laughed, and then shuddered as the cloth began to wipe his battered flesh again.

"Soldiers?" he rasped out.

"You are dead to them. They left two days ago."

Two days? He remembered none of it.

"*Am* I dead?" he asked.

The woman chuckled under her breath. "Very much so, to Roman eyes."

He tried to process that, but didn't get far. "Thank you," he whispered then. God, but his throat was sore, as if he had screamed for an entire night...no...he wasn't going to let himself go there. He didn't want to remember any of it.

The woman named Droichead finally sat back as if satisfied with her work and patted his shoulder. "You flew well for a man who has also held a gladius," she said, and he found himself startled by the odd mix of reverence and pity in her voice.

"What's a gladius?" Oh, of course. His mind immediately coughed up the image of a Roman short sword.

Droichead laughed softly. "You are *not* still flying, remember."

"Tired," he whispered.

"Then rest now, and in time, we'll see what way we might point your feet rather than your wings."

Chapter 65

In the end, I could barely stray from his side. The data rolled in, fast, anxiously, if data could be viewed that way. We were close now, his worlds bumping and colliding. I waited to see when to intervene, when to push end on the program he was creating for us all.

-E

Ciaran stared at Tess. Why had the Gaelic spilled from her like that, crow and fly, right when the craft was airborne? Who or what was the crow, though? Himself?

The bridge program is malfunctioning. The words came up sharp and clear in his own mind. He tried to remember where he had heard them, but only found a hall of mirrors, echoing his own face back to him. So he framed the words again, clear in his own head.

The bridge program is malfunctioning.

Nothing. The silence of his mind was nudged only by the sound of the air transport, the gentle rocking of the vehicle. He waited, trying to be patient, hoping for some thread he might pick up and trace back to a shadowy origin.

"The bridge program is malfunctioning," he said again, aloud this time.

"I am Droichead," Tess muttered under her breath. "To malfunction is to finally live."

He snapped his eyes to her face, but she was still staring down at the metal floor, her hands resting on each thigh. "What did you say?"

"I am the bridge," she repeated, in a voice not entirely her own.

He held his breath for a moment, and then let it out in a long sigh, pressing back in his confinement, his eyebrows puckering hard enough to cause a flare of pain.

"What's the function of a bridge, Tess?"

One of the officers shifted then, his blank faceplate snapping toward Ciaran. "Shut. Up." he grated.

She raised her head then, and gave it a gentle shake as if coming back from a daydream. But her eyes were troubled, the skin at their corners pulling down, her lips fluttering. She wanted to speak to him, he knew. But now was not the place or time.

The craft shuddered, and then a harder thump of landing pads hitting the ground rang through the cargo hold. The officers were on their feet at once, one cop going ahead, the other lingering as Tess leaned forward to free Ciaran from his harness. She pulled him to his feet again, but her grip, ferocious looking as it might be, was quite gentle.

He hadn't known what to expect as he stepped down the ramp. The city reared around them, and off in a corner of the landing area, he caught a glimpse of a tiny Japanese garden and teahouse. It didn't fit; and with a start, he realized it reminded him of Tess, as if she could have moved into that miniature garden and people would have barely noticed her puttering amongst the moss and koi.

They pressed forward then, rapid over the wet cement to a security door gleaming with EM safeguard warnings all lit up in bright yellow and black. The scanning tunnel was short, and they passed through without incident.

As the inner door shifted away, he felt a rush of vertigo. And then a lancing rush of fear raced through his mind, hot and terrible. For one moment, he remembered pressing himself into the corner of his apartment, the knife held in his stiff grip, the machine-kind EMTs closing in on him. Screaming, his mind coming apart, that too, he remembered. He stumbled into Tess, and she clutched at him, helping him keep his feet. "Ciaran?"

"I can't go through," he muttered. "Don't. Don't make me go through." He averted his gaze, wanting to look at something, anything but ahead.

"It's just the Harbor." Tess murmured. "See?" Her voice was gentle, her hand stroking the back of his head like he was a child.

He lifted his eyes and turned, but instead of a room of computers stations and intake workplaces that would have graced a governmental installation, the gentle curve of the ocean lapped upon a rocky shore. Small boats had been pulled up and away from the tidal line, and racks of fish were drying. The smell wafted up and into the security tunnel—decay and seaweed, salt and smoky wood fires, people and damp dogs.

When the officers passed through, their outfits fell away and in their place, Daithi and Ashling continued down toward the water without glancing back.

Ciaran groaned, feeling the lintel between the two realities with a terrible clarity. "Do you see it?" he asked her.

Tess held him even tighter, her head against his chest, her hand stroking. "Yes. I see it. It's just a script bleed. You've explained to me that this has been happening all along."

The memories from that other script rushed in— the blindness, the cold water closing over his head, Daithi's terrible and too-intelligent eyes. "I won't go down there. I won't continue this," he said. He broke away from her and started back up the tunnel. He could sense her beside him, keeping pace but giving him room. "I won't continue this, do you hear me!" he yelled, and the narrow security path both echoed and added volume to his voice.

He broke back into the landing area and stopped dead. The grass began only a few feet away from the tunnel, the cement crumbling and falling into black dirt at its edges. Beyond, only the wind-trembled branches of a forest greeted him. He backed up a few steps and bumped up against Tess. He wheeled on her then.

"Kill me."

"Excuse me?"

"Exit me, right now! Do it!" he shoved hard at her chest, his wrists stiff, and his fingers like claws. "Do it, Tess!" He struck at her again, the unnamed fear eating at any last bits of sanity he'd thought he'd found.

He tried hard not to look at her face as he beat at her, but the confusion and hurt bled through in rapid snatches even as she effortlessly held him at arm's length. Abruptly, she caught hold of one flailing arm and folded around him, holding him tightly.

"I can't...I can't...can't," he panted, feeling his heart ripping through the cords in his throat.

"Tess." The voice came out of the forest, calm and a little sad. Tess jerked them both around to face the newcomer. The man walking toward them was chubby, his hair thin and his eyes an indistinct hazel. He rubbed at his nose as he walked forward, his shirt half-tucked and his thin street shoes muddy. "It's OK, both of you. I'm exiting us. But I don't want to shock you, Ciaran. I want you to see my face so when you next see me, you'll know you're free of the synap-canvas. Do you understand? Close your eyes, and I'll pause the production."

"I don't want you to pause it. I want you to end it! And who the hell are you anyway?"

"Eric," Tess breathed. "A high-level tech from the Harbor."

"From Flan's reality," Ciaran said.

"Yes." Eric's eyes slid to Tess and he flushed a little. "Inadvertently in play there by the way. Interesting how your mind works, Ciaran. Barest intuition and off you go, proverbial hound on the fox. You wrote me right into one of your story lines. Although this body," he gestured down the round length of himself, "is rather comical, don't you think?"

"Now you sound like Bear." Ciaran struggled against the cage of Tess' arms and she finally released him, but hovered close. "How do I know you are not he?"

"Indeed, how would you know? That's how your mind works— messy, too many questions, conundrums. All I can do is talk to you someplace other than here and hope you recognize reality for what it is. And hope you know that by exiting us all, I may have a different sort of power than what you're used to." Eric shifted in his soaked shoes. "May I suggest we go now? This is not the place to talk, with your mind creating images that match your mood. It makes me far too uncomfortable."

Ciaran tipped his head, feeling his own eyes become cautious slits. He studied the man before him long and hard. Eric was right, though. He didn't know how to cut through the knot of his own production.

"Do it," he said at last.

Chapter 66

Attachment and aversion—it was the fuel behind all of his work. So often I would see him start to make a connection, to lean toward a kind of happiness so full and hungry and then his mind would tear it all apart. It was so incredibly perverse in its own way.

-E

Flan lifted his face to the sun, one hand braced on the frame of the little conical hut. Droichead stood close by his shoulder, her arms wrapped around a new tunic she had prepared for him. He could feel her studying him, evaluating his health as she had for the past weeks. He finally dropped his eyes to her delicate face and smiled. "I feel almost myself, thanks to you."

"And now you must fly? Is the crow still so much with you?" she breathed. He could hear the hurt and longing in her voice, and he reached out to cup her face. She wasn't real; she couldn't be, none of this could be. But he bent his head anyway and kissed the edge of her mouth in answer.

"That is no reason," she murmured, drawing back.

"If I stay, I endanger you," he replied, trying hard to explain. "There will be more Romans—the land will flood with them. I know...from my history lessons, I know."

"You do not look Roman," she replied. "They will not know you were once among them."

"But I speak like them. I move like them. I cannot take the chance they will hurt you or pull me back into the legion, not after all the kindness you have shown me."

"Is it only kindness you see?" she asked, her voice small.

He shook his head, mute.

"Then why not take me with you?"

Flan had to look away then, letting his eyes lift to sky and tree. "You can't go where I have to go."

"Walker between worlds," she said. "But walkers always return, Caróg."

Except for the crazy ones, he thought. He shook his head. "My name is Flan."

"Not to me."

Her voice hurt him, deep in his gut. He couldn't explain to her this terrible drive to move, to run; it had been growing within him as he healed, like the scars on his back were pushing him into motion.

"This is not my world at all," he said.

"You are not Sidhe, those who live in the hollow hills."

"Perhaps you are wrong. Perhaps that is exactly what I am," he replied, smiling to soften his comment.

The scream that ripped into them then, jerked them both around. The trees batted the sound back and forth, but already the gatekeeper of the tiny settlement was waving a piece of cloth, his face red with emotion. "Romans!"

Flan grasped Droichead, driving her into the hut. "Armor? Sword?"

She beckoned to the rough-hewn chest pressed up against one wall. He released her and flung up the top. There, in neatly arranged piles, rested a Roman breastplate and helmet and gladius, even the bright red tunic of the legions. He wanted to slam the lid shut again, but already he could hear men running for the walls, the creak of the old gate shutting against the invaders. Another voice screamed from the narrow swath of fields, this one female. Flan cursed and ripped the armor out of the chest.

She deftly fitted it all to him, helped him tie the leather laces, the last one beneath his chin so tight he winced as it bit into his flesh. He pointed to the bed where he had lain for so many days. "Hide behind it. So help me God, I won't let them pass, even if it's the last thing I do here."

"They will fire this place," she said quietly. Instead, she reached beneath the bed-frame, and pulled out an old and rusted sword nearly as large as herself.

"Droichead..." he groaned.

"It is our way, Flan-Crow. We are not soft like the Roman women. I fight beside you."

Chapter 67

I had to bring him out of the production more and more toward the end of the template creation. I hated those times, perhaps because I am a programmed healer. I could see what this work was costing him. No. I could feel it.

-E

The exit was different, a struggle to surface, and then, a long lingering behind his eyelids. Everything dragged here, his breath, his mind, and he could feel each synap-contact like the touch of fire all over his body. The effort to finally open his eyes seemed monumental, and even then, it took a long time for his vision to behave and focus.

"Are you with me now, Ciaran?" Eric's voice, but cleaner somehow, sharper.

More mechanical.

He tipped his head to the side, coming face to face with a truly handsome example of machine-kind. The man's eyes were a deep forest green, wholly fabricated but still striking. His hair waved over his broad forehead, more ginger than brown. The tattoo of a high-level med-tech, the ancient symbol of the caduceus, glowed against his tanned skin.

"You're a bit prettier than I expected," Ciaran ground out. His voice sounded as if it had not been used for a very long time.

"I was surprised at first to be part of your production," Eric said with a small smile. "Although, I did find your rendering of me very comfortable, actually, in a round and lazy sort of way. Most entertaining, as always."

Ciaran swallowed, trying to summon some moisture up into his mouth. "Where are we?" The room seemed small to his bleary eyes, small and bare except for the wall of synapjock support machinery.

"Where you've essentially been for the past four years. I wake you now and then, but you don't hold on to that memory. It's part of the problem I've had restoring your basic functionality as a human."

At first the words didn't sink in. Then his eyes traveled his body. The length of it he knew, but this form was slender to the point of emaciation. He ran one hand over his chest feeling his ribs and the implanted port. Even that movement was difficult, tiring. He let his arm fall. "What happened?"

"You were left for dead in a public synap-shop. After you were brought in, a few good teams tried to work with you and got nowhere. Finally, a human co-worker of mine decided there was nothing more anyone could do for you and asked if I wanted to give it a go before they pulled your plug."

"Nothing to lose."

"No. Nothing to lose."

"So we're in a...a hospital?"

Eric hesitated, an interesting glitch for a machine-kind. Usually they were smooth to a fault. "In the basement of the Tri-County Brain Center, actually. They didn't want to spare the room upstairs, but you kept *not* dying."

"How inconvenient of me," Ciaran murmured. "So the whole thing, the template..."

"Is quite real. At least, it's what you and I have been creating together."

That admission made him blink again, revelation piled on revelation. "What?"

"The template that you are helping me refine started out as something I hoped would bring you back to life as it were, whole and functional. And then the project parameters changed over time. I do have your signed agreements, if you are curious. When you are finally released from the facility, I imagine you'll be a rather wealthy man if it catches on at the programming facilities. I have no need of such funds of course."

Ciaran shut his eyes, his groggy brain trying to put the pieces together. "Salmindra...Bear...Clara?"

"All your design. And they were not precisely how I thought a bio might view us. There were times when I thought it best to shut the project down. But I have not given up hope quite yet."

"And Tess?"

The silence went on long enough that Ciaran opened his eyes again. Eric look pensive, and even ran one hand back through his hair like a human. "She comes every day, you know. She was the officer on duty who found you. I stopped trying to figure out why she keeps showing up a long time ago."

"She's human."

"No," Eric said, his voice sounding rather embarrassed.

"But you're machine-kind. How could you..."?

"She became *familiar* to me, the space around her hinting at her presence. And after a while," Eric shrugged expressively, "I could actually see her. It was the beginning of our work together. I hoped I could use your skills to create a template that would..."

"...That would let her see *you*."

"Evolution is built on such things."

"You love her."

Eric raised his eyebrows a little, his handsome face falling into the lines of a lost child. "Do I?"

"That's what it sounds like to me," Ciaran said.

"I doubt it is anything quite that simple."

Ciaran smiled then. "Only machine-kind would label love as something simple." He shook his head, feeling the pillow beneath his head crinkle. "But the Tess in my production, she wasn't part of the script. She's a bridge, she said, which implies she overlays the script somehow. A bridge for what?"

"Not what. Whom."

Ciaran opened his hand, asking for more information.

Eric looked for a moment like he might turn away. "For the fragments of you, the pieces disrupted in your accident at the public synap-shop. You gave the bridge program her face, a personality, everything. The insert was meant to put all the pieces of you back together, but it malfunctioned. It couldn't achieve that objective because you made Tess something quite different from the original intent of the bridge."

"So Tess, the real one who comes here, is the model for the character I superimposed over the bridge program you wrote as part of my what? Rehabilitation? She's not technically part of the template, then."

"Yes. Your grasp of all of this is remarkably clear."

"I don't feel clear," he murmured. "In any case, I seem to be functioning fine now. Maybe you can move me upstairs again since I am so busy not dying?" Ciaran couldn't help let a little bit of bite creep into his words.

Eric gave him sad smile and shook his head. "Now is the operative word. Until the last two pieces of your personality are rejoined, you will not stay one personality, Ciaran Dolan. The bridge program did unite the vice cop and Roman soldier characters within you, but this composite piece of your personality called Flan, he is nearly as stable as you. And he will come out again. You are not nearly as fragmented as before, but you are not healed. In fact, the bridge may have made things worse. The part called Flan is in love and he will fight to stay with the Bridge."

"And if I'm not healed, you can't let me go," Ciaran said tiredly. "Because if a Roman soldier came out in the middle of a street of personal transports, he might make a scene. And we can't have that in our ordered and neat society."

"Essentially, yes. That, and the template must be closed. Your unification is part of that closure."

"Closed?"

"Completed and packaged for dispersal. For that, I still have need of you."

"I don't understand what you are asking of me."

"This, I'm afraid, *would* be beyond your grasp were I to explain," Eric said gently.

Ciaran shifted his eyes to the gray cement-block walls, the long light tubes casting an even and ugly light over his small cubicle. "How do I fix myself? Is that even possible?"

"And that," Eric said in a very small voice "is something currently beyond *my* grasp."

Chapter 68

I knew what was killing him—even exited, his secondary personas never really unplugged and they awoke with him. How is a body supposed to handle the simultaneous sensory input of many different people, times, places? It cannot. It must have, even with the chorus of inner voices, a single guiding principle, and that was wholly shattered in Ciaran.

-E

Flan, who they called the Crow, ran hard through the woods, his breath whistling, his legs shaking with each stride. But he could not outrun the memories— the way limbs fell away from bodies in sheets of red, the way a man screamed so high and piercing that he sounded more animal than human. And the faces, distorted by rage or pain, they were the worst, backlit by the fire and black smoke and the smells. God, the smells. They would never leave him.

Like ancient postcards, the images kept fanning through his brain, and no matter how hard he pressed himself, they kept flipping up, horrific still photographs, to the point where sometimes his arm batted at the air to keep them away.

To keep one image in particular away—the moment *she* had died, the blade slicing across her face before her body twisted and fell. He could not get to her, and without her, it made no sense to fight anymore.

No. He could only run.

A root, hidden by forest debris, caught the edge of his toe, and he tumbled, cartwheeling down an embankment and full into the icy waters of a creek at its base. It wasn't deep, and he pulled himself to his feet, finally shedding the breastplate into the water with a loud splash. He stumbled to the far shore, and half-crawled up the hill, slipping and grasping at anything more anchored than leaves and chunks of rock.

His body wanted him to stop, to go flat at last, but then the memories would find him and devour him whole. He fell again, dragged himself to his feet, stumbled and went down one more time. For a moment he rested there, his chest heaving, the water shivering his skin in the deeply slanting daylight. But her face, her beautiful and broken face, burned in his brain. He shoved himself up and wobbled forward, like a drunkard, from tree to tree, his limbs barely at his command.

When he hit a small open field, he could go no further. He let himself fall, let the ground hit his head hard enough to explode all those memories in a burst of light and a deep-bell peal.

Chapter 69

It was hardest of all to lie to him, to pretend that I had cared for him as an individual and wanted only to see him healthy. In truth, the project was wholly selfish, which, I have come to understand, is the dark and never-toasted genius of any creative act.

-E

Ciaran heard the door hiss open, and he tipped his head to look beyond Eric's hovering frame. The machine kind that entered was very like Tess—same long, dark hair and slanted eyes. But her features were a little more rounded, her body bigger and muscular. She smiled at him brightly. "You're awake this evening."

Something of a cloud passed over Eric's face, and he slipped back so Tess could stand in his place. Ciaran noticed the medtech studying her, as hungry and full of yearning as any human male.

Not unlike the look in her eyes for him. Ciaran smiled at her, his lips tight over his teeth. "Seems I owe you my life."

"Every time you're awake you say that," she murmured.

"I don't remember."

"I know." She let a little silence build between as if she were fully comfortable being with him that way.

"May I ask you a question?"

"Of course."

"Why do you come here everyday?"

Her face fell a little, but with a quick blink she smiled again at him. "Where else would I go?"

Ciaran stared at her a moment, feeling the heaviness of his body against the bed. "I...I don't know how to answer that question. Where do machine-kind go when they're off duty?"

She gave him a pained look. "Where-ever they wish."

"Tess..." he began.

And the look on her face halted his words in his throat. She blinked rapidly, her face flushing. "That's not my name. You know that."

"Not your name..." Ciaran glanced at Eric, but the medtech was staring at the floor, his jaw bunched, his arms tight around his gut.

"Ciaran, I'm Lynnie. Your legal life partner."

He half pushed himself up from the bed then, fighting against the awful pull of gravity. "What did you just say?"

"Your wife, for lack of a better term. For over ten years now." She swallowed hard, an affectation of human discomfort. "You're not getting better, are you? It's getting worse."

"Are you trying to tell me I'm partnered with a...a...machine?" he sputtered.

She took a step back, her arms stiff at her sides, her fingers clenched into fists. And then, the tension ran out of her, her shoulders folded forward and she seemed to shrink into herself. She looked him in the eye for a long moment, and then shook her head. "I can't do this tonight." And before he could call her back, she stumbled out of the room.

A machine stumbled, as if with grief.

Ciaran lay back, and turned his head toward Eric, who still stared at the floor. The medtech shifted uncomfortably.

"You don't love her, not like she needs to be loved," Eric finally murmured. "She was convenient for you to be with, nothing more. No human woman would live with the life you chose for yourself."

"Do you have any idea how fucked up this feels?"

Eric raised his eyes then. "At least as much as you."

"Lynnie is a machine? And if she's my legal wife, surely that means I cared for her at some level. Why can't I remember that? Why am I not climbing out of this bed to punch you in that perfect nose for that matter? None of this feels real." Gods, but he was tired now, losing focus, his hands and feet going numb. And when Eric didn't answer him immediately, he almost didn't care.

Lynnie was not dead. She was still his wife.

And she was a machine.

"You've been deeply conflicted about feeling anything for machine-kind, about showing anything that even approaches affection," Eric murmured. "It runs through your production, through both of your primary personalities. And yet, you legally married Lynnie before your accident. So the emotions must be there, somewhere."

"And you want them, is that it?" Ciaran asked tiredly. "So you can give them to her? So she can see you and fall in love with one of her own kind?" The numbness had spread now, deep into his thighs and biceps, like his whole body was slinking back to his heart. "This doesn't feel real. This *can't* be real. "

"Four years, Ciaran. Four years inside your own head, creating a life in there. Of course it will feel more real than all of this."

"*This* is just another creation, Eric." His words were slurring now, his vision tunneling.

"It's not. I have to put you back in now, do you understand? It's what keeps you alive."

Ciaran couldn't even nod. Instead, he shut his eyes and let go.

Chapter 70

When something is wholly fragmented, only few options remain—repair, discard or live with the flaw. Surely I can only honor his interior choice as his own.

-E

Ciaran leaned up against an oak tree, his leather pack resting against its rough bark, his hip braced to steady his bow arm. The Roman had fallen again. They'd both been here before, maybe had been here many times. But *this* time, the event playing through him frightened him.

The man called out for help.

It was like his own voice, run ragged with fatigue and pain.

Ciaran shook his head, trying to focus, trying to find the right way forward.

And from the forest, a woman ran toward the downed man, her clothing torn and muddied, and blood smeared over a long gash in her face. "Flan!" she cried out, and even from his cover, he could see the total disbelief on the soldier's face, the look of someone who has had a person taken from them and then suddenly, impossibly, that person returned. She collapsed beside him, drawing him up to her, shaking and wild. "My crow. My crow." He could see the soldier struggle to hold her, his helmet almost blocking their frantic kisses.

Ciaran put his bow down, laying the arrow beside it. He started walking toward them then, no idea what he would do when he confronted the other part of his personality, only that he knew it all must end somehow, indeed, must end now.

The man named Flan saw him over the woman's shoulder, and his eyes widened. Ciaran tipped his head, his hands wide and free of weapons. He knew what the soldier saw—a Celtic man, long tangle of reddish-brown hair and eyes that had seen too much. But perhaps he also saw himself walking forward, step by step, his chest sprung open with the kind of fearlessness that comes when there are simply no other choices.

He was near now, so near that he could smell the stench of their fear and their long race through the woods, could smell the death that clung to them both, rippled through with hints of acrid smoke. The woman still had not turned, but the Roman had gone perfectly still, his breath coming in sharp little tugs.

He heard the soldier's sword slide free, but even then he did not lower his arms and was only a little surprised when Flan's lover spun low on the earth. He had only a passing impression of the flash of metal rising to meet him and then the punch in his chest, not any worse than a blow he might have taken on the rugby field on a bad day. He stopped, looking down at her bared teeth, her arm stiff and clinging to wooden shaft of the weapon. A face that was both Lynnie and Tess run together into something almost feral.

He could also see the shaft turning red with his own blood.

His knees gave out, and it seemed his breath had been punched out through his spine. It was OK he tried to tell her with his eyes. "I'm sorry Lynnie." He wasn't sure he said it or simply thought it.

The ground came up hard on his right side, and for one moment all was silence, his eyes carried to the fanning of the tree branches in the lightest of winds.

Peaceful.

Finished.

Whole.

Final Thoughts

I held the completed template in my hand, a little chemical package barely larger than my thumbnail, the light rippling through the material as if I had dipped it fresh from a salt-water aquarium tank. I had shut down all the production equipment, except for the life support systems for one Ciaran Dolan, synapjock.

Afterwards, I could go no further than my lab chair.

I had been sitting there for nearly two hours.

In the end, I had hoped for a raw clarity, a completion that would logically point the way forward for my kind. But I was more deeply conflicted than when I had begun the project. I could have stopped it at any time. Maybe should have stopped it years ago. Still wasn't sure I wanted to admit it was over, even now, after all I had learned.

The confusion this project caused me had been unforeseeable; and now the responsibility of the choice I had to make unbearable. I would not be able to control the outcomes of this small change in our operating templates any more than I could control the trajectory of one human's creative mind.

I personally wanted this thing I held in my hand, wanted it badly for a machine named Lynnie. And I also wanted to crush it beneath my heel, erase my research and fall back into the routines that any of thousands of medtechs moved through each day, day after day, for all the long years of their lives. But I was already awake, was I not? I would have to watch them around me, eddying, my own kind not ever really seeing me.

Yet to awaken them like this—was it a kindness to them? To a machine like Lynnie who came each day to look on a human face and thinks she really loves it? Was Ciaran's reaction to her not proof enough that our society was not quite as progressive and knit together as it liked to believe?

A warning bell went off near Ciaran and in my own mind. Both expected me to take action. I let the insistent message in again: 12:44 alert. Patient is crashing. Do we begin standard resuscitation measures or do we abort?

It really was the question, was it not?

About the Author

K.B. Nelson holds a master's degree in comparative religion and loves teaching yoga, qigong and adult education classes when she is not writing, crafting fiber art or running after the sheep in her backyard. "My grandfather once said he was a jack of all trades and master of none. I think I have managed to live into that same sentiment my whole life, and I can't say it has ever disappointed me." Kim has authored three non-fiction titles and six science fiction works and her poetry has appeared in both national anthologies and national magazines.